BEYOND

TWO SUNS

MAUREEN A. MILLER

BEYOND

SERIES

PROLOGUE

Less than two days after her high school graduation, Aimee Patterson walked her Cocker Spaniel by the pond on her parent's farm. When Ziggy charged into the woods on the other side, Aimee was paralyzed with indecision. The forest was scary–a dark lair she had avoided since childhood. But she was not a child anymore, and something had caught the dog's attention. Trailing after him into that bleak stockade... Aimee disappeared from this planet.

She woke up on a spaceship so grand and so far from Earth, never imagining that her adventure in space would last five years. In that time she learned new technology, visited a foreign planet, battled aliens, encountered disease—and cured it. Most importantly, though, she fell in love.

When the adventure was over, Aimee was

twenty-two years old and confronted with a monumental decision. Should she remain in the stars with Zak and start their life together, or should she return to Earth to lead a normal existence and comfort the parents who never knew the fate of their missing daughter?

Aimee's heart yearned for one future, but the burden of responsibility argued for another. The truth was that in order for her and Zak to spend a life together without regrets, they both needed to evolve—to mature.

For half a decade, Aimee walked the routine journey of life—always waiting—always looking to the stars—knowing, hoping, that one day he would return for her.

Today was that day...

Five years.

Five long years.

Aimee stared through her hands at the pine needles blanketing the ground below. Beneath her loafers the packed earth altered, transitioning from brown, to gray, to obsidian–until finally the turf was gone and her leather shoes reformed atop a marble floor.

For a moment she was afraid to look up.

Five years.

Five years ago today she stood in this exact same spot, saying goodbye to the man she loved. It was a moment filled with anguish barely diminished over time. In that period, doubt grew into a behemoth monster that warned daily that she would never see him again. To protect her heart, she had tried to move on, but no man could connect with her as *he* did. And, every night the pendant around her neck burned his memory into her dreams...

Five years.

Only moments ago, she stood in the woods behind her pond as her heart drilled with the fear that he would not come back for her—and yet, the beam had appeared from above. A sign of faith. A sign of love. He was back. He wanted her. She bled happiness at the thought of being with him.

Zak.

Yes, time had passed, but in space the hands of the clock grew fuzzy. Here she was, once again aboard the Guardianship HORUS, about to be reunited with the man of her dreams.

At last, Aimee lifted her head.

With a spontaneous burst of delight at the sight of Vodu's creased face, she leapt off the pedestal and enveloped him in a fierce hug.

"Welcome back, Aimee Patterson." His

embrace was strong. His voice deep. Still with a face grooved like a road map, the man was nonetheless ageless.

Aimee stepped back to accept the next set of arms that wrapped around her. *Raja.*

Drawn tight into this embrace, Aimee's fingers lodged into the golden hair spilling down Raja's slim back. She could smell a sweet hint of something botanic, and heard emotion deep in the declaration, "Aimee. I'm so glad you're here."

Aimee, I'm so glad you're here.

Not, *Aimee, I missed you.* Not, *Aimee, I'm so glad you're back.*

Aimee withdrew and detected a flash of trepidation in Raja's green eyes, but the wide smile did its best to conceal that bantam shadow.

As delighted as she was to see Raja, Aimee was already looking over the woman's shoulder. Save for these two individuals, the transport room was empty. Maybe he was waiting elsewhere. Maybe he was planning a surprise.

Her anxiety could not be masked, particularly when the faces staring at her began to lose their mirth.

Aimee retreated so that she could see them both simultaneously.

"Where is he?" her voice cracked.

Raja clasped her hands together and

pressed her lips tight, turning towards Vodu. Maybe age moved at a snail's pace aboard the HORUS, but youth was external. The eyes revealed all–and right now the years tallied up inside Vodu's blue gaze.

"Aimee, let's go somewhere where we can sit down."

On cue, her legs weakened. She reached out and Raja was there, sustaining her with a strong grip.

"*Where is he?*" Aimee repeated, desperation lassoing around her throat.

Vodu winced and cast his glance towards the stars outside. "Aimee, Zak–"

"Zak what?" *Oh my God.* She could feel panic inching up the back of her neck—red hot fingers worming their way up her scalp.

"Not too long after you returned to Earth, Zak left for his planet, Ziratak, as planned."

Aimee wasn't even aware that Raja's arm had slipped behind her back for additional support.

"He–" Vodu hesitated, "–he missed his rendezvous with the HORUS. We lost communication with him."

The old commander read her despairing expression, but continued. "We sent reconnaissance missions for as long as we could before the HORUS pulled out of range. The *terra angels* no longer had the capacity to make it back to us. It would have been a one-way mission if any more took off."

"And no one volunteered?" she cried. "For a man that was your best Warrior? A man this entire ship idolized only second to you! No one volunteered for a one-way mission?"

Vodu's face pinched in pain. "Aimee–"

Now it looked like he was the one who required a chair. "The reports that came back from those last recon missions were dismal at best. The Korons, who we believed were leaving Ziratak, in fact returned ten-fold. The rebels that Zak was intending to unite with, did not even exist, or had been wiped out quite some time ago."

Blood drained from Aimee's face. She began to feel dizzy, but blinked back the assault. "Zak?" She could manage no more than that single plea.

"They found his ship." Vodu swiped a gnarled hand across his face. "It had been gutted to the point of inoperable. There were tracks around the craft–" he closed his eyes, "–not human."

"There was nothing to send that one-way mission to," he defended. "Nothing encouraging enough to warrant it. Zak was like my own. I would have flown to him if I could, but our window to reach Ziratak had closed. We have to wait another *ren* until we can return. And we *will* return."

"So, if Zak left the HORUS shortly after me," a spark of hope ignited, "then we are getting close. I've been gone a full *ren*."

A *ren,* she recalled, was a span of five Earth years.

Vodu nodded, but he possessed no spark. "Aimee. We have to be honest with ourselves. We have to accept the fact that Zak has most likely been–"

He couldn't say the words, and she sure didn't want to hear them.

Vodu's lips thinned with strain. "You have a choice now. Our *terra angels* have made some upgrades. We are close enough to Earth that we can take you home and still afford your pilot enough time to make it back to the HORUS." He paused. "I think it is wise for you to go back."

Aimee flinched. "You brought me up here. I didn't beam myself up. Why would you do that? Just so you could tell me this horrendous news and then dispatch me back to my world—left to always wonder?"

"I did not bring you up here," Vodu

declared, his condemning eyes cast over her shoulder. "*She* hit the button."

Aimee recoiled from the embrace around her back and pivoted to capture the wide glance that eluded hers.

"Raja?"

CHAPTER ONE

A lump worked its way down Raja's pale throat. She closed her eyes. "It was an impulsive gesture," she admitted in a husky tone.

Vodu shook his head in disapproval.

"So you see," he inserted. "As much as we are happy to have you back with us, we also think it's in your best interest to return home. This ship may hold too much grief for you."

Aimee glanced at Vodu whose expression was grave and remorseful. She switched her attention back to Raja, whose countenance was evasive. The woman was hiding something.

"How long do I have to make this decision?"

The rustle of silver fabric sounded as Vodu crossed his arms. "Not long, but there is definitely time for a welcome feast."

A welcome feast.

How festive.

Her world was in bedlam. All she wanted was to be reunited with the man whose touch lingered with her for the past five years. She did not want to *eat.*

She would go to their feast. After all, they were extended family. At this moment, her own family had read her letter and was coming to terms with her decision to leave. In an epic note, she had tried her best to assure her parents that she would be safe and happy, and would one day return to them. But not this day. Not this year.

For now, she would attend their feast, if only to be courteous.

And, then she would find Zak.

For such a gap in time, little had changed aboard the HORUS. One fact was glaringly apparent, though. There were far fewer personnel on board.

"You went back to Anthum?" she asked Raja who nodded in response.

Aimee recalled sitting in her college dorm room at night, staring out the small window as she thought about the residents of the HORUS, hoping that they had been able to return to their planet and start anew after the virus that nearly destroyed them.

Vodu extended his arm, inviting her into the next chamber. For a moment, she stared at the stark white wall, angry that she was unable to see behind the pearly mask. Had she lost her skills over the five-year hiatus? Was she unable to discern the images woven into this enigmatic fabric? Or was it that Zak was not here to calm her?

Relax, Aimee. Try it again.

Composure was undermined by the denial roiling inside her. Zak could not be dead. He simply could not be dead. She would *never* accept that. He was a survivor. He was a Warrior.

Relax, Aimee. Try it again.

Listening to that memory, she took a deep breath, watching as the white wall blended with intricate designs and three-dimensional imageries to reveal the symbols that identified Vodu's private quarters.

With little fanfare, he waved his arm at the door, allowing them to pass through into an opulent conference room. This was Vodu's personal meeting space for visiting dignitaries. A long oval table made of a composite similar to black marble was surrounded by twelve spherical-based chairs.

"Excuse me as I step out and collect the guests," he said. "I also need to contact the food hall and alert the Warriors of the impending trip back to Earth."

After a pause, he looked at Aimee. "You have hardly changed, Aimee, and yet you are more beautiful than ever."

Bowing slightly, Vodu waved his hand at the wall and stepped through it.

Aimee turned towards Raja who was lowering herself into a chair.

"Who was that man?" Aimee gaped.

A sad smile dusted across the woman's lips. "He has not been the same since Zak disappeared. He tries so hard to put on a positive front."

It was more than that, though. It was more than the feast, or Vodu's oddly exuberant behavior. Vodu was not the type of man to suggest *a feast*. Vodu commanded the HORUS. He led. He charged. And, he did it all with an intellect that humbled Aimee. He did not plan feasts.

Wasting no time, Aimee slipped into the seat across from Raja. She splayed her palms atop the cool amalgam surface and leaned in. "Tell me the truth. Why did you press that button against Vodu's wishes? Tell me that Zak is alive."

Raja's glance fell. Her shoulders trembled as if a chill coursed through her. She opened her mouth to speak, but her body deflated again.

"Raja, *please.*"

"Aimee, you have to accept that Zak is most likely gone," she pleaded.

"No," Aimee sat back. "No, I don't."

Raja's hand curled into a fist on the table and she shook her head to cast aside an inner conflict.

"There were rumors from some of the returning recon Warriors," she started.

Aimee tensed.

"They–they reported having seen Zak. They could not positively identify him, but they felt certain it was him by his stature, his hair, and yet–"

"And yet?"

"And yet," Raja hesitated. "They could not be certain, because he had...changed."

"Changed?" Aimee's eyebrows furrowed. "Changed how?"

"Aimee," Raja's elbows jutted out when she leaned in. "If the man they saw was Zak–he–he opened fire on them. He used a Koron's solar ray. One of the Warriors came back injured and one came back blinded. If it was Zak, he would certainly not fire on his own."

"I want to speak to these Warriors."

Raja frowned and sat up. "You're going to completely discount what I just said, and you're going to extract from it the only piece of information you want to hear...that Zak is alive."

Aimee gauged Raja. They had both grown out of their youth. Raja was now an elegant woman with catwalk model looks. Shiny golden hair slid over her shoulders and nestled across her chest. Wide blue-green eyes with a veil of dark lashes studied Aimee, awaiting her retort. Instead, Aimee held her tongue for a moment.

"Raja—" she began softly, "you never answered the question."

Raja's glance clashed with hers. "What do you mean?"

"*Why did you push that button?*" Aimee enunciated each word, because suddenly the answer was of the utmost importance.

Splicing fingers into her hair, Raja cupped the sides of her head. In this stark conference room this seemed like an inquisition.

"Just before Zak left, he pulled me aside." An anxious eye peeked out from the silken hair. "He said, *If I'm not here when the HORUS returns to Earth–and if by some miracle Aimee is waiting for me behind that pond–*" Raja hesitated, "*—bring her here. I will find a way back to her.*"

Aimee's throat clenched. It was so tight it brought tears to her eyes. She tried to clear her throat to remove the obstruction.

"My dear Raja," she looked at the woman through a bleary veil, "I do believe that you are a romantic."

Raja tugged at the collar of her shirt. "The translator on these new garments is failing. What is a romantic?"

It was the first time that Aimee noticed that the mandatory silver suit was gone. Raja wore actual pants and a short-sleeved blouse. Granted, the material was stellar—a synthetic that Earth could never produce. Yet, the style looked remarkably familiar. The pants were tight, made from a dark-blue fabric, and the blouse was white. Opalescent. The similarity finally registered and Aimee proclaimed, "Your outfit. It looks like something from Earth. The blue material could pass for jeans, and you could almost get away with the white clingy blouse on Earth."

"We needed a change." Raja blushed. "I had some input in the design of these garments."

"There is no need to light up organ failure on your suits anymore?" Aimee asked, knowing that the plague that assaulted these lovely nomads had finally been eradicated.

"We could never let go of that paranoia. The illumination of these garments is slightly more discreet." Raja's golden eyebrows hefted.

"Romantic!" she exclaimed as the definition finally came to her. "*Idealistic. Passionate. Lover.*" Her high cheekbones glowed with a flush that her outfit could never produce. She hesitated and regrouped.

"He missed you so much, Aimee. He was a lost soul after you left. He poured himself into his goal and rarely spoke to anyone. When he pulled me aside to deliver that last message—well, it wasn't something I could dismiss. Zak never had a request in his life. I had to heed this one."

Raja slumped back in her chair. "But, what if I've brought you up here and there is no hope that he is alive? I have taken you from your family." She glanced up imploringly. "Please consider Vodu's offer to have the Warriors take you back to Earth."

Not likely.

But Aimee did feel bad for the position Raja had placed herself in. She knew the woman was conflicted. Above all else, though, she was grateful to Raja for heeding Zak's last command.

"Thank you, Raja." Aimee's gratitude was so tremendous it squeezed her throat again when she tried to speak. "Thank you so much for listening to him." She coughed into her curled fist. "Exactly how long do we have until we reach Ziratak?"

Raja cocked her head. "Half of a *renna*. Ummm, a little over one of your rotations."

A little over a year.

Quick to recall her formula for time in space, Aimee calculated that to be a few months. After a five-year sojourn, the pain of waiting several more months slapped her in the face. It would be an interminable delay, but she was already scheming. If Zak was in trouble, he did not need a weak, lovelorn woman from Earth to come save him.

He needed a Warrior.

"Raja, I'm going to need your help."

Retaining composure during Vodu's feast, Aimee finally convinced the commander that she was prepared to stay on board the HORUS until its next pass to Earth.

Five years. A ren.

Time. What was time? Time could now only be measured by the seconds, the heartbeats—each breath until she reached Ziratak.

She had to find Zak.

Alive.

CHAPTER TWO

Ziratak

They were coming. It wasn't so much the sound that revealed them. It was the subtle vibration of the ground beneath his feet, like the percussion of a distant explosion. It was *their* march. The dead tread of stone against sand. A ghostly gait of menace.

Zak swiped his forearm across his brow. The sun showed no mercy, and this desert vista offered little refuge in which to hide.

Judging by the increased reverberation and the trickle of sand cascading down the closest dune, he guessed them to be on the other side of the knoll. Hefting the burdensome solar ray, he aimed it at the line where shadow met light, waiting for their grotesque silhouettes to appear. He would use their own weapon against them and depending on how many of the Korons there were, he would destroy each one until they claimed his life.

Perspiration trickled into his eyes, clashing with the glare of the suns. The deadly blend blinded him as thousands of diamonds cascaded across his field of vision. In that shower of gems he saw someone approach. It was a feminine silhouette. Lean. Tall. Beautiful. His body jerked in shock as the sun radiated off the flowing auburn hair.

"*Aimee,*" he whispered with desperation.

She was exquisite, as if the suns had stirred the sand into over five feet of gold, and rendered this woman that he had missed so fiercely. He took a faltering step towards her.

Aimee could take his exhaustion away. She could take the pain away. Her touch would make him feel whole again. How desperately he wanted her touch.

"Aimee," he called, his voice hoarse from thirst.

Zak blinked only to find that the phantom was a trick of the light, another bantam effect of the madness that wormed into his soul.

Aimee was gone, and in her place the shadows grew. They became tall, macabre caricatures of men, deformed and still increasing in size until the suns were obliterated and only blackness remained.

Zak held tight his weapon.

Aimee had a plan. And at the moment there was only one person—*or thing*—that she could trust to assist her. But, where the heck was he?

In the past she couldn't take two steps without bumping into one of the floating computers named JOH. JOH was an advanced, nearly life-like version of the internet on the HORUS. His bright blue face passed through corridors eager to assist with information and impart his own spin on the goings-on of the ship.

Feigning fatigue from stress, Aimee escaped Vodu and Raja's supervision by retiring to her assigned quarters. Marching down the stark white corridor, she was astounded to have not yet run into one of the ubiquitous blue-faced tablets.

As she was about to cross through an intersection and enter the linear transport, a metal skeletal leg stepped out from the junction to her right. Its clawed aluminum foot hit the marble with a chilling screech. It startled her because they didn't have skeletal robots when she was here five years ago.

When the second leg rounded the corner

there was no torso atop it. There were no arms, no neck, and no head. There was merely a familiar computer tablet with two legs protruding from beneath it.

"What the—" she whispered.

The metal legs halted. The monitor resting atop them flashed a blue orb, something akin to a vibrant crystal skull. Inside that skull, black sockets grew larger by the second.

"Aimeeeeeeeeee!"

The legs kicked into action. *Clang. Clang. Clang.* His movement was as fluid as a rusted gate.

"Aimee, I just found out you were on board. Raja tampered with my data feed." His black mouth puckered into a pout. "I knew we were above your planet, but she scrambled my packets so that I could not tell you had been beamed up. Why would she do that, Aimee?"

"JOH, you have legs!"

Aimee still gawked at the metal limbs that looked straight out of *Terminator.*

JOH lifted one leg and wiggled his three celluloid toes. "Before you left, you told me I needed legs." He bent his metal kneecap. "I'm still trying to figure out what benefit these things hold. They slow my progress tremendously."

Crossing her arms, Aimee gave him a

bemused smile. "They make you look more—grounded."

"Grounded." Black eyes blinked. "The curse of gravity. Not every JOH has been encumbered with these anchors. Only a few betas." His enthusiasm returned. "I am so happy you have returned!" And then his mirth waned. "Zak was never the same after you left."

It wasn't like the old days where she could lift this JOH to eye-level, so she hunched over to whisper into the monitor.

"What do you know of Zak, JOH? Did he say anything to you before he left?"

Obsidian orbs sliced left and then right before returning to her. "He said he would be back. He lied. He is not back."

Aimee surged her fingers into her hair, drawing it away from her face as if it could ease some of the strain. The strength in her legs failed and she tucked against the wall, sliding down it until she sat on the floor with her face in her hands.

"I want him back," she whispered. "I want Zak."

There was a soft scrape of metal as JOH zeroed in, hovering over her on his crooked legs.

"In half a *renna* we will be in Ziratak's solar system. They are going to send out a search

26

party to find him, but the mission will be set up for failure again."

Through blurred vision she glanced up at the blue face. "Why so?" she challenged.

JOH's legs flexed as he peered around the corner and jerked back before her. "Even though the *terra angels* have been redesigned for long distance hauls, Ziratak is a big planet. A diminutive search party will not be able to check everywhere in the limited time they are offered. It will be just like last time. Unless they get extremely lucky and locate Zak immediately, they will be forced to withdraw."

Withdraw.

There was only one choice.

"JOH, I want to be on board one of those search missions."

Azure crystals chimed as they scattered and reformed into a face—a face cast in disapproval. "Not possible," he admonished.

Hoisting her back up the wall, Aimee rose to look down at the three-foot figure. "I have waited five years to be back with the man I love. I have had my body ripped into millions of pieces and transported through the stars only to reform here on the HORUS and be told that it is *not possible* for me to go after Zak. Maybe something got lost in the translation, but I did not *ask*, JOH.

I *am* going to be aboard one of those missions. I *am* going to find Zak and bring him back here with me. It's not up for negotiation."

JOH tapped one of his aluminum toes. It might have been comical if she wasn't so charged with anxiety and adrenaline.

Onyx orbs stared at her. She could see her worried expression reflected in them. Even in that brief glimpse, she recognized the deluge of tears that waited to be shed later.

"Aimee," he began in a cajoling tone. "There is only one *terra angel* with the capabilities to spend an extended period away from the HORUS. That ship will be staffed by two of the most efficient Warriors we have. It is not big enough to accommodate more."

Before she could interject, he continued. "Any other ships joining in the mission will have the period of one of Ziratak's rotations—several days before they are forced to return. If—*if*—we could get you on one of those recons, that is all the time you would have." Again he interrupted her. "Vodu will forbid it, you know. And you do not have the training needed for such a mission."

Aimee crossed her arms and waited. "Are you through?"

JOH blinked several times. "For now."

"I thought you all were supposed to be

technologically advanced. What type of lame spacecraft can only stay away for one lousy rotation of a planet?"

There was no time to recognize the absurdity in her disparaging observation. She wanted answers.

JOH's eyes narrowed. "You combine the time it takes for that huge planet to rotate— Ziratak is much larger than Earth," he was quick to add. "And then you equate the progress of the HORUS itself."

It's not as if the HORUS is going to pull up in a parking space and wait...

Zak's words, and the recollection of his grin distracted her. She focused on JOH's litany.

"We use an ore that is artificially produced in the Jay-four satellite to fuel our crafts. It is an abundant mineral on Anthum, but easily manufactured here."

Manufacturing. Now, he was talking her language. After graduation from college, she had spent a year as a project engineer in an automotive manufacturing plant. It was a position that made her father proud.

"JOH, can you take me to your manufacturing satellite?"

The change in her demeanor startled the computer. His black eyes narrowed.

"Might I recommend visiting the Jay-four satellite *after* you have had a decent rest? You look a bit—"

Her eyebrows hefted in challenge.

"You look lovely," he quickly added.

Aimee nearly laughed. How many computers had charm? Tact aside, perhaps JOH was right. Ready to head a one-woman militia to save Zak, she recognized that she needed to think clearly. Being irrational was not going to save him. And, no matter what obstacle presented itself, that was what she was going to do.

Save Zak.

Alone.

JOH had returned Aimee to the very same accommodations she occupied during her previous tenure on the HORUS. Disregarding the tiny pool that shimmered behind opulent columns, she walked directly towards the bowl-shaped window and placed her palms flat against the glass surface. She leaned forward, resting her forehead there. It was neither warm nor cold to the touch. The wondrous vista of stars and celestial marvels seemed bleak to her. She searched the closest planets, a pair of crimson orbs that played tag behind the HORUS.

What did Ziratak look like? She needed to know because every night she was going to stand here and search for it.

There was no audience now. No feasts. No censures.

She was alone, staring at the stars, left to wonder and worry about Zak. These very same tasks consumed her every night on Earth, but there, she was helpless. Here, she was closer. She would find him, and she would not accept any of the wordless fears expressed on the pale faces of these citizens. Zak was alive. The alternative was too grim to accept.

In the glass she witnessed tears coursing down her cheeks. The burning liquid illuminated her eyes, or perhaps it was the reflection of a thousand stars.

What had the poet said? "Do not go quietly into the night..."

As beautiful as the perpetual night of space was...she would not go quietly into it. She would fight for the man she loved, and she would bring him back.

CHAPTER THREE

A soft staccato against her door roused Aimee. She was already awake, and had been for some time, but the new garments proved an obstacle. The slim, sparkling blue pants slipped up her thighs and hugged low on her hips showing off her runner's body. She was not the awkward adolescent that once walked the opalescent corridors of the HORUS. Tall and thin, Aimee now looked more like an athlete, and the slim pants made her legs seem endless. It was the top that was giving her a battle. She stood in her cotton bra and stared at her frown in the bathroom mirror.

The staccato rhythm at the door repeated.

You're just going to have to wait, whoever you are. It was probably JOH. JOH had not evolved from his puppy-like enthusiasm.

Aimee's forearms were stuck in the tight sleeves of the blouse. Again she hiked the garment over her head and tried to shimmy it past her shoulders. Her skull poked out, and her auburn hair swayed to a static waltz above her head.

"Aimee?"

Raja. Thank God.

With her arms still stuck in the shirt, Aimee walked behind the door and jerked her hand to open it, quickly stepping aside so as not be seen.

Raja entered, casting a curious glimpse around. Her sloe-eyes landed on the misfit in the corner, and she let loose a very unladylike snort.

"Are you stuck?" she asked the obvious.

Aimee wrinkled her nose at the amusement on her face, and offered her arms up in defeat.

"Help."

Raja waited until the door snapped shut and walked over with a smile.

"The garments need to be form-fitting in order to get the most accurate reading of your vital statistics." She crossed behind Aimee and reached for the hemline of the garment. "Now duck your head."

Obeying, Aimee grunted as she felt Raja tug the shirt over her head and down her back. When the dreaded task was complete, she could feel the static electricity wreaking havoc with her hair.

"Seriously, how does anyone manage that by themselves? Does everyone have an assistant to get them dressed? Or is JOH about to sprout arms and take over the deed?"

Raja chuckled and studied her. "You have lost weight."

Aimee glanced down at the shiny navy pants and tight white shirt. "These things suck in about ten pounds of body weight. Of course I look thin."

Taking a moment to appreciate the glitter in the material, Aimee looked up. "Don't you ever just want to throw on something loose?"

Raja looked wistful. "This is all I know. I've seen old paintings of Anthum, where women wore flowing gowns sometimes, but that was a costume associated with the affluent, and my parents were simple physicians."

Raja had never known her parents, Aimee recalled. She was born on the HORUS. Her mother survived long enough to achieve the birth, but was finally claimed by the deadly virus in the Jay-nine—the satellite where everyone infected went to die.

"They would be so proud of you," Aimee said softly.

Raja's pale hair slid across her shoulders as she jerked her gaze towards the windows. "I am nothing but an assistant. I haven't done anything to make anyone proud."

"You helped to save my life. You stopped Sal—"

Aimee's lips clamped shut. She did not want to say the name. Was he still locked away? Actually, she did not want to know what became of the evil scientist that had nearly dissected her.

Ignorance is bliss, right?

Astute eyes saw through her, though. Raja studied her thoughtfully, but held her tongue. After a measured pause she took a deep breath and asked, "Okay, Aimee Patterson. What is it that you need my help with?"

The blunt phrasing and use of her full name made Aimee smile. She decided to be equally as direct.

"I want to be a Warrior."

Expecting laughter, maybe even shock, Aimee was startled by Raja's measured nod.

"I'm not surprised," Raja stated.

"You're not? Why?"

"Well, nothing really surprises me when it comes to you. If you want something bad enough you don't recognize obstacles or barriers. I envy you that trait."

"You are no different than me," Aimee countered.

"I am still an assistant."

"Are you? You took control when the virus broke out on this ship. You did not report to anyone."

"Most of the scientists had fallen ill," Raja argued. "I had no choice."

"You had fallen ill as well, and yet you refused to accept it. Without your guidance that situation could have turned into chaos."

"Without your saliva we would all be dead."

"Enough." Aimee's knees buckled and she flopped down into the closest chair. "The recollection still bothers me. Right now I have one goal, and you are absolutely right—I refuse to accept any obstacles or barriers." She looked up plaintively. "I want him back, Raja."

Raja's eyes rounded. "I know you do. That is why I brought you up here. And that is why I am going to help you."

Overwhelmed by Raja's sincerity and the anxiety of Zak's disappearance, Aimee dipped her face into her open hands. She did not weep. She would not weep in front of Raja. Both women fought public displays of vulnerability. It was an unwritten rule, and a sign of mutual respect.

There were many similarities between her and Raja. They both were quiet. It was not shyness per se, but rather that they were always thinking. Physically, they had similarities in age and stature. Both women were slim and tall. Their only contradiction came in hair color. Raja possessed beautiful, gleaming blonde tresses and Aimee was crowned with shiny auburn locks. The styles were similar, worn long—well below their shoulders. Aimee was going to have to introduce Raja to the concept of a ponytail. They both had blue eyes, but the shades differed. Raja possessed orbs the color of a Caribbean sky, while Aimee's bore the dark hue of the ocean depths.

"There is one other who seeks Warrior training," Raja mentioned. "Like you, he is not qualified to be in the program. Most Warriors are descendants of Warriors. Genetically they are the best gifted for the program."

"Genetics," Aimee snorted with her face still down. "It's all about genetics around here. Zak was not the son of a Warrior, but I guess his genetics were too hard to pass up."

An image of his muscular shoulders and the recollection of the rugged band of muscles across his abdomen validated her notion.

"I agree. Those stereotypes did not exist on Anthum, I am told. They were born by discrimination on the tight quarters of the HORUS."

"Tight quarters! This ship is the size of New York City."

Raja smiled. "I know what New York City is. I asked JOH. And, as big as it may be, it is still a spec on a planet."

Peeking out of her bangs, Aimee managed a slight grin. "Well, when you use that perspective–" She sat back up. "Who is this other one that seeks Warrior training?"

Instead of glancing at a watch or a clock on the wall—neither of which existed on this ship—Raja stared through the huge plate of glass as if the alignment of the stars could give her a perspective on time.

"Hurry," she encouraged. "I need to get you both to Corluss."

"Corluss?" Aimee hastened after her. "Is that a person or a planet?"

Whipping along the exterior wall of the HORUS in a linear transport, Aimee glanced down at her wrist. A silver-faced watch still hugged it, but the device had stopped ticking the moment she arrived aboard the Guardianship. Even after changing into the new clothes, she had neglected to remove the timepiece. Now it was a perpetual reminder of the time she departed Earth.

12:26pm.

"Where are we going?" she asked, peering curiously through the window. "We're almost at the back end of the ship."

Raja tapped her fingers on the console as the chamber gradually decreased its speed.

"You haven't been to our training center. It's huge. It spans multiple levels. Some levels require special access only permitted to the highest-ranking Warriors. Even *Watchers* are trained back here."

As the doors to the transport slid open, Aimee's eyes widened in awe. A two-story grand arch of beveled stone marked the entrance to an amphitheater. This vestibule looked gothic, like something you might find on the grounds of a historic university. As she passed beneath it, she marveled at the texture of the chiseled rocks, scarred with veins of blue and green.

The sound of men in combat drew her attention. On a stage at the center of the arena, two men in silver lustrous suits exacted moves akin to karate. Their prowess in such a tight space was well choreographed. This was not a fight. This was an exercise in training—a flamboyant dance of skills.

Captivated, Aimee drew closer, studying their synchronized moves, but a hand tugged on her arm.

"No," Raja cautioned in a hushed whisper. "It is better not to draw attention. You do not belong here, remember? Your training is to remain concealed."

Aimee swallowed down a protest and joined Raja in hugging the shadows along the back wall of the amphitheater. Passing rows of empty seats, Aimee continued to watch the men in combat from afar. It was a form of art, a ballet of strength and finesse. She could easily imagine Zak overpowering anyone who ventured into that ring.

Wherever you are, Zak, if anyone dares to touch you...fight them. Fight them and stay safe.

"This way."

Raja's call startled Aimee as she jogged to catch up. Ahead, the fair-haired woman slipped into a doorway. They were now ensconced in a narrow corridor, walking single-file to the sound of their heels snapping against marble.

Aimee drew in a deep breath and searched the stark white walls, relieved to see the outlines of shadowed chambers behind them. She had not lost her touch.

"Where—"

Raja's hand flipped up to curtail her. She turned to face Aimee in the tight quarters.

Stress manifested on the woman's face in a series of fine lines creeping from her eyes and lips. "Listen to me," she whispered with urgency. "This is serious. You are *not* a Warrior. You are the furthest thing imaginable from it."

Aimee frowned.

"Aside from not being bred into it," Raja explained, "you are a female. Neither of us is permitted back here. I may be able to get away with it by claiming that I was beckoned for medical services, but you—"

"Why can't a woman be a Warrior?"

Raja sighed, although the hint of a smile lingered. "That is all you could take away from my warning?"

Aimee's forehead wrinkled stubbornly. "Yes. I find it absurd that there is a sector of the ship where women aren't allowed. How archaic. You all think you're so advanced up here."

"Trust me, the inhabitants of this training center find the fact that you are not a Warrior more offensive than your gender. This is a tight society, and their camaraderie is justified. These men exist to protect us. Who are we to tamper with that?"

"But," The concept still irked her. "Zak was not like this. He wasn't so arrogant. He did not portray himself as being from a select caste." It still pained her to utter his name.

In respect to that distress, Raja glanced down and nodded. "I think we've established that Zak is different."

Tears pressed against the back of Aimee's eyes. "Yes. That we did."

"Come on," Raja urged. "Let's get inside and then we can talk freely."

Feeling the tug on her arm, Aimee followed Raja into darkness as the door slipped shut behind them.

It took a moment for her eyes to acclimate. In the distance was a faint glow. They shuffled through the shadows until that light expanded into an open arena as spacious as a basketball court. One wall was made of glass, and through it a majestic vista of the cosmos provided a formidable backdrop for the solitary figure in silver.

In her periphery, Aimee caught Raja holding her finger up to her lips to indicate silence. Together, they watched the man raise a weapon—a laser of sorts—and aim it at a JOH standing on its two metal legs, its blue face nonplussed by the task.

"He's going to shoot a JOH?" Aimee whispered incredulously.

"Shhh. It is a mock *star laser* used for training."

As he assumed a practiced stance—even from this distance, Aimee could tell the young man was lean and sinewy beneath his snug silver suit. His pale hair was cropped short, in military style. He looked every part the Warrior as he leveled his *star laser* and prepared to fire.

After a slight jerk of his wrist, the diaphanous wave shot from the gun and drove a hole in the pliable wall five feet adjacent to JOH. The black crystals that made up JOH's mouth emitted a sigh, and the young man let loose a curse, holding the weapon up to his face as if it was the culprit for his poor aim.

"You try too hard, Gordeelum," Raja admonished.

"Gordy?" Aimee cried out.

Flinching, he turned. At that moment she caught the resemblance in his maturing face. When last she had seen Gordy, he was a boy giggling with a playful JOH. Now, a tall young man in his late teens approached her, his keen blue eyes probing her face as intently as she searched his.

"Aimee?"

Where was the young voice?

This was the deep timbre of a man.

To hell with it. She launched her arms around his shoulders. "Gordy, it's so good to see you!"

His frame remained rigid until she heard him chuckle, and a ghost of the boy returned. "I wish you didn't have to see that. I really *am* getting better."

As he stepped back there was a blush across his prominent cheekbones.

Five years might have passed, and Gordy was not a child anymore, but youthful defenses still beat strong.

"Well heck, if I tried to fire that thing I'd probably shoot my foot off," she laughed.

Gordy shook his head, torn between frustration at his wayward aim, and enthusiasm at seeing her. "I doubt that."

Still marveling at how Gordy had matured, she realized that his smile had dropped.

"You came back for him."

It wasn't a question.

Aimee's throat constricted. "Yes."

A discreet glance passed between Raja and Gordy. Aimee caught the collusion there.

"What?" she snapped. "What was that look? Stop regarding this as a lost cause. I refuse to believe that."

Distracting herself with the onyx canvas of space, Aimee played connect-the-dots with a string of stars in the distance. Maybe they weren't stars. Maybe one of them was Ziratak.

Would they even tell her if it was?

"My *look* wasn't what you think, Aimee," Raja cautioned. She glanced at Gordy and sighed. "Gordeelum, meet your new training partner."

Gordy's jaw dropped. "What? That's impossible. *She* can't be a Warrior."

Crossing her arms, Raja cocked an eyebrow. "And why is that?"

"She's—she's—" he stammered, "—a girl."

Aimee felt both sets of eyes converge on her.

"Ummm, I'm almost twenty-seven now. Hardly a girl anymore."

"Twenty-seven what?" Gordy frowned and then nodded. "Oh, of your planet's rotations? Yeah, well, I'm not quite sure what that means, but the point is that only *men* are Warriors."

Calculating, Aimee quickly volleyed, "Raja, you said that I was joining one other who was not qualified to be a Warrior. I gather I am not qualified due to my gender." Her eyes narrowed on Gordy. "But, if this is the other who is engaging in illicit training, what is his disqualification?"

The furrow of agitation across the bridge of Gordy's nose revealed his adolescence.

"Age," Raja explained. "Heredity."

"Bah," Aimee dismissed both ranks. "Technicalities."

"Exactly," Gordy agreed. Dispirited, he glanced down at the *star laser* in his hand. "Okay, so neither of us are qualified to be Warriors, but the ones that *are* qualified aren't doing their jobs."

"What do you mean?" Aimee came alert.

"I mean that they aren't out there trying to find Zak," he condemned. "Zak was our hero. Without him, the HORUS is just—vulnerable."

Cursed tears. They were undermining her again. Aimee cleared her throat. "So it's you and me? *We* are Zak's rescue team?"

Raja tipped her head back and made a silent plea to the lofted ceiling. "Don't be so critical of our Warriors." Though she was defending them, her tone lacked conviction. "They *tried*. And, in the end, they had to obey Vodu's orders. Do you really think Vodu would not have exhausted every effort to retrieve Zak?"

"No." Gordy evaded her eyes.

"No," Aimee echoed.

"Good." Raja nodded. "If you choose to

train for this mission, you are doing so without Vodu's consent. You are doing this irrespective of the Warriors that will be returning to Ziratak. You do this out of—"

Love.

"Respect and frustration," Raja continued. "You do this at your own risk, acknowledging that you will never reach the caliber of our highly skilled Warriors."

In Gordy's expression Aimee saw her own belligerence reflected. Before either could protest, Raja hastened on.

"You are sworn to secrecy to never share the names of those who have assisted you."

Compelled to raise her hand and pledge her allegiance, Aimee instead asked, "Raja, are you going to get in trouble for this?"

"Not if you never saw me here." Raja winked. Sobering, she added, "Listen to me." Her eyes narrowed. "I mean *really* listen to me. Gordy, you are too young. And Aimee, as much as you think you can conquer anything, you are simply not strong enough for a hand-to—umm, if you had to engage in a personal battle."

"But I took on those tree creatures on Bordran."

"No." Raja was adamant. "You did not. You used cunning perhaps, but you did not *take them on*." She eased up slightly. "As biased as they may sound, there is a reason the Warriors are such an elite crew. Only the strongest and most-skilled will survive. What good does it do to send in a fleet of Warriors and have half of them die from frailty and ineptitude?"

Gordy snorted and Raja scowled. "Do you have something to say, Gordeelum?"

He tapped the tip of his boot on the marble floor and then stood erect, looking her in the eye. "Yes." He squared his shoulders. "I am not frail. My youth is an asset. I have more stamina than some of the elder Warriors."

"And if a Koron was standing ten feet in front of you, would you be as accurate with the *star laser* as you were just now?"

Opening his mouth to retort, Raja didn't allow him the opportunity. "No, because you would already be dead if a Koron was standing ten feet in front of you. Or blind."

Trumped, the young man remained mute.

"And you," Raja rounded on Aimee. "If you found Zak, and he was injured...would your judgment be clouded?" Disallowing a response, she inserted, "Of course it would. But a Warrior's judgment cannot be."

Pain curled up into a fist behind Aimee's ribcage. It must have been evident on her face because Raja's expression softened. "I am being harsh. But I pack the punch of a *sumpum* compared to the man you are about to meet. You want to train to be Warriors? Then you shelve your emotions. Anger. Depression. They are all weaknesses. I am only trying to prepare you, or offer you a chance to reconsider."

Aimee felt Gordy's eyes on her. They were two misfits resolved to their fates.

JOH's metal toes clanged against the floor. "He is coming." The black crystal orbs shifted towards the doorway.

Who?

Aimee held her breath in anticipation.

CHAPTER FOUR

A whisper like the breeze over autumn leaves alerted that a portal had opened. Heavy footsteps fell as a formidable figure emerged from the shadows. A man. Tall. Middle-aged—although age was hard to estimate with the clean-shaven head and mirrored glasses that wrapped completely about his blushed skull. With the lack of hair, Aimee could discern muscles flex across his cranium. The man's build was athletic inside his dark blue uniform made of the same fabric as her pants. A squared, clean-shaven jaw wrapped around a mouth set in a grim line.

He stepped up alongside Raja and asked in a hoarse tone, "Did he hit the JOH?"

"No." Raja folded her hands across her abdomen. "But he was very close."

A snort sounded from the man's flat nose. "You lie as bad as he shoots."

Aimee could not see the eyes behind the

reflective shield, but she could tell that she was the subject of his next question.

"And the other one?"

"Aimee," Raja offered. "She has yet to try."

"She," he muttered and shook his head. "What will you bring me next, a *swallor* droid?"

Clang. Clang. Clang. "*Swallor* droids are only good for menial maintenance duties," JOH stated with obvious disdain. "Namely, latrine services."

Swallor droids were janitors, Aimee concluded, distracted by the stark man. He extended his hand towards Gordy and curled his fingers in demand. Obligingly, Gordy surrendered the *star laser*.

In an unexpected move, the bald man swung his arm and blasted the ray in JOH's direction, suspending the computer by the tips of its metal toes for a second before releasing the trigger.

JOH's black eyes bulged and then righted themselves. "Was that necessary?" he asked in a droll voice. "Could you not locate a *swallor* droid for your games?"

"It's more fun to aggravate you." The man nearly smirked.

"Aimee, this is Corluss."

Aimee held out her hand, startled when

Corluss held out his...about six inches in the wrong direction. There was an awkward pause in which she maneuvered to clasp his firm shake.

"Corluss was blinded by a fleet of Koron solar rays," Raja explained.

Beside her, Gordy frowned and stated the obvious. "And *he* is going to train us?"

Raja sighed. "Corluss, this is Gordeelum."

Corluss thrust his hand out in Gordy's general vicinity. The young man glanced at Aimee and then Raja, and finally down at the sinewy hand, which he shook with indecision.

"Who hit the JOH?" Corluss challenged.

"Who hit the JOH?" JOH mimicked, his crystal lips flapping in exasperation.

He was ignored.

Gordy's cheeks began to burn. "I was distracted. I heard the door opening."

"What about the last eight tries—"

"Quiet!" Gordy cut JOH off.

"Corluss was a famous Warrior who protected us during the Koron invasion." Raja explained to Aimee. "The Koron invasion was a concentrated attack of several hundred of their fleet. It took all the armada we had to fight them off. We lost many men in that coup, but thanks to Corluss and other brave Warriors like him, so did the Korons. And Korons do not reproduce easily."

"Thank you for the accolades, Raja," Corluss said, "but these two have no idea what the Koron invasion was like, and they just think I'm an old, blind man."

Gordy nodded, knowing full well the man could not see the gesture.

"I feel air rhythms, Gordeelum. I can feel the pattern that indicates you are shaking your head in agreement."

Gordy's jaw dropped.

"One thing I have learned is that sight breeds apathy." Corluss reached for the silver band around his eyes and hoisted it off his head.

Aimee gasped.

Corluss had irises, but they were pallid, blending with the whites of his eyes. The pupils, if there were any, were mere black specks.

"Put these on," he instructed Gordy.

Hesitant, Gordy held the reflective ring up to the light.

"Do it, Gordeelum," Corluss ordered.

Hauling the silver ring over his head, Gordy rested it atop his ears as it was slightly loose. "What good is this thing...I can't see through it."

"Oh, I hadn't noticed that." Corluss deadpanned.

Gordy tilted his head back, no doubt trying to peek through the loose gap at the bottom of the frame.

"Keep your head straight. You don't need to see."

Corluss stepped forward, his white eyes were like cue balls, shifting but not focusing. He grabbed Gordy's hand and pressed the *star laser* into his palm.

"Shoot the JOH."

"What?" Gordy cried. "I don't even know where he is now."

"Why is that?" Corluss crossed his arms, which transformed his shoulders into beefy mountains. "Is that because you were not paying attention to him? His location was not important enough to you, so you lost track?"

JOH blinked, but remained still beside Aimee. She considered taking a judicious step away from him, but the gun was a powerless replica. Neither of them was in any danger. Right?

For as tall as Gordy was, Corluss dwarfed him. Taking Gordy by the arm, Corluss pivoted him into position and then raised the point of the *star laser* directly at JOH. JOH wobbled slightly but held his ground in affront.

"This is impossible," Gordy challenged.

"How can *you* find the JOH if you are blind?"

"Stop talking and listen."

"To what? Unless JOH is speaking or moving...you can't hear him."

Aimee glanced at JOH and his black eyes flicked in her direction. She swore she detected a grin on the ambiguous mouth.

"Stop talking." Corluss tilted Gordy's head in the proper trajectory. "Feel the vibration."

"What vibra—"

"Silence!" The top of Corluss's head turned red. Composing himself, he continued subdued. "JOH emits a very low frequency. Extremely low. You may not notice it unless you were resting your ear on top of him, or perhaps setting your palm flat against his bottom."

JOH frowned and his eyes slid up behind his frame for a second before falling back into place. The dark crystals that formed his lips moved to speak, but he clamped them into a straight line as if he was holding his breath.

"I can't hear it," Gordy whispered.

There was no outburst from Corluss this time. He lowered Gordy's arm and spoke in a low tone. "There is no miracle here. Sometimes you simply have to take a—guess."

He clamped his hand over Gordy's and pressed the release on the laser. A charge volleyed through the air. It was like watching a still photo of a jet stream.

Aimee felt a breeze brush her forearm. Beside her, JOH swung his flat face to the right.

"It went right between us," she marveled aloud.

Whipping the silver band from his eyes, Gordy gaped at the path between them. "Really?"

"I felt it. Thank God it was a fake *star laser* or you would have burned my arm off."

"You always say that, Aimee," JOH injected. "You always say, *Thank God,* but you never tell me which of the 9023 gods that I am supposed to thank."

Aimee hesitated seeing that Corluss was studying her with his translucent gaze. It gave her chills, but there seemed nothing malevolent about this man. Yes, he was overbearing, and indeed quite athletic, but she prided herself on being able to detect menace in people. In this man she found none.

"Aimee."

The sharp call nearly made her snap a salute. "Yes?"

"Why do you want to be a Warrior?"

Bravado fled on the wings of that simple question.

Why?

"Zak." It was a strangled cry.

She turned away, refusing to disclose her emotions to a blind man who saw all.

"Ahh, Zak." His voice gentled. "A great Warrior. His skills stemmed from a strong mental discipline. He had patience and cunning, as well the physical power to back them up. I was honored to be a part of his training."

"You trained Zak?" She glanced back.

"He sought me out. I am not an approved tutor as you can imagine, but Zak wanted more than his daily lessons. When most Warriors would be exhausted after a full drill, Zak wanted to keep going. Since they would not accommodate him, he came to me." Corluss' arm swept wide. "And in this very chamber we spent hours developing his agility and prowess."

It was easy to imagine Zak in here now. His onyx suit melding with the black void of space beyond the glass. A dominant figure with dark hair and golden eyes that clashed with the inhabitants of the HORUS.

Longing for him, Aimee conjured up memories. Memories of his pensive face as he paced across the marble. He would turn and spot her, and his grin would elicit a small dimple.

"What if I asked you to stay?" his voice was rough. "What if I did something totally

selfish and asked you to stay?"

Tears burned behind her eyes at the recollection.

"I volunteered for the mission to Ziratak," Corluss cut into her thoughts.

"You're blind."

Perhaps it was tactless to point that out, but she was in pain.

A quick adjustment of his spine revealed her comment had scored.

"I could have been a passenger," he defended. "I could have helped."

Aimee's head cocked to the side as she considered this brawny, bald, middle-aged man with the silver halo around his head.

"Look," she cleared her throat. "Gordy and I want to be on the mission to Ziratak. We will do whatever we have to." A quick glimpse at the young man beside her produced an agreeing nod. "And I think," she continued, directing her words to the blind man, "you are just the man to make it happen."

Brooding as Corluss was, she swore his lips quirked.

"I agree." Gordy closed the gap and offered an enthusiastic smile.

"Well, then–" Corluss' lip hiked up at the corner.

"–Ziratak, here we come," Gordy finished for him, and thrust his hand out flat in the air.

Hesitating just a second, Aimee laid her palm atop it. With a tip of her head, she invited Raja to participate. Studying the joint hands, Raja finally stepped up and placed hers on top of Aimee's.

Clang. Clang. JOH ambled up, his black eyes big inside his blue face. "I'm in," he announced.

All eyes turned to Corluss whose chiseled profile stared straight ahead.

In a hoarse tone he echoed, "Ziratak, here we come."

With a swift thrust, he extended his fist about three inches over theirs. After a second's hesitation, he uncurled that fist and dropped his hand to clamp down over theirs.

"Zak."

Cool air dusted across his skin. He dared not open his eyes. This was just another phantom here to tempt him. Sometimes it was family. Often he saw his father, a young, confident, and patient man. Curse the Korons to have deprived him of this man's guidance through life.

But most of the time it was *her.*

She beguiled him with her dark glossy hair and eyes the color of the horizon. All that had ever kept him going was the hope that they would be together again. Dazed or not, he was lucid enough to realize that the window to her solar system had come and gone. Did she hate him? Did she think he had not returned for her?

No. He did not want to open his eyes.

"Zak. You piece of *Zull* dung, I know you're awake. Open your eyes."

His eyes were prone to deceiving him, but his ears were sharp...and that wasn't Aimee.

"They fail me, so I would prefer to keep them closed."

There. That should dissuade the heavy-breathing ogre by his side.

"You were attacked by a band of eight Korons and survived. Are you really going to lie there and complain about your eyes?"

"I was not complaining. I was stating a fact," Zak offered mildly.

"Fine. Wallow in your misery. I'm sure you don't care what those blasted piles of sand and rock are up to now."

Zak arched his brow but kept his eyes shut. "What?"

Silence.

"Dammit, what?" he repeated.

Silence.

In a lurch, Zak swung his legs off the stone pedestal and glared at the mangy man before him.

"What, Zuttah? I am up. My eyes are open. I am looking at your ugly face and your toothless mouth, which is *not* telling me what the Korons are doing."

Zuttah reached up to his bearded chin and rubbed muddy fingers over his lips. "I have teeth." He grinned and flashed a mouthful of molars that had been ground down to half their size by his nasty habit of gnawing on rocks when he was nervous.

It took a moment for Zak to focus on his burly friend. After a few blinks for confirmation, he was able to discern the man in tattered *Zull* furs resting his rump against a nearby boulder. Wild hair framed a leathered face with cheeks so large they reduced the yellow eyes to mere slits.

Sun poured through the cave entrance and Zak winced at the assault.

"They still hurt?" Zuttah's mirth ebbed.

"Yeah. How long was I out? When is nightfall?" He nodded to himself. "The night will make it better."

"You say that every night," Zuttah pointed out, bending over to retrieve a round pebble and pop it into his mouth. His face scrunched up with effort as he started to grind.

"That is disgusting." Zak shook his head and used the cave wall for leverage as he rose on shaky legs.

"There's water in the jar." Zuttah tipped his nose back into the shadows.

Ah, the blissful relief of the dark. Zak delved into it, asking over his shoulder, "Now will you fill me in?"

"On what?" Zuttah muttered, "Oh yes, those hulking piles of rubble."

"Or, as you might call them, *dessert*."

"I do not *eat* rocks, Zak. I chew them. There is a big difference." Pouting, Zuttah's grin quickly emerged. It disappeared just as fast. "They seized ten more rebels at daybreak."

Blood throbbed in Zak's temples. He pressed his fingertips against them.

"Are they still alive?" There was a threat in his voice.

Undaunted by the tone, Zuttah spit out his rock and declared, "Last I knew, yes. But it's just a matter of time."

"*Gayat*," Zak cursed.

"Anyone out in the desert trying to make it to the mountains for safety can't get past the Korons."

"I did."

"And you were beaten and blinded, and you see ghosts," Zuttah pointed out.

Ghosts. "I am not blind. My eyes just hurt."

Zuttah snorted. "Whatever the case, soon the Korons will control the entire desert and have us contained here in the mountains. And then what?"

Ziratak was primarily a desert planet—arid and sandy. In the far north, however, lie a small mountain range that grew to high elevations with snow-capped peaks. Two nearby suns toyed with those snow-covered vistas, melting them at will. Through fissures and streams, this condensation spilled out into the desert in a single depression that became the Zargoll River. Though the banks of the Zargoll remained barren, they had once been inhabited and nurtured through an in intricate irrigation system.

Zak and his family lived along the Zargoll. When the Korons came, their home was destroyed along with the rest of the community. The irrigation system was blasted away and the banks of the Zargoll were now occupied by Korons, waiting for desert-trapped rebels to seek the sustenance of water.

A large contingent of rebels lived safely in

the mountains, which the Korons avoided due to the rain. But to reach that safe haven, any rebels left lingering in the desert were inevitably drawn to the river where the Korons lie in wait.

"We need to gather all the men we can," Zak stated. "There are still citizens stranded in the desert to rescue."

"Zak." Zuttah turned serious. "You need to stay here and rest."

"I don't need rest."

Admittedly, Zak held a fatalistic view. Without the promise of seeing Aimee again–with his sight failing–with his mind failing–there was little concern for self-preservation. His only motivation now was to save his race.

Death was a beast with no teeth.

He did not fear death.

CHAPTER FIVE

Damn, the *star laser* was heavy.

It was no larger than a hair brush, but she might as well be clutching a steel brick. Leveling her hand with the target on the far wall, Aimee felt the tension in her forearm. She adjusted the boomerang-shaped weapon to align the tip with the symbol illustrated there.

Peace.

That was the supposed translation for the gold-embossed mushroom carved five feet above the floor.

Peace.

She was a big fan of irony.

Alone in this training chamber, she was distracted by her reflection in the window. The view beyond was that of a system of planets bound so tightly together that they looked like someone had just broken a rack of pool balls. In that melee of colors she saw her silhouette. Long.

Lean. Poised for the attack of an enemy that was not there. Instead, she was shooting at a symbol that translated to *peace*.

Without Zak, her peace had been shattered.

Aimee focused and caressed the underside of the crescent. Gone was the need to squint. That had been a physical crutch for an awkward teenager. Aimee, the woman, had clear vision. She tugged with her pointer finger and the faux charge projected across the twenty-foot span, illuminating a baseball-sized circle several inches away from the mushroom.

Sighing, she lowered her arm.

A handclap from behind jerked her into a full pivot. It was a vaulted chamber capable of producing thunderous echoes, but she swore the sound emanated from directly behind her.

Having snuck in here for a private session, there had been no need to tamper with the lighting. Instead, she relied on the ambient glow of the HORUS through the bank of glass. Now she wished she had stopped to turn on an illumination bar or two. The limited light betrayed her, leaving the recesses of the training chamber cloaked in shadows.

Aimee stood still. She refused to call out. The weapon in her hand mocked her. It was incapable of damaging anything, and even if it were real, she had just demonstrated how bad her aim was to whoever lurked in the dark.

A footfall sounded. *To her left? To her right?*

It repeated, and she instinctively swerved the star laser towards the left...towards the deepest shadows.

Who's there?

She refused to voice that plea. Although, if this ended up being Gordy playing games she was going to line him up three inches to the side of the mushroom.

"You need to work on your aim, Aim*ee*."

Her blood ran cold. The *star laser* trembled in her quaking hand.

"Your enemy could be standing right in front of you, and you would not even be able to shoot him."

The first thing she saw was the blue glow of the ship against pale blond hair. A suit of silver emerged from the shadows as the figure approached on a muffled tread.

"That target was almost thirty feet away," she argued softly. "You are only ten feet away, Salvan."

Light from the entryway landed on the aquiline nose and the sinister grin.

"A bold statement from a woman with an impotent laser."

Quivers of fear wormed down her legs. Could he see her shake?

"They let you out, I gather?" She tried to sound calm. "On good behavior, was it?"

"My value is in the lab, not a detention chamber. They came to their senses."

It had been five years, but the voice had not changed. A nasal whistle caused a slight lilt to the end of some words. And, the sharp arrogance still rang true.

Aimee's eyes flicked towards the doorway. It was the only way in, and the only way out— and Salvan stood in her path.

He took another step forward and cocked his head to the side. Ashen hair hugged hollowed cheeks, the celestial light rendering him as a skeleton with little flesh. It was her nerves that produced the drama, though. Another glimpse and he looked remarkably the same as he did when he stood above her with a luminous rod ready to dissect her in the name of science.

"What do you want, Salvan? My body no longer holds any appeal to you."

Tepid blue eyes dipped down her chest. She could see the pale eyelashes as his gaze traveled lower. When his gaze finally returned to hers she shivered at the glacier lurking there.

"I wouldn't say that," he smirked.

To her horror, he took another few steps until he stood directly before her. She would not flinch. She would not flee. Her chin hefted, depriving him the satisfaction of her fear.

Up close, she could see his porcelain skin, nearly translucent.

Salvan's lips were pursed in consideration and his eyes roved over her in slow motion as she felt the revulsion build up deep in her throat.

"You have become quite an attractive woman, Aimee." Reaching up, he traced the backs of his fingers against her hair. When she jerked away from his touch, it amused him.

The blatant trek of that cold scrutiny down her throat and across the swell of her breasts gave her the impulse to gag.

"I don't want to slice into you Aimee," he whispered. "We have conquered our plague."

No thanks to you.

"I want to touch you, though. You have always fascinated me."

I do not fear this man.

"Salvan, I am done here. I suggest you step aside."

"And if I don't? Are you going to call your Warrior?" Salvan leaned in close as if to share a confidence. "Oh wait—he's dead."

Aimee's finger tugged reflexively on the star laser and the innocuous beam blazed into the floor beside her foot.

"Tsk. Tsk." Salvan reached for her hand, sliding cold, thin fingers around it. "You better let me take that before you hurt yourself."

Yanking her hand from his, she nudged forward and crowded Salvan. "Step back," she warned. "Now."

Slate eyes flicked down to her lips and back up. He smiled. It was the Devil's smile.

"It was a pleasure seeing you again, Aimee." He took a step back. "I'm sure we'll run into each other real soon. With Zak gone, you might consider looking elsewhere for ummm—" his lips pursed in consideration, "—companionship. There is only so much a JOH can handle."

Revulsion made bile rise in her throat.

"Back off." She crowded him again, their eyes locked in a duel.

A familiar flutter of fall leaves marked the opening of the training chamber.

Heavy footfalls sounded, and the flash of a mirror collided with the panorama of stars.

"Is there a problem here?" Corluss asked in a husky tone.

Salvan strode up to him and waved his hand before the silver band around Corluss's head. "What would you know? You are blind and you are old. Do you think you're keeping it a secret that you're training these rejects? Do you think people care?" Salvan's voice pitched. "They pity you. They believe you and your students are pathetic." Stepping aside, he tossed Aimee a cold smile. "So no need to be so secretive. None of you will ever set foot in a *terra angel.*"

On a screech of boot against marble, Salvan turned and marched towards the door. Only after the confirming click that it had closed did Aimee release the adrenaline. It flooded out so fast and so hard she staggered a step, seeking something to hold onto, but there was nothing. Only Corluss, and he looked as congenial as a riled porcupine.

She bent over, planting her hands on her knees as she gulped in a deep breath.

"That's it. One more."

Aimee shot an incredulous glance up at the gleaming scalp.

"One more what?"

"Deep breath. You lost a lot of tension with that last one."

How the hell do you know?

"When you released your breath it was

very ragged, but it smoothed out towards the end," he answered her unvoiced question. "One more and you should reduce some of your blood pressure."

"You're a doctor too?"

She wasn't in the mood for this magician's parlor tricks. The blood he spoke of pounded inside her head, and the beat kept repeating, *he's dead, he's dead*.

"I wouldn't have let him hurt you, but you were doing fine on your own."

"What the hell are you talking about?" She rounded on him.

"I entered the chamber from an alternate access a few minutes ago. I moved to the front door and waited to make my presence known."

Aimee searched the murky walls, but she wasn't in the mood to relax and try to read them. "What alternate entrance? I thought there was only one way in and one way out."

"You thought wrong." He smiled.

She realized it was the first full-fledged smile she had ever seen on Corluss. Too bad she didn't share in his mirth.

"You were spying on me?" she accused.

"No. I had come to see how you were making out with the *star laser* when I realized that scientist was in here. It didn't take a sighted man to pick up the vibes of hostility." Corluss crossed his arms, which yanked his suit tight across his biceps. "I must admit, I wanted to see how you handled yourself."

"Son of a—"

"Excuse me?" He signaled towards the far wall. "Shoot that *vora* symbol, Aimee."

"What?" Anger impaired her hearing.

"Shoot it. Now."

With her feet still planted firmly in the opposite direction, Aimee swung her shoulder back, hefted the *star laser,* and fired at the mushroom. The baseball-sized orb of light fell dead-center of the emblem.

Corluss looked pleased. "Well done."

Dumbfounded, she gazed at the *star laser* and then the tarnished ring inside the mushroom. "I'll be damned," she whispered.

"I would have stopped him." Corluss stared straight ahead. "If he had tried anything more than verbal intimidation, I would have stopped him."

The heavy weapon dropped to her thigh. "You wouldn't have had to."

They shared an unspoken understanding, and then Corluss added, "You will make a good Warrior, Aimee."

"He tried to kill me once." That pulsing

blue wand had come so close to slicing her abdomen.

Corluss let his arms fall. "Yes. I am aware of the history."

"Why did they release him?"

"It just happened recently. His time was up and he was freed from the detention satellite–but with no credentials and no access to the labs. They say he wanders the corridors, talking to himself." Corluss cleared his throat. "It's just a matter of time before he enters the therapy wing."

That didn't pacify her, but a more pressing thought was on her mind. "He said that none of us will ever set foot in a *terra angel*. I realize his words stem from malice, but—"

"I'm not going to lie. It isn't going to be easy to get onto one. We are not far from Ziratak now and the Warriors have met to select their team. There are only a few who have volunteered for the mission."

Her free hand curled into a fist. "How quickly they forget him."

"In their defense, Aimee, there is a good chance that this is a one-way mission."

"Bah." She whirled away and stalked towards the glass wall, searching the conflux of planets for inhabitable signs...clouds...water.

There were none. "You can all keep your negativity. I won't have any of it. I will believe, Corluss. I will believe that I am going to find Zak and bring him back here."

"What if he doesn't want to come back?"

"Five years. Nothing will keep me away. But if you are not in those woods, I will understand. I will understand that you have a new life."

Zak's last declaration haunted her. Had he found a new life? Was that why he did not come back?

"Then I need to hear that from his lips." She turned around and strode up to the blind man. "Find me a *terra angel*—and teach me how to fly it."

To see herself in his reflective lens was disconcerting. Shadows lingered within her normally vibrant eyes. Her cheeks were flushed with anger, and the sparkly white shirt clung to a chest still heaving with anxiety.

Looking into that mirror, it felt as if Corluss was staring back at her—yet, she was painfully aware that the eyes behind this barrier were lifeless.

"Your co-warrior is already ahead of you," his deep tone rumbled.

In the reflection her dark eyebrows

knotted into a frown. "What are you talking about?"

Up close, Aimee realized that Corluss's face wasn't so much old as it was weathered. A beard of tiny white scars circled his jaw as if a pane of glass had exploded in his face, and the bald cranium did not seem a byproduct of age, as it too possessed a cap of precise scars. What could have blinded this man, scarred his face, and nearly destroyed his head?

The Koron's solar ray.

And she was about to put herself in the path of one.

"What are you talking about?" she repeated.

"Gordeelum," Corluss explained. "He has a ship he wants to pilot."

Something about the twist of the man's lips told Aimee that he was suppressing vital information.

"Can you take me to this ship?"

"Of course." Corluss bowed and stepped back.

"How," she challenged. "How do you find your way around if you are blind? Are you even really blind, or is this all a big hoax?"

She regretted the question the second it was out, but she was in pain—emotionally wounded. In that state, little consideration went into her words.

For a moment, all Aimee heard was the sprinkling of pebble-sized meteorites tapping against the glass wall. Celestial snowfall. Then she heard the fabric of Corluss' shirt as he lifted his arm and hefted off his eye shield. Crowding her– stark, lifeless eyes glared at her shoulder. She was grateful for that trajectory because if they had hit their mark, she feared she would have lost her soul in the empty orbs.

Yes, she regretted her question. There was no denying that these eyes were dead. No matter a person's eye color–if you delve into their irises, you will find a thousand distinct specks blending to form the overall hue. Each grain represents a unique thumbprint—a trace of heritage. One's eyes might be blue, but that single brown spot came from a grandmother, or that short sliver of green came from great-grandparents, or the mottled yellow dots wormed their way in from relatives never heard of. No matter what—the iris was a diverse canvas filled with the paint of a thousand generations.

But not in this man. In this man she saw no past. She saw no future. It was a stark white slate. Curse the Korons for taking that beauty away.

"This is no hoax, Aimee." He hauled the silver band back over his eyes, severing that disturbing view. "If you lost an arm, would you not adapt and use your other? If you lost your ears would you not read the breaths across other's lips?"

The band of muscles atop his thin eyebrows relaxed. "We adapt Aimee. It's what we do."

"If I could not fly a *terra angel*," she murmured, "would I not adapt and find another way to get to Ziratak?"

When the smile tugged at the corners of Corluss' lips, Aimee saw the reflection of her own in his mirrored shield.

"Exactly," he nodded. "You have done good here today. Let's go see what your compromise is."

To his credit, Corluss was very adept in the halls. If you passed by him you would never know he was visually impaired—well, except for the bright silver halo across the bridge of his nose like an angel on steroids.

Inside the linear transport she posed a challenge. "How do you know when to stop?"

"You don't have to wait until your

destination symbol scrolls by. You can key your destination in when you board the transport."

Huh? Five years aboard this ship, and all that time she had slammed her hand down on the rapidly scrolling images to catch the one she wanted to disembark at.

"Show me how." Great. She was asking a blind man. What did that say about her skills?

He reached up to the strip of flashing symbols and ran his fingertips along the right-hand rim of the frame. Sliding those fingers in about an inch, he traced a diagonal line. It looked like a backslash. When he pressed on it another horizontal bar appeared with static symbols. Sliding his fingertips down this bar he scanned until he found the image he was looking for and depressed it. The linear transport began to move and was soon sliding alongside the HORUS on its way to—she identified the symbol—the flight deck.

"Sit back and enjoy the ride."

That would be nice, but there were no chairs inside the transport. Instead, Aimee placed her hands on the bar in front of the glass panel and stared out into the black void. The abrupt halt of the transport sent her stumbling sideways. *Dammit.* For all the sophistication of this vessel, couldn't someone have engineered better brakes?

"Follow me, Aimee."

Follow the blind man.

To her left was the entrance to the launch bay. It was marked with murals of past missions. It was also identified by the clamor of power modules and the chorus of orders volleyed in a foreign dialect. At this distance it was just a medley of undertones, but Aimee was anxious to be a part of that activity. For her, the launch bay was a mecca for engineers with its sleek-designed space crafts—the kind not yet conceived on Earth. It was a technology to make her mouth water—an adrenalin rush.

Here, everyone's role was equally important. Each took part in something so epic with the launch of these exquisite vessels. And these men, these talented mechanics, engineers, Warriors…these men had all banded together to save her and Zak when they crash-landed on this very flight deck. Their skills humbled her and she wanted to be out there with them, soaking up their knowledge.

"This way."

Doing a double-take, Aimee was confused when Corluss started off in the opposite direction.

So much for following a blind man.

"Corluss, the launch bay is this way." *How*

could he not hear it?

He didn't bother to turn his head. "We're not going there."

Trailing after him on sluggish steps, she saw a group of three men dressed in sleek silver bodysuits approach from the opposite direction. They were engaged in conversation when one noticed Corluss and Aimee. He nodded at Corluss and then chuckled when the gesture wasn't reciprocated.

"Hanging out with a different crowd, Corluss?" The man eyed Aimee.

Corluss halted. His head inclined and slowly swerved towards the voice. "She's much prettier than any of you."

The group snickered and continued towards the launch bay. Perhaps they represented the utmost in strength and agility. But they weren't Zak.

"Come on," Corluss encouraged.

Aimee lengthened her stride so that she could stand abreast of him.

"They disrespect you? Why? Aren't you a hero?"

The fleshy ridge behind Corluss's ear pumped in spasm. "Warriors are heroes. I am no longer a Warrior. This generation of Warriors does not respect me. They do not know me."

Undeterred, Aimee persisted. "What happened? What happened the day you were injured?"

He laughed. "Injured."

"Blinded, then."

A JOH floated by and called out, "Hello Aimee," as it continued down the corridor.

Distracted, she turned to discover that Corluss was gone. Where the hell did he go? She paused and inhaled deeply, relaxing and taking a second visual sweep of the walls of the long corridor. There, to her left was the hazy blue outline of a portal, and beyond it, the vague silhouette of a man. She reached out and swiped her hand to draw the panel open and immediately located Corluss on the other side.

"Keep up, Aimee. We have deadlines now. Ziratak is approaching."

Aimee hurried inside, barely giving the small alley a second glance in her haste to pursue the man that passed through the narrow channel at a brisk pace.

He stopped so abruptly that she collided with him and mumbled an apology. The momentum was enough to push him off his mark. He reached for the wall and ran his hand down it, and then to the right.

"Here." Aimee reached around him and

swiped the handle, listening to the rustle of the panel as it evaporated to form an open doorway.

"Thanks," he muttered. "Get in."

Aimee followed him into the chamber and almost cried out when she felt motion beneath her feet. The tumble of her stomach indicated they were moving…this time in a vertical ascent.

"Wh-where are we?"

"We're behind the launch bay."

"Where are we going?"

"Up."

Settling into the motion, she responded, "I can tell that, but up to where?"

Slouched in the corner of the tight compartment, he ignored her question and instead broached another topic. "So you want to know about the Koron battle?"

In the curved perspective of his glasses she looked like a dwarf. A confused dwarf.

Crossing her arms, she said, "I gather this means our journey *up* will take a while?"

"It takes two of your seconds for a solar ray to blind a man and destroy his life. We have time."

The bitterness was a show, she determined. This man harbored great sorrow.

"Where did this happen?"

"Out there." He tipped his head.

In this tight chamber and under this harsh lighting, Aimee could peruse the starburst of scars across his face.

"Korons carry solar rays," he recited. "But large-scale models are mounted to the face of their war crafts. Our *terra angels* possess shields to deflect the retina-searing rays. However, in this case, their combat lasers had already battered my windshield. As strong as our screens are, a tiny crack manifested. I was busy readying the oxygen helmet. When the next blast came, it completely shattered the windshield. The explosion ripped through the cabin and destroyed my helmet—and with my face exposed—there was nothing to stop the assault of thousands of shards of *alorium* from raining down on me."

Even as he spoke, she noticed his hand reach up to rub his blemished chin. He continued in a subdued voice. "All it took was that split-second. The pain was so intense, I was shocked into opening my eyes—and that is when the solar ray struck. To this day I don't know if it was the agony, the trauma, or the lack of oxygen that knocked me out. The *terra angels* have sensors to know when the pilot is incapacitated. They are programmed to return to the HORUS in such a state. I guess I made it back in enough time for them to revive me and mend some of the wounds to my face. But to this day, no one has ever been able to correct the damage inflicted by a solar ray."

Aimee jumped when the compartment fell still.

"We're here." Corluss stepped up to the door. Her hand on his arm halted him.

"What happened next?"

He froze and stared straight ahead. A muscle jerked above his temple.

"There is nothing more to add. I was blind, and I would never fly again."

The severity of his tale contradicted that simple assessment.

When the door slipped open Aimee did not follow him. Sensing this with a quirk of his head, he listened and waited.

"Is there a problem?" he asked.

"I am trusting you to teach me how to survive as a Warrior." She watched as his shoulders bunched—his hackles raised. "I don't offer up trust easily. I need to know I am being trained by someone that deserves my confidence."

In a slow pivot, he reached for the doorframe with both his hands. The silver band tilted in her direction. "I was labeled a coward." His lips thinned. "Is that what you want to hear?"

"For heaven's sake, why?" She stood ramrod straight in the back corner of the elevator.

Corluss reached up and massaged the skin just above the lenses.

"I really don't want to talk about it anymore, but you are right. You need to be certain you want to pursue your training with me based on the facts." A deep breath seemed to settle him. "The TA, the *terra angel* behind me was exposed when my craft retreated to the HORUS. The Korons destroyed it."

"How—"

"A Warrior knows the second they are blinded by a solar ray that they are no longer an asset. They are useless for the future. It is never stated, but implied that you should use whatever power you have left to go out with dignity. They felt that I should have overthrown the autopilot and used my *terra angel* as a weapon and crashed into the Koron craft."

"And kill yourself?" Aimee asked, aghast. "My God, you people are not as advanced as I had hoped. You have ridiculously outdated philosophies."

Corluss's neck stiffened. He collected himself and continued. "Perhaps that is true, but a good Warrior, a good man died—" clearing the hoarseness from his voice, he added, "and I did not do everything in my power to save him."

"Bah." *Martyrs. Not Warriors.*

Aimee stepped up to the door, and waited until he got out of her way. Arching his brow, he backed up.

"What is your verdict then, Aimee?"

He was too wide for her to go around him, so instead she glared up into the reflective lenses, seeing the blush of anger flaming across her cheeks.

"I want a man who is not going to teach me to kill myself at the first sign of trouble." She eased up. "No disrespect to your disability, but you do not appear impaired to me in any way. Inconvenienced, perhaps. But, from what I can gauge, you are dependable and still formidable, and most importantly—you are intelligent. And your life was worth preserving. So yes, I would very much like to have you teach me how to be a Warrior."

When there was no response, she gently nudged him aside with her shoulder and added, "But please leave out all the martyr lessons."

"Aimee." The haunting tone stopped her.

"If you had to sacrifice your life to save Zak's—would you do it?"

The blood drained from her face. She

rounded on him. "That is *not* a fair comparison."

"One life is more valuable than another?"

Anger lost its zeal. She searched that silver band that secreted the dead eyes. "You are right."

She would sacrifice everything to be with Zak.

"Teach me to be a Warrior, Corluss." In a final act of submission, she added, "Please."

"I still haven't figured out where we are exactly." Aimee scanned the opalescent walls, frustrated by the vague delineation behind them.

For the most part, everything appeared abandoned. Consoles sat idle with no dancing lights to indicate activity. Spherical chairs remained empty. The ambiance spoke of a forgotten era. A time when technology and architecture were not the forerunning motivators.

"This was the original flight command center of the HORUS," Corluss explained. These chambers used to host our operational managers and our Watchers when they weren't on duty."

On second glance, she could see signs of previous inhabitants. Small, suspended cots for off-duty personnel. Dormant diaphanous panels, relics compared to the three-dimensional monitors located on the main flight deck.

Aimee peered back down the corridor. "There aren't even any JOHs back here."

"No. Maybe one will swing by from time to time out of boredom, but there is nothing—or no one back here anymore."

"Except us."

"Except us," Corluss echoed. "And two more."

"Two more?"

Corluss reached the end of the corridor where there loomed a large entryway. In the distance she could hear the persistent bang of a...*hammer*? No, surely not.

With his hand out, Corluss sought to swing open the door, but missed his mark by inches. On his second attempt, Aimee discreetly reached beside him and flicked the panel open.

"I know you did that," he uttered. "I'm blind, but not clueless."

Aimee grinned. "And that is why I trust you."

Entering into a cylindrical tunnel made of an aluminum alloy, Aimee felt like she was traveling through a sewer system. Her heels thudded with a tinny echo as they progressed towards the light several feet ahead. Corluss' shoulder eclipsed her view, but when they reached the end of the tunnel she was able to step up alongside of him.

"Whoa," she gaped. "Are you serious?"

"Serious about what?"

Shaking her head, she mumbled, "It's just like talking to JOH."

Her words echoed back at her and Corluss turned with a stern ridge on his forehead. "I do *not* sound like JOH."

His rebuttal went unheeded. She stepped past him, transfixed by the view. They were in a hangar, similar to, but smaller than the magnificent launch bay. Several hundred yards in the distance she could see the gaping mouth of space, waiting to be fed. The concave walls to this lofted chamber appeared tarnished as if a giant fireball once blew up in here. The bay itself was bereft of any of the advanced equipment found on the modern deck.

"Where are we?"

"This was the original launch bay when the HORUS was first built."

Something in his voice dragged Aimee's glance from the rustic magnitude back to his face. The scarred head tipped back as if he was looking at the view with her, but she realized he was angling his head and listening to the reverberation of their voices, as if through that din he could visualize his memory.

"This is the bay I launched from," he explained. "I have never *seen* the new one. But, after that first epic battle with the Korons, it was clear that we were sorely deficient in defense. We needed more Warriors. We needed more *terra angels*, and we needed more room to accommodate both."

Extended before her were the familiar platforms that served as runways. The stillness of the bay was disturbing. Normally, the flight deck would bustle with activity. Even when there were no Korons to battle, Warriors were busy with their traditional missions to retrieve plant life from foreign lands. Though their plague had been eradicated, they were not so arrogant as to believe another would not someday develop. Preparation was a way of life for these Anthuniams—these passengers of the HORUS.

"They gutted out the compartments behind this wall and continued to bore their way through to the opposite end of the ship, and that is the giant flight deck that you are accustomed to."

"So this bay was just left here to go to waste?"

"Quite literally," Corluss remarked. "They use this deck to jettison trash. Aside from that, it is left untouched."

A clamor of metal clanging against metal drew her attention. The percussion volleyed off the walls like a chorus of cymbals.

"What is that?" Was it the amplified echo of JOH's new feet?

"That is the reason we are here." Corluss tilted his head, listening to the banging, using the sound to gauge his steps.

Following the blind man again.

As she drew closer, Aimee realized there was a partition in the middle of the runways. From behind that wall the clatter grew louder, and in between each beat was the subtle murmur of conversation. A few steps closer and it was not conversation, but rather, yelling.

"In what galaxy is this going—" The rest of the outburst was obliterated by the strike of a hammer.

To her right, Aimee realized that Corluss sported a full-fledged smile. It made her uneasy.

"If you would just wait a—"

"Wait?" *Bang.* "Waiting—" *Bang.* "—is not—" *Bang.* "—going to fix this." *Bang.*

Reaching the partition, Aimee bent at the waist to peek around it.

"What in God's name is *that?*"

Gordeelum swung around, a short metal

staff jutting out of his clenched fist. His shoulders slumped.

"I told you I wanted to get this finished before you brought her here," he berated Corluss with a frown.

"I am told that you can't keep a woman waiting."

Aimee looked past Gordy's red face at the heap of metal he had undoubtedly been hammering away at. It looked like an elephant taking a nap—with its front feet extended before it, and the rear feet dragging behind. Instead of giant elephant paws though, it had what she surmised were engines. The round hump of the elephant's body was dented and dinged and riddled with scorch marks. A wraparound windshield sat on top, like the turret of a tank.

"Gordy, what is this contraption?"

"Con-trapp-shun?" He cocked his head waiting for the translation to feed in from his suit. "Oh," he smiled. "This is my ship."

Ship?

It was a wilting mastodon.

"*That* is capable of flying?"

Gordy followed her glance and his smile faltered. "Well—it will be." He held up the hammer. "After some work."

Glancing over her shoulder at Corluss,

Aimee sighed when she found him staring sightlessly down the runway. "Was this your idea?" she called, arresting his attention.

Corluss crossed his arms. "I used to operate one of these. They aren't as bad as your tone implies."

"Yeah," Gordy inserted, "but the new *terra angels* can withstand the firepower of a Koron spacecraft. This—this—piece of—" His arm flailed in search of the right analogy. "Well, whatever it is—we have to work on this windshield, and—" dejected, he added, "—the body."

"Not to mention these plasma engines. Archaic, I tell you. How am I going to simulate these old magnetic fields?" A small man emerged from the other side of the ship to kick the rear foot of the elephant.

He was short. Very short. Almost dwarf short. A high forehead was framed with thinning red hair that turned white at the temples. Shaggy red eyebrows capped narrowed green eyes, while a rotund girth was made more evident by the tight silver bodysuit—a fashion statement that did not flatter the figure. All in all, he looked like a cosmic leprechaun.

"I'm Aimee," she asserted when no one seemed inclined to introduce her.

Sharp eyes snapped away from the elephant's foot to scrutinize her. "*Hmmff.* The engineer?"

"Ummm, well, yes. Back on my planet."

"Great," he growled. "Maybe you can make yourself more useful than this idiot with his *cynthian* staff."

"I am trying to get some of the dents out," Gordy defended, his deep voice cracking.

"The only thing that will get the dents out is a pool of liquid *alumium*," the leprechaun countered. "Then, we can recycle this relic and build something that will actually fly."

Aimee recognized the red flare of impatience on Gordy's cheeks. She stepped up between the men.

"Time-out. Can someone tell me what's going on here, and—" she turned to the stout red-head glaring at Gordy. "And can you kindly tell me who *you* are?"

Shoulders drawn back, the man straightened to his full five feet.

"Wando."

He did not extend his hand and Aimee dropped hers to her side.

"It's nice to meet you, Wando."

Wando scratched his nose with the back of his hand and sneezed. "I'm sure it is."

Whoa. Got a winner here.

"Are you helping Gordy with this vessel?"

Remain tolerant.

"No. There is no help with this lump of—"

"*Wando.*" The deep threat of Corluss' voice spooked the little man.

Wando scratched his hair, glanced at the floor and then back up at Aimee. In what was either an epileptic seizure, or a battle to conform, his facial muscles hiked into something that could pass for a smile.

"I am the oldest, rather, most-veteran mechanic on the HORUS. In my day, I designed state-of-the-art *terra dusters* on Anthum, and was renowned for my expertise." He cleared his throat, and his smile was growing painful to watch. "Now, my technology from Anthum is outdated. These new *terra angels* designed by the HORUS engineers put my skills to shame—or so they tell me. Still, you would think they could have found a role for me here—"

"Will you quit your pouting?" Corluss interrupted. "Aren't you working on the ion drives for the new line of *sky crawlers*?"

"Assembly line maintenance!" Wando scoffed. "Plug the square peg into the square hole. A *sumpum* could do that."

"Kind of hard with those squishy feet of

theirs," Gordy chimed in.

Wando glared at him.

"Anyway," Corluss injected, turning towards Aimee, "Wando had some free time. He also has some familiarity with this old craft—the only one of its kind. We can work on it in peace here without anyone knowing what we're up to. And Wando will not tell because—because he is one of us."

Vexed, the leprechaun mumbled his contempt as he executed an about-face and hunkered around the other side of the vessel.

Aimee turned towards Corluss and raised her eyebrows in a silent inquiry, and then realized the gesture went unseen.

It didn't take a rocket scientist to conclude that *us* was a band of rejects.

CHAPTER SIX

Night brought reprieve to the oppressive
heat. But night on this planet was short-lived.
Where one sun disappeared, the other would
soon replace it.

Adorned in *Zull*-skin pants, Zak left the
similarly-sewn vest behind in the cave. He did
not need it in the desert. Here, under the light of
their single moon his arms glowed blue, as did
the waves of sand he hunkered down against.
Torches burned in the distance. Those of the
Koron guards.

Zak traveled alone. Zuttah was waiting for
a rendezvous on the other side of the river. His
last words before they split up had been to berate
Zak for this perceived suicide mission.

Yes, the odds were abysmal at best, but
what role did odds play when it came to saving
lives? Odds did not matter.

Zak inched closer, tensing when he saw

the outline of three rebels tied to posts in the sand. Two men and a woman—prisoners on their own land.

In his palm, the solar ray burned with promise. For what he had planned, though, it was useless until he was in close range. Continuing his methodical approach on all fours, hoping to blend with the ripple of shadows produced by the wind-strewn sand, he aimed for the torches.

Now, close enough to hear the guttural dialect of the stone creatures, Zak studied their hideous silhouettes. Unlike a human form, their bodies possessed no curves. Solid lines formed inflexible abdomens and rigid legs. Segments of rock linked to form arms, and the embryonic sculpture of the head offered a crude resemblance to a human face, but the features were static. Lips did not move. The nose did not inhale. Eyes did not shift. Lifeless.

Despite these outward appearances, they still possessed a morsel of intelligence. Even now, one craned its head into the wind. Had Zak revealed himself? Anxious, he flattened against the sand and remained immobile for nearly an hour until he felt it was safe to resume his progress.

Drawing near the circle of light cast by the flickering torches, Zak could now distinguish the two men with their wrists and feet bound to wooden poles driven deep into the ground. Blood mingled with welts beneath the braided shackles, and old blood stains scarred their *Zull*-skin garb. To the right of them, the woman rested on the ground, either asleep or unconscious.

Zak pressed his lips tight together and tried to blow air out through the taut line of his mouth. It was a trick his sister, Zari, had taught him. He was impersonating the warning call of the *Zull*.

From this hazardous perspective, he could hear the grate of stone and rock as the Korons marched the perimeter, peering into the night with vacant eyes. There were only three guards stationed near the prisoners. Ahead, sporadic pockets of rock creatures could be seen further down the river. Nocturnal sentinels, communicating in hushed guttural tones.

Zull, the sloth-like creatures of the foothills, roamed the desert at night while it was cool. They needed the sustenance of the river as much as humans, but the Korons ignored the indigenous creatures. Korons did not need meat. They did not have blood to grow cold, so *Zull*-skin or any other attribute the beast provided was of no benefit. At the sound of the animal, the closest Koron merely cocked his head and then turned away, disinterested.

Zak licked his lips and repeated the call. This time the Korons barely gave it heed.

Good. Gullible towers of rock.

One more time, Zak mastered the low wail of the *Zull*, but in this instance he integrated an ancient word of warning from the Ziratak dialect. It was so subtle, it would be impossible for the Korons to detect it. Even the rebels themselves did not pick up on the subliminal inflection. He tried again, challenging the limits of articulation, and this time caught a rebel's head quirk. Edgily, the man glanced at the Korons and then swung his gaze back towards the dark.

Attempting one more faint call, Zak scored when he saw the frown blossom on the rebel's face. This rebel was a middle-aged man with a full brown beard and thinning long hair. A leather strap drew the hair back from his face so that Zak could glimpse the eager eyes searching the night, scanning the shadows with a rare blend of unease and hope.

Zak rolled onto his side and then back into place. It was a motion, if caught from the corner of an inhuman eye that could be mistaken for a *Zull* satisfying an itch. The sharp focus of the rebel was neither bestial, nor casual. Walking to the furthest extent of his bindings, the man cast a cautious glimpse over his shoulder before resuming his scrutiny of the shadows.

Gyrating to his right again, Zak noticed that the second male rebel perked up and joined in the surveillance. Across the dark plain, Zak made eye contact with this elder man. There was something amiss with that connection—a sheen to the eyes that indicated possible fallout from a solar ray blast. Regardless, the man acknowledged his presence and judiciously sat down, leaning back against the very pole that restricted him.

These men recognized the need for discretion. Had they both walked to the extent of their ropes it would have drawn attention. Anticipation of escape sharpened their judgment.

The man standing cast a brief glimpse down at the prone woman. With a meaningful look extended into the night, he gave a very discreet shake of his head.

She was either injured or incapacitated.

It was a minor setback. Digging his knee into the cool sand, Zak crawled to the perimeter of the torchlight, still maintaining eye-contact with the unshorn rebel. Zak hauled the solar ray up and then dug it into the ground, its flared tube aimed at the Korons seated fifteen yards away. For the plan he had in mind, he needed to draw them into close range.

The attack was a gamble. He wasn't even certain the solar ray was going to work. But this was also the only chance he had to free the rebels.

Unable to convey his intent, Zak looked into the somber eyes of the long-haired man. A silent nod of consent was all Zak required to set his plan into motion.

There it was. A quick jerk of the chin.

Pressing his lips tight, Zak blew through them with the soft trumpeting call of a hungry *Zull*. One of the Korons rose to investigate. From the stone-faced expression it was hard to gauge if the alien sensed danger or was merely bored.

A few more steps and the Koron would spot Zak. Readying his solar ray, Zak held his breath. It had been his intention to draw in all three rock soldiers at once, but the other two were still engaged in grating communication.

Across from him, Zak noticed that the rebel knelt to consult with his companion. Both men rose and advanced until their ropes drew taut.

The Koron cast them a disinterested glance and clumped another step closer to the shadows. Each solid impact of that tread reverberated through Zak's body. At the edge of light, the stone guard grew alert. Its head swiveled abrasively, and when it detected Zak's presence, its stout arm lunged with remarkable agility to engage its weapon.

Zak was quicker.

Under the anxious eyes of the rebels, Zak jerked his palm and fired the solar ray. Instead of the debilitating blast of radiation, a burst of water shot out, showering the Koron with what might as well have been acid. A guttural scream attracted the other guards as they charged forward on distended legs. Zak waited until they were close enough and then spattered them with an eviscerating dose of liquid.

On impact, the water transformed rock to sand as the Korons seeped into puddles absorbed by Ziratak's copper terrain. Slack-jawed, the rebels gawked at the empty spot where three monsters had just stood. Their daze was temporary as they quickly rallied and looked towards the man approaching them from the depths of night.

Zak withdrew the blade from his belt. With a few quick slashes, he freed them from their bindings. Though they suffered from malnourishment, the promise of freedom afforded them new strength.

"Hurry, before the others notice," Zak

warned.

Their heads bobbed eagerly.

"How will we get Zasha out unnoticed?" The long-haired man inquired, his troubled gaze evident in the torchlight. "Her fever is so high."

Crouching down, Zak leaned in close to the woman and ordered, "Help put her over my shoulder."

With little debate, the man assisted until Zak was once again erect, bearing the unconscious woman across his left shoulder, and the solar ray in his right hand. There was very little water left in the chamber, but it was enough to take down one more Koron—perhaps.

Dipping his head into the dark, he instructed, "Follow me."

At first, Zak thought it would be a successful escape into the night, but the elder rebel stumbled on the discarded rope. He fell to his knees and his muffled cry of pain was enough to alert a Koron stationed further down the river. The plodding steps approached, their thunderous beat rippling the ground beneath Zak's feet.

One more. He could take out one more.

"Run!" he hissed.

With a doleful glance at the woman draped over Zak's shoulder, the long-haired man grabbed the elder rebel's arm. In an awkward tandem, they charged into the dark.

Immediately afterwards, the Koron lumbered into range, his solar ray aimed into Zak's eyes.

"No," Zak whispered. "You will not take my sight. And you will definitely not take my life."

His palm constricted and the stream of water hit its mark. It scored a line across the Koron's abdomen, severing him before the ensuing spray disintegrated his granite carcass. At that moment, the stream from Zak's solar ray dribbled to a halt. There was no time to see if others were approaching. With a jerk of his shoulder, he righted the woman into a more secure position and trailed after the rebels.

Zuttah corralled the two men running aimlessly through the desert. When Zak joined them, he pivoted to ensure that they were at a safe distance from the Koron camp.

"I know how we're going to exterminate them," he declared with a breathless laugh.

Zuttah's beady eyes were lost under the curtain of night, but his skeptical tone was distinct. "With your water rays? They can only carry enough to take out a few. There must be thousands stationed along these banks."

"Exactly." Zak grinned.

The second sun had begun to bloom on the horizon. A single ray of light scored Zuttah's dubious face. "It is time to get you back to the caves, my friend. Your madness is returning."

He was not mad. He had a plan.

However, the one person with the insight to pull off that strategy was on a planet far far away.

"Aimee," he whispered. "I need you."

"No disrespect, but we are already tinkering with plasma engines on Earth, so that must make this technology pretty old for the HORUS."

"*No disrespect, but we are already tinkering with plasma engines on Urrrth.*" Wando mimicked like a patronizing parrot.

Aimee glared at him.

"*Of course* it is old technology!" Wando shouted. He hobbled around the leg of the elephant, battering it with his metal cane. "But you seem to know all there is to know in the entire conflux of universes, so why don't you share with me how we are going to get our hands on an impulse engine?"

"If you're going to just stand there and make fun of me, I'm not about to answer any of your questions." It took effort, but Aimee managed not to shake her finger at the belligerent troll.

"You are under the mistaken opinion that I care about your answers."

"Eeeeyah." Gordy clapped his hands over his ears and shook his head. "Is it going to be like this up until departure?"

"Departure?" Wando shrieked. "This piece of scrap metal can't depart its own shadow."

Gordy frowned, trying to assimilate that image. He looked to Aimee, awaiting her rebuttal.

Rather than let anger get the best of her, Aimee drew in a deep breath. Dealing with this opinionated dwarf was no different than clashing with the plant manager who had been, *"at his position for twenty-three years, when she was no more than a toddler"*, as he always recited.

"You might as well forget this ridiculous plan of yours," Wando interrupted her thoughts. "I don't know how you convinced me to be a part of it."

Corluss stepped up alongside her. His posture was so rigid it made his chest look impossibly huge. A voice of authority added to the overall effect. "You volunteered when I reminded you that the HBC was in need of repair."

Wando winced.

"What is the HBC?" Aimee asked.

The red-headed mechanic ambled away, with the click of his cane echoing in the empty launch bay.

Apparently, he wasn't going to answer. She tipped her head up towards Corluss.

"The HORUS Baling Center," he supplied.

"Baling...as in crops? Hay?"

"It's our garbage system, Aimee." Gordy explained, distracted by the *star laser* he had aimed at a beam suspended from the vaulted ceiling. In profile, he was a fit young man, closing in on six feet in height. With his blond good looks, he reminded Aimee of an emerging superhero one might find in the movies.

Gordy fired the laser as the nook five feet to the right lit up. Raising the weapon even with his eyes, he glared at it. "I bet the real *star laser* is more accurate."

So much for the super hero.

Aimee closed her eyes. Had they lost sight of what the goal was here? Finding Zak. Bringing him back alive. Spending eternity with him.

Okay, perhaps the last was a personal goal, but still...

"Corluss," she whispered exclusively to

him. "Are we wasting our time here? Will we make it to Ziratak? Should we trust in the Warriors...that they will bring him back to me—us?"

"You are asking a former Warrior," he pointed out quietly. "I will tell you the answer from our heart. That answer is that a Warrior will do everything in his power to save one of his brothers," he hesitated, "even if it means taking one's own life."

Pain lanced his words, but he continued. "And I will tell you the answer from our mind. We are machines, taught from the earliest age to obey commands. That indoctrination is so strong it overrules the heart." He nodded. "If the command comes to return to the HORUS—*and it will*—the Warriors will leave Zak behind."

After a moment of shared silence, Aimee announced, "Then, thank God I'm not a Warrior yet."

Crouched behind the bulbous rear left foot of the sleeping elephant, Aimee analyzed the blackened chambers for any sign of promise.

"So, what is it that you do on your planet that makes you even remotely qualified to supply intelligent input?"

With a sigh, she sat back against her heels.

Approaching her, Wando's fuzzy red-haired cap bobbed with each awkward step. From this level she realized the source of the gimp was unequal leg lengths. Wando simply had one leg that was an inch longer than the other. Over the years his body had found a comfortable slouch to accommodate the anomaly. Bitter wrinkles framed a pinched mouth and fluffy red and white eyebrows capped the cagey eyes.

"Look," she sighed. "We have to work together. If you feel that you can get this machine into space on your own, then I will step back. But, if there is anything I can assist with, I am more than happy to help, and I don't see anyone else lined up offering to do so."

She could tell he had expected belligerence. Her compliance startled him. Perhaps it was her imagination, but the lines around his eyes relaxed a fraction.

"I asked you what it was you do on your planet."

Score a point for me.

He had yielded. It was evident in his subdued voice. Maybe it was only a slight triumph, but the victory was still sweet.

"I am a product engineer in an automotive plant."

"Aww-toe-moh-tuv," Wando enunciated with a frown. "Spacecrafts?"

"Umm, no, but I aspire towards that. You could consider automobiles planet-bound crafts."

"Oh, like *terra dusters*?" He glanced up at the elephant.

"Probably." Aimee agreed, following his gaze. "What did your *terra dusters* use for propellant?"

Wando scratched his nose with the back of his hand. "Plasma mostly." He took the same hand and patted the elephant's fuselage. "Like this. But, I was working on an ion drive with more power before they took me off the project and replaced me with someone younger and more knowledgeable."

"Is that why you don't like me?" she mused. "Because I am younger? Trust me, I am *not* more knowledgeable than you."

Stroking his ego seemed to work. Plus, as much as Wando would probably care not to admit, he and Aimee had a lot in common.

Distracted, he now reached up to scratch his hair, weaving a bird's nest in the coppery patch above his ear.

"I don't like anyone," he declared, but there was a hint of a grin in his vow. "Now, what is it you use to propel your awww-toe-mohtuvs?"

"Petroleum, but we are slowly—way too slowly—moving to electricity. I have been spending quite an extensive amount of time researching green options."

"Green?"

She could see it on his face when the translation kicked in.

"All your *terra dusters* are colored green?" he asked. Then, considering it for a moment, he added, "Is your planet fertile? Is this for camouflage?"

Aimee smiled. "No, *green* for us means using materials that are safe for our planet. Our current methods are destroying our ozone layer."

Wando's nod was exaggerated. "Ohhhh. Yes. Yes. I ran up against similar problems."

"But, you were working on an ion drive? An ion drive is electronic propulsion. I am very interested in that. Is it something that we can implement in this monster?" She patted the tin shell.

Wando's fingers wrapped around his chin in consideration. "We could, but the problem is that ion thrusters have very short bursts of energy. We would be back to the original plight of the Warriors—a one-way mission. We wouldn't have enough power to catch up to the

HORUS on our return. But—" he hesitated, "if we could make one of those thrusts powerful enough–if the charge/mass ratio of the ions was just right, we can create a high enough exhaust velocity–we just might be able to do it."

A glimmer of hope bloomed inside her, but the practical engineer reared its ugly head. "What about the launch? From what limited knowledge I have of ion drives from our novice space program, they work well in deep space, but what will power us for the launch?"

"Yes, yes." Wando was enthused by her knowledge. "It is true that ion thrusters work best in an environment void of other ionized particles–" he glanced at the gaping void at the end of the deck, "—like out there. But, I've been tinkering with the idea of creating a vacuum *inside* this launch bay."

Aimee brightened at the notion.

"It could be possible," Wando continued. "With this facility being out of operation. The active launch bay behind us needs oxygen and assorted gasses, but with this being one craft and just a handful of people...possibly, just possibly, we could suck out such luxuries."

Yes, oxygen would be considered a luxury.

"Right. Air is an insulator. It keeps electricity from flowing. But a human can't exist in a vacuum for more than 10 seconds? We would need external oxygen."

"Yes, yes." He waved that off. "We will pressurize the inside of this old *duster*, and we will have oxygen packs." Bulbous cheeks boosted. "It could work."

Caught up in the enthusiasm, Aimee's smile nonetheless fell. "That would get us off the HORUS. How would we take off from Ziratak?"

Wando hobbled in a circle, his cane clicking against the metal floor. He began to curse, or so she imagined by the outburst of strange words. He smacked down the cane in frustration. "We need that cursed JOH, although he will probably be miserably inept as usual." He paused. "But, if he could give us an accurate rundown of the topography of Ziratak—"

Glancing around, Aimee saw Corluss working with Gordy on his shooting skills. That task seemed as insurmountable as their plight with the elephant. Her search broadened to the long empty platforms and the vast portal into space beyond it. Right now an arsenal of oxygen and other gasses held that obsidian world at bay. In a vacuum, the black lava would seep into this hangar and steal all life with it.

"I don't see any JOHs in here," she observed.

"Meh, I chase them all away. If one comes in, I swat it with my cane."

"Wando," she cried, "why would you do that?"

"They are a nuisance. They think they know more than everyone."

"Well...they do."

"Meh," he repeated. "It is best if *you* go get one, because they sure aren't going to listen to me."

The thought actually made him grin, and Aimee felt her lips tickle in response. She looked at the tarnished elephant and considered all the obstacles ahead of them, and suggested, "Would it just be easier to steal a *terra angel*, or stow away on one?"

Wando considered this. "Maybe—but not nearly as fun." His mirth dissipated. "Honestly, neither option is viable. Apparently, there was a stowaway once on a *terra angel*. They reduced the size of the cabins to physically disallow that. And as far as stealing a *terra angel*—well—who is going to teach you to fly it? I don't know how to run those fancy ships. This monster," he hit the *terra duster* with his cane, "this, I can teach you. Plus, by the time we are done with the work we have to do...you will know it inside and out."

Oh! I hadn't even considered that. I'm

going to be the pilot!

It made sense now. Who was going to do it, the blind man? Gordy possibly? Her expertise, even if it was from the technology of another planet trumped whatever Gordy could offer.

"What about you? Are you coming with us?"

Wando snorted and screwed up his face like he had sucked a lemon. "No. This is as far as I get when it comes to adventures. You have to possess a certain amount of death-lust to do this sort of thing."

Death-lust. Wonderful.

"Now—" he looked towards the door. "Go get me that JOH."

"I'm not going in there." JOH's eyes widened with fear.

"Why?" Aimee asked.

"He'll hit me. He has a big cane."

"But you have legs now," she argued.

The black crystal orbs blinked and then swept down as one metal appendage lifted at the knee. He tested out a jerky kick. It was a maneuver a sloth could evade.

"Good," Aimee encouraged. "Now let's go."

"I don't think this is a good idea,

Aimeeeee."

"JOH, you are about as tall as Wando now...and you are much more intelligent."

Computer or man, both thrived on flattery. JOH took a step forward and paused, his crystal face shifting as far as it could to see if Aimee followed.

"You first," he offered.

"How gallant," she smirked.

Behind her, the clang of JOH's clawed feet reverberated through the launch bay. It was echoed by the clash of the hammer used to wake the sleeping elephant.

Gordy noticed them crossing the deck, and jogged over.

"We've made some headway. I applied a coat of *zelenium* to the exterior." He scrunched his nose. "That stuff smells awful."

Falling in stride with Aimee, he continued, "I cleaned up the interior and worked with Wando on some of the circuitry. Aimee, the controls are functional now!"

Great! Now she just needed to learn how to operate them.

"Thank you, Gordy. That's all very helpful, but have you been keeping up on your lessons with Corluss?"

His enthusiasm waned.

"I have." Conflicted, he waited and then leaned in closer. "I'm frustrated. What if I fail when we get there? If I fail, Aimee, we—"

Aimee halted and felt JOH crash into her. She turned to straighten him and looked Gordy in the eyes. "What was one of the key factors for you not being a Warrior?"

"My family. I am not of Warrior blood."

"No," she replied. "Your age. Gordy, the truth is that this might be too much for you. And if you have any reservations at all, I don't want you to go with me. I want you to stay here and be safe. There will be another mission...and you will be ready for it."

Blond eyebrows furrowed. "You didn't tell me to give up on the *tak wand*, Aimee. You encouraged me to try harder. Why would you change your attitude now?"

Gordy was a painting still in progress. He was taller than her. His face had matured from the plump-cheeked young boy to a sculpted young man. His alert blue eyes pierced her with their dedication, and burgeoning biceps flexed from the motion of his hand clenching into a fist. *And yet...*

"Gordy, I'm afraid for you."

"Ahh," he shook his head and crossed his arms. "I've acquired yet another mother. My mother, my sister—they are *afraid* for me. I thought you might be different."

Instead of the anger that she anticipated, he let out a prolonged breath. There was fatigue in his expression. Perhaps he was maturing.

"This is not worth risking your life over."

"And it's worth you risking yours?" he countered.

"*Yes.* But this is personal for me and you know it."

Some of the tension eased from Gordy's face. His crossed-arms slackened. "I am not going to get into a debate over who has a more noble cause." He turned to look down the runway at the blanket of space. "We don't have much time and you don't have the luxury of coming up with someone else, so you are pretty much stuck with me." Those bright eyes challenged her. "We will both achieve more than we give ourselves credit for. I'm sure of it."

What a fine young man he had grown up to be.

"When we land, you will obey every word I say, right?" She cocked her eyebrow in threat.

"Every word," he chuckled. "At least you said, *when*, and not *if.*"

He tipped his chin at the JOH cowering behind her. "What's he doing in here? I didn't think they came to this part of the ship."

Aimee glanced over her shoulder. "It took some coaxing."

Big black eyes blinked up at her as the metal legs crooked so that his flat face could peer around her hip.

"I owe him a detailed explanation of the presidential election procedures on our planet, plus a brief overview of the game of golf."

"Hole in one," JOH quoted to no one in particular.

Gordy nodded, bemused. "Ah, feeding his insatiable databanks again? You never know what stray communication signals he will latch onto. They produce the strangest questions."

"The election process on every planet intrigues me," JOH said in affront. "One would think the concept is simple, and yet every planet makes it so complicated."

"Yes, well," Aimee clapped her hands together, "right now JOH is going to help us pick our landing spot."

JOH's mouth stretched into a thin line. "So I have been told."

"Don't you want to help?" she asked.

"Help? It is fortunate for you that I execute whatever is asked of me. Let us clarify that I am not *helping*. I am doing my job."

A large clang followed by a brief grunt announced the arrival of Wando from behind the *terra duster.* Wiping off his hands, he reached for his cane as the group jumped when he smacked the metal tip against the fuselage.

JOH shrank back behind Aimee.

"Well, look," Wando huffed. "The cowardly analog has made his way into my domain...hiding behind a woman nonetheless."

Aimee could see JOH's face crinkle and cascade between trepidation and anger. The latter won out and he stomped his metal feet around her.

"I was beckoned here to *help.*"

Wando snorted and pivoted back towards the ship.

"Is he really the best you could come up with?" JOH glanced up at Aimee.

"Be good, JOH. We need him."

"I could easily recite the circuitry of a *terra duster.*"

"Yes, and I will be coming to you with questions, but JOH, until you get hands, you can't give us *hands-on* experience."

"Hands!" He glanced down at his feet. "You want hands now?"

"Where will the Warriors land on Ziratak?" Aimee asked the blueberry gemstone face that continued to cast nervous glances at the mechanic straddling a discarded engine shell.

Wando wasn't actually seated. He leaned his rear against it and balanced himself with his cane. Corluss stood behind him with arms crossed, the twosome looking as congenial as undertakers.

Aimee rolled an engine shell over and squatted down on it, close enough to JOH that she could see her reflection in his flat face. Beside her, Gordy crouched down to his knees for a better perspective.

As soon as JOH confirmed he had everyone's attention, his blue face disappeared and an image of sand dunes replaced it.

"Ziratak." His voice continued as the desert played across his monitor. "What you see here is mostly what you get with this planet. Its life-source comes from a small mountain range near its polar cap."

The image changed. Craggy, snow-capped cliffs poked at a brilliant blue sky. At first Aimee thought she was seeing a reflection from the snow, but on second glance, it was clear that there were *two* radiant suns hovering over the mountain chain.

"This range feeds the Zargoll River which was once majestic—the artery to numerous waterfront cities."

A thin band of water with red clay embankments mocked JOH's depiction.

"When the Korons came, they destroyed those cities. The few inhabitants they did *not* kill were used as slaves to haul sand from the desert and fill in the Zargoll. These are the last images I have of the river, but I can only assume that the situation has grown worse."

"Where did you get these pictures, or your information?" Aimee asked.

"They were recorded from Zak's eye shield." The images faded and JOH's blue face reappeared.

Wincing at the name, Aimee collected herself. "When?"

"The last time he returned from Ziratak, so it has been quite some time. Our Warriors," JOH continued, narrating without the images, "will land in the south, at the furthest reaches of the Zargoll—far away from the mountain range and its turbulent winds. They will hike the river's perimeter. If Zak is alive, he is most likely lingering near the water for sustenance. If the river is dried up, their search will be quick."

Desperate visions flooded her head. She

could not yield to them. She had to stay sharp.

This river's source was the mountain. The mountain offered cover. It offered asylum— whereas, the desert was barren. If Zak was there, she would bet he was in the mountains.

"We need to land near the mountains."

JOH's eyes thinned into straight lines. "Not a good plan."

"Why," she challenged, "the winds?"

"I hate to agree with this walking font of useless knowledge," Wando inserted, "but JOH is right."

A tremulous smile gouged the blue orb. "I am?"

Wando leaned forward and smacked the chassis with his cane.

"Unlike the new *terra angels*, this alloy is very light. Flimsy, might be a word you would recognize. Originally, the idea was that it would make it faster. Later, that idea was refuted when the craft had no stability and wobbled its way into atmospheres. A strong wind could likely cast this craft back out into the desert like it had been slapped."

"Right," Aimee nodded. "So we try it, and the worst case is that we end up landing in the desert anyway."

Wando's bushy eyebrows vaulted. "There

is a big difference between *landing* and being cast like a wingless *monawk* into the sand. The latter will leave you battered, and most likely disable the craft and remove any chance of getting it back up in the air again."

Aimee considered this and turned to JOH. "Then you better come up with the track of least resistance near the mountains."

"But Aimee—"

"No, listen. We can't afford the time it would take to hike across the desert. It could be days...weeks, who knows. This is why previous Warriors failed. The HORUS was pulling out of range before they ever got near the mountains. They ran out of time. We will not."

"No, you'll just die." Wando scoffed.

Beside her, Aimee noticed Gordy scowl. "We can do it."

Corluss cleared his throat. "It's nice of you all to ask, but I landed on Ziratak once."

Three sets of eyes, and a JOH swung towards the blind man.

"Oh gee," Wando swiveled around on his engine shell. "Where the heck were you while we had to watch this terminal on stilts dazzle us with pointless data?"

Clang. Clang. JOH took two steps towards the mechanic. Wando cast him a disinterested glance before tilting his head up at Corluss again.

"The Korons had already invaded Ziratak," Corluss explained, "but had yet to attack the HORUS. When we landed on Ziratak we set down in the desert and gave them a wide birth. Vodu had warned us about them and what they had done to the inhabitants of the planet."

Zak's family. Aimee's heart ached for Zak's tragic loss.

"Ours was just a mission to see what they were up to. The desert was barren and they spotted us shortly after we landed. We barely made it back to our ships...and they sent an armada after us."

"And the mountains," Wando encouraged. "Did you see the mountain range, or fly over it...I'm assuming there is some purpose for you to share this information with us right now."

Deaf to his sarcasm, Corluss continued, "We felt the mountain jet streams as we were coming in, but it posed little concern because we had no intention of landing in the highlands. It might be difficult—but if you ride the wind, you could use it to your advantage and glide to a safe landing."

"There." Gordy thumped his knee. "Now that this debate is over, let's get back to work."

Wando shook his head, the fabric around

his neck rustling.

"Do you have something to add, Wando?" Aimee questioned.

"No. You're all a bunch of reckless fools. Not much for me to add to that."

No. There wasn't much left to add.

It was time to act.

CHAPTER SEVEN

"We are close." Raja's reflection was sober.

She stood in Aimee's room, staring out the window at the conflux of asteroids creating a ribbon between two crater-pocked planets. Turning away, she faced Aimee.

"I shouldn't have encouraged this," she sighed.

Aimee shook her head before Raja finished.

"We both know that what you did was right." Aimee sank onto the edge of her bed and gazed into space. "Raja, I have to find him. I have to—"

In three strides, Raja was at her side. "I know. And that was the only confession of weakness that I will reveal. I am behind you all the way." She forced a smile.

It was easy to read the fear in that smile. "Don't worry," Aimee allayed. "I will be back very soon."

Spine straight and eyes clear, Raja said, "I know you will."

Glancing at Raja's clenched hand, Aimee just now realized that the woman was clutching a glass vial.

Raja followed her eyes. "Take this with you." Her voice trembled.

"What is that?" Aimee reached for the tube. It was the size of a lipstick container.

"If—" Raja hesitated, "—if you should be struck by one of their solar rays—" her throat caught.

"What—"

"Madness follows quickly. It abates after the brain has had time to heal, but besides blinding a person, the flash traumatizes the mind." She nodded at the vial. "This will ease the symptoms."

"What type of symptoms?"

"The brain doesn't catch up with the fact that you have been blinded and it creates sight for you. It contrives images that aren't there. If not addressed quickly, they will make a person go mad. That serum will help." She waited for Aimee to acknowledge, and hastened to add, "Promise me you will take that with you and use it if need be. It has other healing qualities, but I haven't had time to test them all out...but, I am certain it is safe."

"How does it work? On our planet everything they give you just makes you sleepy. I don't want to be sleepy."

"Sleep would be the best thing for you under those circumstances, but no, it brings clarity. It sharpens your cognizance so that you can recognize what is real. It can only be used in minimal doses or else a reverse effect occurs. I've been tinkering with some other healing attributes that were included, but there was no time to test those."

"I fully intend to wear my eye shields, so I hope to never need this—" She twisted the clear vial around. "But, I will take this with me."

"Good." Raja relaxed. "And Gordeelum? You will see to it that his eyes are protected?"

"Absolutely, but I am going to do my best to keep Gordy *inside* the ship. I'm already extremely nervous about bringing him along. If anything happens to him—"

"He is a bright young man. He is skilled. And he cares about you and Zak. He was preparing for this long before you came back aboard the HORUS. Believe me, I have done nothing short of drug him to dissuade him, but he is a man now—no matter how much we choose not to accept that."

Aimee laughed. "Yes, I guess we are getting old, Raja."

Raja's lips curled up. "That we are." She sobered. "Vodu still knows nothing of this. He will not be pleased."

"An understatement. I am sorry you will be left behind to deal with that. Will you get in trouble?"

"Me?" Raja fluttered her long eyelashes. "I know nothing."

Aimee jumped up from the bed to hug her. "Back home I was too busy and—well—too withdrawn to spend much time socializing. I had one childhood friend who moved to California." She looked Raja in the eye. "You are my only girlfriend."

Surprise and delight mingled in Raja's eyes. With an understanding nod, she admitted, "I am also too busy and too reclusive to have friends." She grinned coyly. "But, I have you."

They shared another quick hug and Raja ordered with a hoarse voice, "So come back safe, okay? I don't want to lose my only friend."

"I will come back. And I will bring Zak with me, who is also your friend." Aimee vowed. "And then we will find a man for you."

An uncharacteristic snort slipped from the prim woman. "Men don't look at me. They just see a scientist steeped in tonics and analysis."

"Maybe you're too steeped in tonics and analysis to notice them looking."

They laughed.

Outside, a copper planet appeared as a small spec on the black canvas of space, like a shiny penny on the asphalt.

Ziratak.

The combination had not changed.

Aimee mimicked the symbols on the wall with her hands in the sequence Zak had showed her. With a gratifying hiss, the portal slid open and she was ensconced in a dark tunnel. Cascading water echoed about her as the rippling reflections cast eerie shadows on the wall.

Emerging into the giant vaulted atrium, Aimee tipped her head back and viewed the splendor of night in the glass dome above. Worlds dangled in the distance as if on strings in a giant diorama.

Before her, aisles of plant life paved a forest more grand than the most spirited imagination could contrive. With her boots clicking against the marble floor, she passed by a waterfall and paused to watch the fish dart beneath the surface like aquatic fireflies.

So many memories assaulted her in this haven of exotic trees and foreign flora. In between a tangle of purple branches, she caught a glimpse of black and white fur. She crouched down and whispered, "Come here, boy."

The fluffy black-tipped ears of a *sumpum* emerged. His face was covered in white fur, but somehow he saw her through that nest of fuzz and sneezed before retreating back into the forest.

Aimee stood and continued to her goal. Four alleys down—just through the crosswalk—a single palm tree stood amidst a conflux of alien plants. It was her link with Earth. It was also the spot where Zak had told her that he loved her. Tears welled up in the corners of her eyes. Oh, how she wanted him to emerge from the shadows again. How she wanted to feel him step up behind her and slip his strong arms around her.

Soon.

He had to be alive. *He had to.*

Glancing up beyond the bushy fronds of the palm tree and through the glass-domed ceiling, Aimee could see the copper planet. It was now the size of a beach ball and flanked by two bright stars, like a pair of celestial eyes.

Ziratak. Zak's home.

It was close enough to begin to discern shadows and wispy contours on the surface, and the bright green and white band across the top. So innocent it looked. So innocent. So beautiful. And, so deceptive.

It was time to go.

She climbed the dirt embankment and dusted her palm against the coarse trunk of the palm tree. This lone tree was her talisman. Touching it would bring her luck. Glancing up, she discovered a plump coconut suspended above. She smiled at it, squared her shoulders, and headed back towards the exit.

Recounting Wando's operational instructions in her head, Aimee was distracted as she disembarked the linear transport. She was not looking ahead and crashed directly into someone walking the opposite way.

"I'm sorry," she mumbled, steeped in her mental checklist.

"Where are you going in such a hurry?"

A bucket of ice water might as well have been poured over her, such was the chill produced by that voice. Aimee looked up into glacial eyes as her throat constricted.

Salvan.

"I have a—class."

"A class?" He cocked his head, a sweep of pale hair falling to the side. "It must be an awfully important one at the pace you were moving."

"It is." She wished these pants had pockets so that she could hide her trembling fingers.

"Well then," Salvan stepped aside. "I wouldn't want to keep you."

Air rushed from her lips. "Thanks," she muttered, hastening forward with her head down.

"Oh, Aimee?" Salvan called.

Aimee froze. She didn't look back.

"It's interesting that the classrooms are in the other direction—" he paused, "and about the only thing ahead of you is the old launch bay."

"Not that it's any of your business," she rounded, "but I am meeting with a mechanic to review future enhancements to the *terra angels*."

Salvan crossed his arms. His smug smile reminded her of the neighborhood cat that carried a bird carcass in its clenched jaw.

"All the mechanics work in the new wing."

There was no time for this debate. Aimee felt her cheeks scorching. "I understand that the launch bay is very hectic right now. We decided to meet somewhere with less distraction."

"Right. Right." Salvan nodded. "They are preparing for a mission. To Ziratak, right?"

Aimee's stomach fell.

"I guess they're going to make another pathetic attempt to retrieve Zak. I don't know what makes them think they will be successful after all this time has passed. I'm sure they are just going through the motions to appease Vodu." He took a step backwards. "And speaking of Vodu, I was just on my way to see him. I will be sure to commend him on offering you private lessons on the old flight deck."

Son of a —

Aimee's hands curled into fists. Was he bluffing, or was he really going to rat her out to Vodu? If Vodu had any inclination that something was going on in the old launch bay, he would investigate and immediately put an end to their endeavors. She had to move fast.

Her eyes clashed with Salvan's in a silent duel.

"I'm sure your approval will mean a lot to Vodu," she stated and then quickly spun and walked away.

"We have to move fast."

Gordy, Wando, and Corluss turned at the sound of her voice. A legless JOH floated around the back end of the sleeping elephant.

"What happened?" Corluss asked.

"Salvan spotted me coming here and he's on his way to tell Vodu."

The meaty part of Corluss's forehead furrowed. Wando reached up with his cane to push Corluss aside so that he could amble forward. "That old fool will shut us down."

"Vodu is not a fool," Aimee corrected, "which is exactly why he'll shut us down. He is a perfectionist, and this—" her hand flailed to the tarnished *terra duster*, "is far from perfection."

Wando's face twisted with disdain. "She is not pretty, but she will fly, and more importantly, she will bring you back. We just have to move fast." He limped towards the wall and used his cane to open a container on the floor.

"Everyone, grab your masks," the old mechanic ordered. "Aimee, Gordeelum...it's time. I was hoping you would have the luxury of trailing in the Warrior's wake, but it looks like you have to make the first move."

Ambling towards her with a spandex hood that contained a clear plastic face shield, Wando thrust the garment at her. "You should be fine inside the *duster*, but put this on just in case. Wait until you're safe inside the craft before removing it." He shoved another hood at her, and nodded towards Gordy, "for him."

Wando tossed a hood at Corluss. It hit him in the chest and fell to the ground.

"Meh," The old mechanic uttered before donning the garment himself. Tufts of gray hair protruded from the bottom. He looked like a *Q-tip* with rusty, frayed ends. Moisture from his breath condensed on the faceplate, but as soon as he tapped a button embedded outside the hood, the cynical eyes were visible once again.

"Hurry!" he snapped in a tinny voice. "I am shutting down the oxygen. You need to be in that ship and ready to go the second we have reached full vacuum pressure, which will be in about five of your minutes."

Every fallacy with this plan pummeled Aimee in the head. *They were not ready. What if they failed? What if they failed?* The cadence chimed with her pulse.

She turned towards Corluss who had just stooped to feel around the floor for his hood.

"Corluss, are you sure you don't want to come?" Panic laced her words.

"If I am not an asset, then I am of no help whatsoever."

"You've been out there. You can talk me down."

A weary smile played with his pale lips. "I will be in your ears talking you down, Aimee." He reached for her shoulder and squeezed. "But no one is telling you that you have to get in that ship. In fact, you will make everyone's life easier if you don't."

"Hoods!" Wando shouted.

Corluss hauled off the shield around his eyes and pulled the hood over his head. Once he pressed the button atop his ear, his lifeless eyes came into view. They saddened her.

"You say that," She yanked the silver cap over her head, tugging her hair in the process. "And, yet you are helping me."

"If I had my eyes, you know I would be up there with you. Be my eyes, Aimee. Talk to me. Let me see it all again."

A bitter chill possessed her, and it was not just because of Corluss's words. Wando had enacted the vacuum. Oxygen, photons—all energy was depleting. Despite the ventilation provided by the hood, Aimee felt tightness inside her chest. Spasms cramped her limbs as the water in her muscles began to evaporate. Her eyes started to bulge in fear.

Wando's voice sounded in her ear. "Now

would be a good time to get into the ship. We will be in a pressurized chamber at the rear of the flight deck. I will have communication with you the entire time." He hesitated and his normally raspy voice gentled, or maybe it was the gasses leaking in from her hood. "The blind man is right. No one is saying that you have to do this. There is no disrespect in admitting that you are afraid. Just—just—*make a decision*."

That's what she needed. A verbal kick in the ass.

"Gordy!" It was a command. A question. A plea.

His eyes were as large as JOH's behind the mask, but he was already sprinting towards the elephant and there was no time for further discussion.

In the background, Aimee heard the peal of an alarm. Garish lights on the walls flashed in warning.

Gordy slammed the exterior of the *terra duster* with his palm, and the plank that served as a doorway slid open only three-quarters of the way. Already something had failed. She scrambled behind him through the slot. As soon as he was certain she had cleared the entry, Gordy hauled the panel in and jabbed the airlock.

Immediately, the pressure abated. Her

arms no longer felt like they were wrapped in tourniquets, and her eyes didn't feel like tennis balls.

"What's the alarm?" Gordy yelled, tripping into the front seat.

Aimee fell into the chair beside him, the shell curling protectively around her hips. "Salvan must have alerted Vodu, and he's trying to stop us."

At the end of the deck, the portal began to close. It was a behemoth gate. It would take a while. *But, they needed a while.*

"Wando," she cried into her mask, feeling her breath blast a warm surge against her face. "We have to take off now."

"There is still a trace of oxygen in the chamber," Although tinny, his voice sounded calm. "Check the interior. Make sure the atmosphere is stable like I showed you."

Aimee's fingertips dusted across the panel before her. Where the interior of the contemporary *terra angel* was glossy, black and sleek, this predecessor was clunky, gray and bleak. The sensors did not react to her skimming touch so she pressed her fingertips down with force and lights began to flick on.

Digital readouts flooded the wide console. Above that mantle an expansive windshield revealed the daunting progress of the gate.

Despite the controls being marked with Anthumian script, she had reviewed them enough times with Wando to have memorized the function of every switch. Most were stabilizers and auxiliary encoders that could apply to any language. Wando had simulated takeoff with her nearly a hundred times over the past few weeks, but simulation offered a false sense of security.

"The inside of the cabin is stabilized," she declared even as she was tapping the last gauge, waiting for the hologram to materialize.

"Good."

In the background she could hear Gordy engaged in a similar conversation with Corluss and JOH.

"Can I take this hood off now?" she asked Wando.

"Mmmm...yes."

Well, that sounded confident.

Aimee hooked her finger under the bottom of the cap and drew it up over her mouth and nose, taking a few tentative breaths. Satisfied, she yanked the hood off and threw it on the floor beside her seat. For one wild second she noticed that the grooves in the floor were lined with particles of sand. *Anthumian sand?* Cool. How long had that been here?

"The deck is depressurized, Aimee. Start the ion drives."

Perspiration dotted her forehead. She swiped the panels that would initiate the ion drives. In trials, they had reached this state and were satisfied with the results. They had not been able to fully test the thrusters yet. In order to do so they would need to take off. This could be a very short mission.

"Ready here," Gordy called, his hood off now as well.

She glanced at him and saw how flushed his cheeks were, as if he had been running a marathon.

"This is your absolute last chance to back out, Gordy."

His profile revealed a grin.

"I'm doing this with or without you," he vowed. "Considering that you know more about the controls and the ion drives, I'm hoping I'm doing it *with* you."

Aimee smiled as she swiped the initializer. The shell-shaped seat vibrated beneath her. Ahead, the gate proceeded with its slow closure, narrowing the view of space. Alarms went off like flashbulbs on a Hollywood red carpet. In the corner of her eye she noticed a doorway slide open as a host of silver-suited men spilled onto the deck.

"If you're going to do this, Aimee, you have to do it now," Wando called in her ear.

With her free hand, she reached into her collar for the chain and rubbed the pendant with the pad of her thumb.

"Let's see if this elephant can fly," she whispered. "Hold on, Gordy!"

She let go of the pendant and initialized the ion thruster. At first the ship shook like it had just coughed out its last gasp of breath, but then she felt the roar behind her. Power surged through the *terra duster,* yet it only budged a few inches. With the force of the shudder, it felt as if the *duster* was strapped in place.

"The vacuum wasn't clean enough," Wando sounded miffed in her ear, "it will kick in—"

A commotion interfered with her receiver. "Wando?"

"Get your hands off of—"

"Wando?" she cried.

Aimee was flung back into her shell. The magnets in the discharge chamber hit the electrons, enabling voltage to the ion optics. Due to the elephant's sheer size, she felt that they were moving too sluggishly. Outside, the walls of the launch bay began a slow progression.

Black. Gray. Black. Gray. Like the shadow of a banging shutter.

The elephant felt so cumbersome that when she saw the portal into night approaching, she thought for sure they would just tumble off and spiral down into oblivion.

But, the *terra duster* slipped off the edge of the platform into space and to her delight, responded to all the commands on the console.

"I'll be damned," she mumbled. "This is actually working."

"What?" Gordy shouted over the raucous noise.

In a monitor that displayed the rear view, Aimee could see the door to the launch bay draw closed. The giant guardian ship was a feat of engineering and took her breath...literally. She gasped and yelled, "What?"

"What did you say?" Gordy countered.

"You look stable from here—" Wando sounded distracted. Vodu's men must have reached him. "Let back on the thrusters. You will catch up with Ziratak's orbit very soon." A pause. "It's too late," he yelled. "They can't come back until they are ready to."

Aimee realized that the last sentence was directed at someone inside Wando's pressurized booth.

They can't come back.

"What did you say?" Gordy repeated.

Aimee tapped the panel, and the thrusters subsided. There was a nauseous feeling of weightlessness, as if at any second this elephant was going to plummet, but they held their altitude, and according to the holograms, they were on course for Ziratak. Looking away from the transparent image, Aimee gazed through the windshield at the real thing. Ziratak grew at a rapid pace—an imposing sphere resplendent with swirls of milky clouds, and the dark scores of the lowlands. The northern polar cap was covered in a layer of clouds. That haze was no doubt the source of wind that would plague their landing. For some reason it did not concern her. If she made it that far—if she was on the surface of Ziratak—if she was *that close* to Zak—she would succeed. She was certain of it.

"What did you say?" Gordy looked impatient now.

"I said that elephants *can* fly."

"Elephants?" he mouthed, waiting for the translation to pour in from the collar of his white suit. She could tell the moment he received a definition because his face screwed up in distaste. "Eww, god-awful beasts, aren't they? Can they really fly? Are those wings, and not ears?"

A slight tug caught the *terra duster*. It was subtle, but she was sensitive to every anomaly right now. On the three-dimensional display before her, she could see that Ziratak's powerful fingers of gravity had latched onto them. They were on their way in. Immediately adjacent to this tableau, the monitor displayed the rear view. Tiny starbursts of light ejected from the mouth of the HORUS. The Warriors were en route.

"Wando," she spoke into the transmitter above, "are they going to reach us before we land?"

Distracted by the speed of the *terra angels* chasing her, Aimee didn't notice the silence at first. "Wando?" she called again.

Gordy shot her an anxious glance. "Corluss?" he cried.

Nothing. Only the groan of the fuselage filled their ears as the elephant entered Ziratak's atmosphere. The external pressure jolted them in their seats as Aimee grabbed the console for stability.

"Aimee, are you going to be able to do this without them?"

She yanked her hair behind her ear.

"Not much of a choice," she muttered.

A deep breath helped. Just make it onto

the planet. Everything after that was at the hands of fate, but landing was all up to her.

"Okay, Gordy, here's what I need you to do."

"Thank you," he rushed. "I need someone to tell me what to do."

The elephant lumbered under the milieu of gasses. Though they were both secured into their shells with pilot straps, they still jerked in tandem with every rattle of the craft.

"I have to focus on this landing," she raised her voice as the pitch of the friction against the spacecraft turned into a screech. "But, I know those Warriors are closing in on us. I don't think they will do anything crazy like try to shoot us down, however, they may try to *escort* us to another landing spot. I need you to monitor their status. Tell me if I have to make an evasive maneuver. Keep me posted on what they're up to."

"On it!" he shouted. And then a second later, he added, "They are fast. They're already approaching the atmosphere."

Aimee heard him, but she was distracted. There was no way to increase the speed of this relic. *Hah. Relic.* As old as this *terra duster* may be to the Anthumians, it was advanced beyond anything Earth had ever designed.

At this point, she had little control over the trajectory of the elephant. The craft was at the whim of Ziratak's drag. Once they pulled through the stratosphere, then perhaps she would gain some command...if the wind did not whisk them away in the process. Right now they were flying blind, lost in a thick web of clouds through which brief glimpses of daylight tormented them with promise.

"I lost them," Gordy announced, his voice warbled by the acceleration.

"I can see daylight," she cried. "We're coming through. We might even be able to land before they break from the clouds."

"The Warriors aren't stupid," he pointed out. "They know where we are."

"They are not stupid, but they are disciplined. If they were instructed to land in the desert...that is where they will go." She hesitated. "*Then,* they will come look for us—maybe."

The clouds began to diminish.

"Shields on!" she yelled.

Gordy snapped the silver band over his eyes. In the act of drawing on her own, she caught a glimpse of him. With the intimidating shield, the intense set of his profile, and the strain in his shoulders, he looked like the Warrior he aspired to be.

Please let him stay safe.

"Are you secured?" she asked the obvious, but in this case, concern overruled the apparent.

"Yes." Frustration made his voice pitch.

Roll your eyes at me all you want, Gordeelum. At least they'll be safe.

The elephant bucked one last time as they broke through to a cobalt sky. At first, all she could distinguish was a fierce clash of red and blue on the horizon. The coral surface looked barren and hot under the luminous sky and brilliant suns. Even through her eye shields, she had to squint to scan the desert.

Wando's instructions came rushing back.

Don't look out the window. Trust the controls. The controls will not be tainted by glare or indecision.

As she glanced down, small bubbles of light floated behind her eyes. Sun glare. In a moment they dissipated. Atop the panel, the hologram displayed the horizon just as if she were looking out the windshield. They were speeding across a flat desert at—aww hell, she tried to remember the ratio, but it was too complex a math problem.

They were about 20,000 feet above the surface. This display was more than a hologram. It was like a living picture, complete with color and texture. In the midst of the endless desert loomed a thin scar. Pinching her pointer finger and thumb above the display caused it to zoom in on the feeble remnants of a river. This was the mighty *Zargoll?*

Looking ahead she observed a mountain crest in the distance. Wando informed her that everything would be on autopilot until they reached the foothills, when the merciless winds would attack. It would not be long now. She wished she had something as mundane as a steering wheel to grab onto, but the *terra duster* was controlled by the dexterity of her fingers. After that, it was just a cunning joust of woman versus wind.

CHAPTER EIGHT

It was evident the moment the initial lick of a breeze tickled their belly. It was like riding the swell of a wave that gently lobbed them back into place. The next assault was not so mild. The craft shuddered, which jerked Aimee's hand, causing the *terra duster* to drop rapidly. She drew her fingers tight together over the panel and hauled the ship back up to a safe elevation.

Whew. This was a maneuver she could not simulate in the security of the launch bay. It gave her a boost of confidence to know that it had worked.

"We're still clear in back," Gordy announced in a shaky voice. "I don't know where they went. You would think you could see them by now. Maybe you're right. Maybe we'll be down before they break through."

Confidence was missing from that assessment.

"Forget what's behind us for now. Wando told me to keep focused on the panel images, but

I still trust eyes over gauges. You look out that window and tell me if we are about to hit something."

Wind sheared the *terra duster* as the fuselage rattled like a tin roof in a tornado.

"Well, we're going to hit the side of a mountain very soon."

It was a remarkably calm assessment. She hoped that composure meant he had faith in her.

Belligerent currents funneled around the craft, hauling it like a lassoed cow towards the starboard side. On that side, an austere granite mountain face loomed closer. Instinct dictated that she should veer left, out of the path of danger—but instead, she relaxed her fingers and surrendered to the wrench of the wind.

"Uhh, Aimee, what are you doing?"

"Gambling."

"Gambling?" he hesitated. "Now is not a good time to *gamble*."

The elephant began to spiral—an evil harbinger. Aimee was resolved with her decision, though. Steadfast fingers remained flat above the grid. *Hold the course.*

Another lesson you could not simulate was how to land this craft. Wando had been over it with her time and time again, but just like parallel parking—until you executed it yourself, there was no way to gauge where the vehicle would end up. And as with every attempt to parallel park, she was afraid she was going to hit something.

It was plausible that they could crash and still survive—but this old *terra duster* was their transportation back to the HORUS. If it was damaged, then they were stuck.

"Anything behind us?"

"Still clear."

Strange.

There was no time to think. The wind sucked them into a downward plunge. Her hand trembled with the effort to keep the elephant level.

"Aimee, the mountain!"

Perspiration clung to her neck. It made her collar itch. Ahead, the broad face of the volcanic mountain looked like a yawning mouth, ready to swallow. According to the calculations on the screen, if she was to hold her course, they would slip just around the edge.

For poor Gordy who was staring agape at the stark palisade, she didn't think he cared about calculations. As imperceptible as they may be, she was beginning to see results on the monitor, though. The elephant battled the winds and held its starboard position. On the hologram, empty sky formed at the far right side of the grid. She locked onto that, using her left hand to grab her seat and hold her steady. The effort made her arms tremble, but the *terra duster* began to clear the rotund base of the mountain.

Trees dotted the foothills like green leopard fur. At the end of the fir line, golden-grassed knolls sloped down to meet the desert. This was the best she was going to get. Yes, the flat bed of desert sand would have made an easier runway, but if there was vegetation here—then *here* is where she would find life.

"You cleared it!" Gordy yelled. "Wooooo!" He punched the air.

Aimee allowed herself one brief smile.

"Alright," she said, composed. "We're going in. Make sure you are secure."

"Yes, mother. You've only said that to me five times now."

She squeezed her hand into a fist and the elephant responded by decreasing its speed. For as much as the *terra duster* obeyed her orders, the wind tried its best to undermine her. Clasping her fist tighter, the spacecraft shook with the effort to respond, but it was still moving too fast to land.

Aimee jolted when she felt a hand on top of hers.

Gordy had reached across the space between them and he was squeezing her fist. The combined effort was working. The duster began to reduce its speed. In a gradual descent, she lowered their joint grasp towards the black panel. In response, the elephant dipped close to the surface—maybe only a hundred feet above the grassy knolls.

Down. Down. *Slow.* Down.

Cold air hit her hand as the fingers clasped about hers slackened.

"You've got it, Aim."

Down.

The fleshy ball of her palm grazed the grid and the *terra duster* skidded over a flat patch of grass. She opened her hand and laid it palm-down on the black surface. A slight jolt shook the craft as it connected with the ground. Aimee eyed the windshield. To her left lie the slope of the mountain. Before her was a crop of spindly trees with tufts of ferns that looked like dust mops. Silence possessed the craft, and for a moment they sat in that void, listening only to their erratic breaths.

Reality finally sunk in.

They were safe.

"Aaaaaahhh," Aimee screamed. "Oh my! We did it."

She reached over to give Gordy a high-five. He looked quizzically up at her hand.

"Smack it," she instructed. "It's a gesture of celebration."

Gordy reached up and slapped her hand. He laughed and then slapped it again.

"Aimee, you'd make a fine Warrior."

"I couldn't have done it without your help." Her smile fell. She had so wanted to be able to achieve this one feat.

"It's called a team," Gordy grinned, his eyes secreted behind the silver shield. "Had we been out on the desert you could have brought it down by yourself, which was exactly what the Warriors did. They couldn't have landed here because they don't travel in teams."

Hmmm. "When did you get to be so smart, Gordeelum?"

"I've always been smart," he replied smugly.

Aimee laughed. With a tremulous quiver, she withdrew her hand from the control panel. In response, the engines shut down, and the grids fell dark. In the shadows, one panel still throbbed a green light. It was the communication system.

She called out, knowing it picked up on their speech.

"Hello, is anyone there?"

"Aim—ee. Vo—du here. —you—alright?"

"Vodu! Yes. We are safe."

"—will talk about this—you return. Start take-off procedures."

She glanced up through the windshield again. In order to launch, they needed a vacuum.

"Umm, that is not possible right now."

There was a long pause.

"—sure your location sensor is on." His deep voice was filled with static. "Will—Warriors find you."

Aimee stared down at the blinking beacon. Her eyes slid towards Gordy. After a pause, he nodded.

"It is not functioning," she announced. "We lost it in the landing."

"Say—again."

She cleared her throat. "We lost the sensor in the landing."

Silence.

Gordy scratched the back of his head.

"—do not leave—ship."

Wavering over the sensor, her finger dipped. The blinking ceased. The elephant was silent.

For a moment Aimee and Gordy stared forward, grasping the magnitude of their next step.

"Well—" Gordy drew in a deep breath, "—let's go find Zak."

And just like that, the weight abated.

They were on Ziratak.

Zak's planet.

The last place he had been seen by anyone—

"Yes," she agreed. "Let's do that."

"There's no doubt in my mind that you have gone completely mad," Zuttah muttered.

The claim disturbed Zak because he felt it might be valid.

They were nearing the foothills. It was a good thing too, because the sun was wreaking havoc on his sight. Even with the aid of the shield, he still had to squint. He hated the obstruction of the shield, but one more solar ray blast would mark the end for him. Still, he rationalized that once he reached the foothills it would be safe to haul the gadget off.

Zak held a hand over his eyes as an additional visor. Walking backwards, he scanned the desert to ensure the rebels were still in tow. Zuttah carried the inert woman over his shoulder. Her pallor concerned Zak, but she could not be looked after until they reached the safety of the caves. The younger rebel, who he estimated to be about his age, crossed the desert with surprising agility considering his malnourished state. The older man trailed a few steps behind. It was hard to gauge his age. His body was remarkably fit, perhaps a result of self-preservation. But, the gray strands in his shaggy hair, and the scores of pain that lined his face revealed his maturity.

Zak glanced again at the unconscious woman. Her long black hair cascaded over Zuttah's shoulder. It reminded him of Aimee's—

"Zak," Zuttah cut into his thoughts, "did you hear that?"

Wind kissed the sand with a soft whistle like the sigh of a *zere* serpent.

"Hear what?"

"I swore I heard a ship."

"A ship," Zak snorted. "Who's gone mad now?"

To be certain, he sought the faces of the two men. The older man stared off into the desert, while the younger one shrugged as if to say, *I heard nothing.*

The desert was taking its toll. They needed to reach the cave…*soon.*

"I'm thirsty."

"We haven't even been gone from the *duster* for more than a half hour," Aimee huffed as she stumbled up a pebble-strewn slope.

"I'm not sure what a *half hour* is, but it sounds long," Gordy griped.

Reaching the top of the hillock, she held her hand to her brow, searching the land below. An orange blanket stretched as far as she could see until it meshed with the cobalt horizon. Behind her lie the austere slate face of the mountain—a 10,000-foot obstacle. There was no route to scale it, and the slopes that flanked it were made impassable with scattered boulders the size of office buildings.

"We're going to have to ration our water, Gordy. As best as I can see, we need to climb down to the bottom of this slope and hopefully come back up on the other side of these boulders."

Gordy's short blond hair withstood the assault of wind. The silver ring around his temples concealed his eyes, but she could tell from the angle of his head he was seeking options other than her suggestion.

"I guess you're right," he conceded.

Flanking the tumbled rocks for stability and camouflage, they hiked down the hillside. At any moment some granite creature might bound from the shadows for all she knew. Aimee refused to relinquish her eye shield. It was not her intention to come this far and lose to a solar ray.

"Look at that," Gordy whispered in awe. "It looks like a sea of blood."

Indeed, that is what the flat surface of the desert looked like in the distance.

"When did you get so poetic?" she mumbled. "Or macabre?"

"Huh?"

"Never mind. The boulders are getting smaller. Maybe we'll reach the bottom soon."

"Aimee, you told me the mountains were the safest place in your opinion—that the Korons wouldn't climb them. And yet, here we are hiking down to meet them."

Aimee turned around and searched over his shoulder. "Do you see a way to go up?"

He followed her gaze. "No."

"Do you see Zak?"

His head swiveled back towards her. "No."

"Then this is our only option."

In several hours, futility began to settle in. They had reached the base of the mountain. As Aimee had hoped, the avenue on the other side of the avalanche was better, but not without obstacle. It was a rugged hike, loaded with loose rocks, narrow cliffs, and no sign of life.

Even with the shield on, Aimee could see the lines of dismay around Gordy's mouth.

In tandem they turned towards the desert, a red tongue that licked at their feet. It shimmered under the heat of the two suns. Where it had been chilly in the high foothills— here the perspiration wormed between Aimee's shoulder blades, amplifying her unease.

Deception lurked in the sand. She understood mirages now. On that gleaming stretch imagination manifested creatures of all shapes and sizes.

"Are there people out there?" Gordy asked beside her.

She squinted, but the heat undulated wave upon wave of mystical layers.

"I don't think so. It just looks flat."

"No. Really—look."

Oh well heck, if she stared long and hard enough she could perceive a thousand monsters with five heads lurking out there.

Wait. Maybe not a thousand. Maybe something like twenty, or ten, or...

"Yeah, maybe I do see something."

Murky shadows. Anomalies of the desert. As they grew closer, her estimate of them dwindled. Were they Korons?

"Gordy, you have your *star laser* ready?"

"Y-yes."

"Let's climb back up behind that last boulder and wait this out. There's still a chance we're both seeing things."

"Okay."

Her heart was racing. Clumsy hands tried to pull the small weapon from her belt. It came loose, but fell to the ground. Instinctively she recoiled, fearing the impact would make it go off.

"It doesn't work that way," Gordy stooped to retrieve it and hand it to her like it was a candy bar. In his shield she could see tension etched on her face.

"It only reacts to the stroke of your finger," he added.

It was a great blessing that he knew about this stuff. She had concentrated so much on making an elephant fly. Her lessons on galactic artillery were few and far between. Still, something about holding the sleek weapon in her hand restored a sense of control. She just prayed she didn't have to use it.

Reprieve from the heat was welcome in the shadows of the lofty boulder. When Gordy moved to scan the desert, she restrained him with a touch of the hand. Instead, she leaned forward for a glimpse.

"You have to let me look," he whispered, "I'm supposedly the better marksmen of the two of us."

God help us.

She was older. She was in charge. As delusional as her intentions may be, she wanted the Korons to get past *her* in order to reach the teenager.

Poking out from behind the boulder, she squinted against the assault of the two suns. On second glimpse, the approaching figures did not look as tall as she originally estimated. Maybe their lengthy shadows cast across the sand enhanced their height. These figures appeared human, and nowhere near the number she had originally counted. Now she calculated maybe ten...possibly less.

"Okay," she whispered. "Look out there. Be careful. Don't let them see you...but tell me if you think they're human, ummm, *mecaws.*"

Gordy peered around her shoulder. His head snapped back. "Yeah, they look human— well, except one appears deformed...maybe not a *mecaw.*" After a second, he added, "What do we do?"

What indeed?

Aimee crouched down with her back

against the granite. One was not human. A Koron? Could the creature hold five or ten people hostage single-handedly? She swung her head out into the sun. Some of the shadows stumbled. Had they been blinded? Is that how the monster controlled them?

Okay, she was liking her odds better. One beast. Counting her and Gordy, there had to be at least ten humans. Blind or not, there was strength in numbers, right?

They drew closer, altering the wake of their shadows. *Damn!*

"Gordy, look again. Tell me how many you see."

He moved to gaze beyond her and she grabbed his arm. "Careful!"

"Careful. Careful," he muttered. He slipped half of his face into the sun and snapped it back. "There's only about three or four of them. I thought it was an army."

"The suns. They cast opposite shadows. Two shadows per person." Damn, she wanted to take the shield off. It itched where it rubbed against the crest of her cheekbone. "So three or four humans—and a monster. Did one of the humans look armed to you?"

"Probably out of ammunition," Gordy suggested. "That Koron is just making him carry it."

"Maybe. Either way, we have to be careful. No matter what you do, do not take that shield off, Gordeelum."

Had the shield been off, she would have probably caught his exasperated glance.

"I'm the better shot. You wait behind me." He shifted into position.

Aimee slipped around the other side of the rock.

"Where are you going?" Gordy called.

"The boulders are smaller down here. If we time it just right, we can push together and roll one of these into him...or at least create a big enough distraction."

Gordy opened his mouth to refute her plan, but considered it with a growing grin. "It definitely would be a distraction." He nodded. "I like it."

They crept in tandem behind the quarry until the monoliths were of a negotiable size.

"The guy in the lead is armed, but the Koron is still taking up the rear. It only looks like maybe two or three people between them now," Gordy chronicled.

Aimee agreed. The man in the lead was taller than the rest. Perhaps he was a young Koron? Whatever the case, these strangers were approaching, drawing close enough that she could see—

She gasped.

"Aimee, are you okay?" Gordy whirled, concerned.

Could it be? Or were the suns playing tricks on her eyes?

Every step he took drew his attributes into focus. Tall. Dark hair. Slightly longer. It was impossible to see his eyes behind the tarnished shield. This man was shirtless, and even from this distance she could see how rugged his chest was—his arms bulging from the weight of the weapon in his hands. Skin bronzed from the sun glistened with a slight sheen of perspiration. Whoever this man was, he exuded strength and conviction, and he made her ache with the memory of Zak.

"Hey," Gordy whispered at her side, "that isn't Zak, is it?"

She couldn't imagine Zak traveling within steps of a Koron. She couldn't conceive him ever being held captive by his worst enemy.

Dragging her attention from the foremost figure, she noticed two men directly behind him. They too were shirtless, but their shoulders were slumped from fatigue and famine. Their waning strength made them trudge through the sand.

Finally, she scrutinized the monster in the rear. Far enough away, the sun hugged his grotesque silhouette in a shimmering glove.

"What do we do?" Gordy jarred her. "They're getting close. We have to shove this rock pretty soon."

Aimee placed her palm on the cool stone. It was the size of a refrigerator. Enough to make a statement. Taking a discrete step to her left she gauged the trajectory of the hunk of granite.

"What are the chances of us sneaking up behind them after they have passed?"

Gordy snorted. "And do what…tap them on the shoulder and say, hello? No, we need an advantage."

"Alright." This was a stupid idea. This boulder wasn't a bowling ball. And the targets were moving pins. "We shove for all we're worth. If you feel the rock start to budge—"

She heard voices.

The group below was speaking. Barking was more like it. From the rear, the monster shouted orders. The dark-haired man in front turned his head, but otherwise seemed unaffected. They drew closer, and the time for Aimee and Gordy to make their move was imminent.

…and yet, she hesitated.

"If we're going to do something, we have to do it now," Gordy whispered. "They're heading for this hillside and they'll see us soon—even if we run."

"Shhh."

"*Sock. Nud—stup—wahtah.*"

Was it the language of the Korons? Zak had told her that they didn't speak. They communicated telepathically, with the exception of a few grunts. They used weapons to communicate with everyone else.

From the rear, the brute repeated his plea. "*Sock. Need—stop—water.*"

Aimee's chest heaved as the talons of vertigo wormed into her head.

Not *Sock*.

Zak.

It had to be the lack of blood flowing to her brain that accounted for her irrational reaction. Stumbling out from behind the boulder, she was vaguely aware of Gordy's cry of alarm.

"Aimee!" Gordy shouted.

But it was too late. She was in the open, lurching down the hillside.

Below, the group halted like a pack of startled gazelle, staring up at her. The man in the lead took a step forward and hesitated. Initially, he struck a combative stance with his weapon raised. His step faltered, however, and the aim of his laser dropped.

Aimee's muscles twitched. Only twenty yards separated her from the clan. Her chest heaved like each breath was her last. Was there enough oxygen on this planet?

In a silent face-off, she stared down the leader. Curse his shield for obscuring his eyes. But everything else was visible...and familiar. The broad shoulders, the long legs, the rich, dark hair gleaming under the dual suns. It was Zak. Never was she more certain of a single fact. His body had matured, and the bare, tan chest looked sculpted with a power that could crush her.

Dammit, take off the shield.

He reached up and hefted the silver band onto his forehead.

Zak.

She whimpered as she connected with those familiar eyes. Gold, like the blazing surface of the sand.

So long. She had waited *so long*.

Zak's athletic frame jerked when he saw her. He staggered a step in her direction. Then, still swaying, he dropped to his knee. Aimee rushed towards him, but froze when he raised his weapon—and aimed it at her.

CHAPTER NINE

Not again.

He thought that he was healing—that the desert dreams had ceased. But here she was, descending towards him from the suns on a bridge of diamonds. Curse the Korons for toying with his sight... *with his mind*. The mere thought that it could possibly be her staggered him. It sapped his strength as he fell to his knee. For all he knew, it was one of *them* standing before him, their grotesque shape reformed by a trick of the light.

They would not destroy him. He would not go down without a fight.

Zak hauled the shield back over his eyes, hoping it would shatter the mirage, but still, she remained. Raising his solar ray, he was prepared to use the last trickle of ammunition to abolish this demon. The mountain was close. Refuge in the cave was a short hike away. This specter would not stop him.

Zak's finger grasped the arch of the cylinder.

"Zak!"

What? Now his hearing was going as well?

He raised the solar ray.

"Zak, no. It's *me*. It's Aimee."

His head twitched. He wanted to wipe the sweat from his brow, but he dared not lose his grip on the solar ray. Dropping his glance to the hands of the wraith before him, he noticed the weapon...a *pulse slayer*, maybe?

The phantom lowered the device, resting it against a sleek thigh clad in a phosphorescent material. The material flattered the feminine curves and made his stomach clench in need.

No! It was not the soft curve of a female thigh. It was a slab of rock hell bent on destruction.

"Zak," the voice gentled and tugged at something deep inside his soul. "It's me." It paused, and then repeated softly, "It's *me*."

"Zak—"

Now it was Zuttah's guttural call he heard from behind. "Lower the ray. She's a *mecaw*."

A mecaw?

A rebel? One of the suns was behind her on its trek behind the mountain. It eclipsed the feminine figure.

Say it again. Speak again. Let me hear your voice.

"It's me," she whispered as she stooped to set her weapon on the sand.

Another figure flanked her. Zak tightened his clutch on the solar ray, but the form was also *mecaw.* Male. Zak's eyes snapped back to the woman. She took a tentative step forward. Gravity on the incline caused her to stumble, but he would not move to assist.

"I don't think I've changed that much," she pointed out. "Maybe I lost a little weight, and my hair is longer. Yeah, I guess it has a lot more red in it since you saw it. My mom said that comes from my great grandmother. She was a stoic old Ukrainian woman who never cracked a smile. My parents took her to Disney World a few years ago. She cried during the *It's A Small World* ride. It was embarrassing—"

Zak lowered his weapon. He hauled the shield off his head.

"Stop." he ordered in a dry voice. "There is only one person I know who talks that much when she is nervous."

The woman's lips smacked tight. She remained motionless, her breath held.

"Come here," he whispered.

Limbs quivered. Hesitant steps turned into

ground-eaters as gravity hauled her down the slope. The impetus landed her with a pronounced smack against his chest.

Cool palms splayed atop his warm skin. He had to close his eyes against the sensual assault. When he opened them, all he saw was his own earnest gaze reflected in the silver band.

"Take your shield off so that I can see you," his voice was hoarse.

Tremulous fingers rose from his chest to yank the reflective band back into thick auburn hair. He wanted to touch that hair—to feel that soft waterfall glide across his fingers, but the shield was gone and he was seized by the view.

Long brown eyelashes rested against high cheekbones. Those lashes flew open and he nearly lost the power in his legs again.

"Aimee," he croaked.

Wide blue eyes gazed up at him. When he had last looked into them, they were filled with tears and declarations of love. It was an image etched in his memory...and now, here she was, standing before him—on *his* planet.

Of course it was a hallucination. It was absurd to even consider otherwise.

"As our leader seems to have lost his tongue, allow me to introduce myself."

Zuttah stepped forward and thrust his

hand out.

Zak noticed Aimee's curious glimpse of the inert form draped across the man's brawny shoulder.

"Zuttah," he introduced in a rough voice.

Aimee accepted the hairy mitt, but no matter where she looked, her eyes always returned to Zak. Still locked on him, she spoke to Zuttah, "You speak my language? Do you have a translator?"

Zak knew she was being polite. The towering pile of *Zull* furs certainly did not harbor the intricate translation system that the HORUS implemented in their uniforms.

"*He* taught me." Zuttah nodded at Zak.

Zak felt the magnetic tug of her gaze. He was afraid to meet it. He was afraid to yield to this vision. It could not be real. It was a rebel communicating with Zuttah, and nothing more.

In his fractured mind, Zak was seeing what he wanted to see.

"Really?" Aimee asked. "He doesn't seem to talk too much, so I can't imagine how you learned."

It was good to know that his fractured mind was still dead on. That would be the blithe type of humor he would expect from Aimee.

Zuttah glanced at him and grunted. "Yes,

well, he is a tad off these days. Your uniform—
where did you come from?"

Before she could respond, Zak was aware
of the approach of the male who had been
eclipsed by sunlight. *No. Could it be?*

"Zak!" Gordy jogged down the hill and
stopped a few feet away with an enthusiastic
grin.

Zak almost felt his lips jerk up in response.

"You people know Zak?" Zuttah asked
with a frown. "You are from his ship then?"

"Yes," Aimee nodded.

Tears began to form in the corners of her
eyes. The sight caused his chest to constrict, but
still, he could not move. He could not speak.

"Wow, Zak. You look different," Gordy
remarked.

*He did? How much different? Was he
repulsive? When had he last seen his reflection?*

"That woman," Aimee nodded at the
unconscious figure on Zuttah's shoulder. "Is she
okay?"

There they were again. Even after focusing
on the ailing female, Aimee's eyes found their
way back to his.

This was all just so impossible. Had he not
lost a bit of his sanity the last time he looked into
those eyes? To have found someone so beautiful,

so perfect—a person he wanted to share his life with—and to watch her go...

"The Korons attacked," Zuttah spoke, but it came to him in echoes. "These rebels were kidnapped. Zak saved them. We need to get this woman to the caves, though."

The echoes grew louder and the shadow realm reached for him with seductive black fingers.

"Zak?" Aimee's voice filled with concern.

That was his Aimee—always worried about him. He closed his eyes. With the light gone, the real world could return. He needed the caves. He needed the dark.

"Zak has not been well," Zuttah's deep timbre returned. "It is important to get back to the caves. Important for you as well. They will be coming soon."

"The Korons?" Gordy inserted.

"Yes, those pieces of rock dung."

Zak's eyes remained closed, but he felt an arm slip under his to wrap around his back. A slender, warm contour splayed against his side. Support. He never had support. There was survival or death. No support. He kept his eyes tightly shut. Opening them might dispel this wonderful sensation.

"Let's go," Aimee stated. "*I have you,*" she

whispered for him alone to hear.

Zak's hand curled around her shoulder. So dainty, and yet so determined. If only she was real. But, he was too tired to fight this bantam being. Zuttah was still speaking calmly. Apparently they were not in danger. Zak kept his eyes shut and enjoyed this dream.

The banter between Zuttah and the others continued as Zak felt the muscles in his thighs contract with the ascent. Already, the temperature dropped, and the air misted with precipitation. He tipped his head back to feel the divine drops. It was not rain. It was a fine haze stirred by the wind across the snow caps.

Beneath his feet came the familiar crunch of gravel and grass. Other treads blended with his, but he listened to his own steps, knowing his proximity to the cave by the alteration of the terrain.

The warm presence still hugged his side, often whispering words of encouragement. *An angel?* His mother had spoken of celestial beings, their bodies as wispy as the clouds that embraced the crater walls. This body felt solid though, and he relied on it as they climbed.

The suns crisscrossed to score an X across

the white peak. Once he had considered that a beautiful sight—nature's emblem, marking the new home of the Ziratak people. Now, that light caused him to recoil. Shortly, the suns would drop behind the peaks of the Zorgon mountain range. The dark was his ally. In the dark, he could hone in on the smallest creature stirring in the distance. In the dark, he could find his way when others would falter. In the dark, he was in control, and the madness abated.

In the dark—he could determine whether this warm presence at his side was truly Aimee.

It was hard not to stare. Hard not to gape at the man she supported with her own weight. His eyes were aimed straight ahead and his expression was intense. Once, his dark hair had been cut so short, almost military style. Now it curled over his ears in a disheveled chocolate blend of strands highlighted from the sun. His jaw, now shadowed with the hint of stubble pumped a familiar muscle. He was nearly six inches taller than her so she gazed up at that chiseled jawline. This was her Zak. A bedraggled, wounded version—but ever the Warrior, and ever-handsome.

She stumbled on loose rocks reminding

her to focus on the path ahead. Had Zak's hand just cupped her waist to assist? Maybe—but other than that, he had done little to indicate that he even recognized her. Heck, he had tried to *shoot* her. It didn't take an engineer to deduce that something was drastically wrong. But, she didn't care. She was here. She was holding him. Zak was alive, and a huge hole in her heart was slowly mending.

As they entered into a narrow channel—a chasm carved between steep slopes, Aimee swore she heard the sound of rushing water. It couldn't possibly be a waterfall. They were locked inside an impenetrable granite stockade, and it appeared as though they were marching to a dead end—a conflux of slate walls adhering into a solid mass. In that juncture, a tiny fissure appeared—a mere slit in the mountain face. The gaping shadow drew taller as they approached it.

"So, you are the woman Zak sees in the suns?"

"Excuse me?" Aimee was startled.

She glanced over her shoulder to find the burly caveman at her side. He maneuvered the narrow channel with grace despite his girth and the burden of the woman in his grasp.

"Ahm-heeee?" He considered aloud, nodding at his recollection.

"Aimee. Yes." A glimpse towards Zak revealed that he was alert and listening, but his eyes were trained forward. She even felt his hastened pace as if the fissure drew him like a thirsty man to water.

Tilting her head away from Zak, she issued a sideward whisper. "What is wrong with him?"

Zuttah leaned in conspiratorially. "Solar ray. He doesn't see well in the light." His voice dipped lower. "And with the head trauma, what he does see—isn't there."

"But his ears work just fine," Zak quipped.

Aimee jerked her head back in his direction.

"Then you can hear your girlfriend," Zuttah barked. "Can't you? You haven't even acknowledged her except to use her as a crutch."

A shiver traveled through Aimee as she connected with Zak's stare. For a moment she saw recognition—and then pain. He wrenched away, slipping his arm from her shoulder to reach out to the tapering walls for support.

"Zak," she pleaded.

She felt a tug on her sleeve. "Give him time," Zuttah soothed.

"We're almost there," Zak spoke over them. "We need to attend to this woman and feed these men—" he glared at the furry giant, "*then* you can go into great detail about my mental state, and then I will come to grips with this vision—" his eyes slid to Aimee, "—that can't be real."

"Zak!" she cried. "I *am* real."

But they were forced into single file by the narrow gap. Aimee glanced up at the sliver of blue sky far above. Like giant fingers, eaves of snow clung to the tops of the ravine. She was no fool. Hollering was likely to jar their precious grip and send that blanket plummeting down on top of them.

Somewhat subdued, she trained her eyes on the broad expanse of Zak's bare shoulders. Five years ago she had thought him so strong, but then he had still been young. Now he had grown into the full range of muscles that ruled his tall physique. Zak had become a man, and she was in awe of him.

When she thought she reached a point where two mountains became one and they would have no choice but to execute an about-face, Zak was swallowed by the shadows—and she was alone.

An arm lunged out of the abyss to latch onto hers. She screamed and fought the tug. In a second she was shrouded in darkness, her eyes struggling to acclimate. Behind her, bodies pressed into the shadows. She felt their breath, heard their grunts of effort, and still the manacle locked onto her wrist. It squeezed once, almost encouragingly, and then it was gone.

Aimee swung around to focus on the gap in the rock and the daylight beyond. The bulky silhouette of Zuttah filled the opening as the others poured in behind him. With relief, she saw the sun glint atop Gordy's blond hair before he fell into the shadows of this secreted cave.

A fire erupted behind her, lighting up the cavern. The smell of sulfur filled her nostrils. The source was a burning pile of kindling and moss heaped near the cave wall. It enabled her to survey her new environment. It was a large cavern with recessed walls that made her suspect there was more than just this grand chamber. Her head tipped back to search the vaulted ceiling. Abnormal rock formations and stalactites, hung like daggers from above.

Another fire erupted in the recesses of the cave, casting animated shadows across the moistened walls. There were others that had been waiting inside the cave. All in all, she could count nearly twenty people.

Zak had delved into the dark. She searched

as far as the flames extended, but could not locate him. About to pursue, she noticed that Zuttah had settled the unconscious woman on a bed of furs and sat back on his heels now staring at Aimee, expectantly. Did he think she was a doctor?

Aimee dropped to her knees beside him. Something had to be done for this poor woman. Aimee placed the back of her hand on the tanned forehead and felt the scorch of fever there.

"She has a high fever. We need to bring it down. Do you have any ice? From the mountain perhaps?"

Zuttah gave her a quizzical look, and then snorted. He hefted up onto his feet and ambled over to a chest sitting up against the wall. Muttering, he grabbed an instrument and returned, squatting down beside the woman. "Just because we live in caves," he scoffed, "doesn't mean that we are cave dwellers."

He stooped over the woman and pressed a small cylinder against her neck. A muscle rebelled against the touch, but the woman's expression seemed to relax. Fine wrinkles around her eyes blended into the olive skin and disappeared. Thin shoulders slackened into the fur. There was even a sigh from her chapped lips.

"She will be okay soon."

Indeed, the woman already looked improved and her eyelids even fluttered open. Brown irises slid about the cave, settling on one of the men who had been marching with them. The man shot forward to be by her side, his hand engulfing hers. As he leaned over, there were warm whispers of encouragement and shy smiles that made Aimee take a step back to offer privacy.

She tipped her head at Zuttah in respect.

Gordy was busy talking to the older rebel who had traveled at the rear of the pack. Occupied with an array of tasks, the group of men and women set about preparing food, honing handmade weapons, and engaging in congenial banter. Dressed in pants of a leather-like fabric, and similar vests, some lined with fur—these rebels looked industrious, and dare she say, *happy*?

With the exception of the three people Zak and Zuttah had escorted in, these men and women looked healthy. Each had dark hair in various states of disarray, while their eyes were all golden in hue. With the woman resting on the furs now coming around, Aimee thought that with some food and water, these three rebels would soon look as healthy.

Her eyes swept over their heads, deeper

into the cave, beyond the flickering scope of the last fire. She stood and made her way in that direction, aware of the curious stares that trailed her.

In a nook created by a flank of large boulders, she found him.

Zak.

Her pulse drilled at the sight of the man reclined atop a flat rock, his head propped on a folded fur. His eyes were closed, but she knew that face. Even now her fingers reached for the charm dangling atop her collarbone. It was a piece of his ship. It was a piece of him. And for the past five years—every time she squeezed it, she saw this face. High cheekbones. A strong chin. Full lips that revealed a quirky dimple when he smiled, and a jaw that jerked in spasm when he concentrated.

Was he asleep? Had he passed out?

She stepped up to what eerily resembled an altar and gazed down at the strength in that broad chest. When last she had seen Zak, he was dressed from head to toe in a black suit that held as many glittering nuances as space itself. Now she could appreciate the tan flesh, the slight sprinkle of dark hair...the muscles. She wanted to touch him—so much so that her hand lifted, balanced an inch above his rising chest.

Aimee yelped as her wrist was snared unexpectedly. That grip hauled her a step closer.

"Who are you?"

His voice was hoarse and his eyes remained shut.

The manacle around her hand was unyielding, but not painful. Heat from his palm engulfed her.

"It's me, Zak. It's Aimee."

Pain lanced his forehead.

"That is not possible."

Still, he did not open his eyes.

"Is it the solar ray, Zak?" With her free hand, her fingers moved from the pendant to dust across the vial Raja had given her. "Did they hurt you?" Her voice cracked on the last word.

Zak remained silent, but he did not let go of her hand.

"If you are a dream," he murmured, "then I do not want to wake up. Let me stay here with you. I waited so long for you. I thought I would be back to the HORUS on time, but—"

The vice around her wrist eased. He continued in that husky voice she had missed so desperately.

"Before I left, I asked Raja to—" his head shook from side, "—to see if you were waiting. I didn't think you would wait. I couldn't blame you if you had moved on. You were so beautiful. A man surely would have claimed you...you couldn't possibly be waiting for me."

She realized that he wasn't talking to her. He was talking aloud—to a memory.

"I waited, Zak. And I was there when Raja brought me back—back to the HORUS."

Zak frowned.

"I am on Ziratak," he declared, more to convince himself. "There is no way you can be here."

If only he would open his eyes. God, she wanted to see them.

"Well, I—" she hesitated because it did sound outlandish, "—I misappropriated an old craft, converted it into something that would fly, and learned to be a pilot so that I could come save you."

"You used to be a vision descending to me on a bridge from the suns." A trace of his dimple appeared. "But you were a *quiet* vision. Now the voice lends some authenticity."

Bah. Enough of this.

Aimee leaned over and dusted her lips across his. She hesitated and then touched them again.

"There," she sounded flustered, "do your visions kiss you?"

Zak shot upright, swinging his long legs off the stone altar. Aimee jumped back, startled.

Finally. Finally, his eyes were open and they looked *oh-so* beautiful. Golden halos around pupils that widened at the sight of her. Deep shadows at their core harbored the wonders of space.

He leaned forward, his shoulders thick with strain. In one quick surge, he lurched towards her, his hands reaching for her face, diving into her hair, cupping her head. And then his mouth was on hers—and she was lost.

It had been five years since she was in this man's arms—and absolutely everything she had done—every decision she had made—was worth it.

He kissed her with urgency as his lips brushed hers, tasting her, testing if she was real. As swift as the assault began, his head snapped back and he stared at her wide-eyed.

"Gayat."

Dammit.

"Wh-what?" Recognizing the curse, her mind was slow, laden with the lingering effects of his warm mouth.

"It can't be you." He touched her hair, his eyes skimming the strands. Calloused fingertips traced her cheek and hooked under her chin to tilt her head back.

"It can't be you," he repeated.

"Do you want me to kiss you again to prove it?" Ah, such bravado, but her voice trembled.

"The thought of kissing you is something I want so badly that it actually scares me. I don't want the illusion to shatter." His palm stroked her throat. "You look—you *feel* so real."

She grabbed his hand and laid it over her thumping heart. Then, she maneuvered his fingers inside the collar of her shirt and wrapped them around her necklace.

A muscle jerked in his jaw. Of its own volition, his hand tightened about her necklace as his knuckles brushed her collarbone.

"It's real, Zak," she whispered. "*I'm* real. Don't let these monsters take this away from you."

Dark lashes descended against his cheekbones as he murmured, "I need to sit down."

Aimee guided him back to the giant rock slab where he rested his rear, but kept his legs splayed out on the ground, ready to bolt.

"Alright," he began. "Fill me in on all the details, and *then* kiss me so I can be sure."

There it was. A phantom glimpse of a grin

she knew so well. Aimee felt tears inch into the corners of her eyes, but she smiled and clapped her hands together and started in.

"Well—I was there in the woods exactly five years to the minute from when you shoved me off the HORUS."

"I did not *shove* you off the HORUS," he defended. "Letting you go that day was one of the hardest things I have ever done in my life...and I've been through some pretty hard times."

Aimee swallowed the lump in her throat and continued. "I thought you weren't going to come back for me. The clock kept ticking and it wasn't until almost ten minutes later that the beam arrived. The next thing I knew, I was on board the HORUS, and Vodu and Raja were hugging me, but—" she frowned at the recollection, "—you weren't there."

Zak nodded. His head down.

When he didn't speak, she proceeded. "Vodu tried to send me back while we were still within range of Earth. He didn't want to see me hurt, as he suspected you were—dea—gone."

Zak looked up, one golden eye watching her from beneath dark bangs—bangs he had not possessed the last time she saw him.

"But Raja had already pulled me aside with her suspicions that you were still alive. She didn't want me to get my hopes up—but as you can imagine, it was all the spark I needed. It was enough to make me devise a plan."

"Yes, I can imagine," he murmured. "And what was your plan, exactly?"

"Quite simple, actually," she beamed. "I was going to become a Warrior."

Zak laughed. He laughed so loud Aimee glanced over her shoulder to see if anyone heard. The others remained unbothered, but his face had flushed from the mirth.

"It wasn't that outlandish." She crossed her arms.

"Men are born as Warriors. It isn't something you choose. It is imposed on you by heredity."

"Said the orphan from another planet."

Now Zak crossed his arms and lowered his eyebrows. "I was an exception."

"You usually are," she grinned and waited as she saw him struggle to suppress his own. "Anyway, I went through training—"

He rose and used his hand against the stone for leverage. Even hunched slightly, he was taller than her. "You went through *training?*" he roared. "With who? The Warriors would *not* let a woman in."

"Oh, you're all so chauvinistic. I got here,

didn't I?"

"*Who* trained you?" he repeated, quirking an eyebrow.

"Corluss, and JOH, and—"

"A blind man? A blind man prepared you for this trip?"

Well, when he put it that way.

"And that chattering box?" he added.

"Did you know that JOH has legs now?" She ignored his goading.

"No." He frowned. "I guess I have been gone awhile."

Shaking his head, Zak continued. "That's all fine. I totally believe you brainwashed, or bullied these people into helping you, but how did you get a *terra angel?* You couldn't have flown with one of the Warriors. They would never let you on board."

"*You* did."

"You stowed away. Did you stow away again? Aimee—"

He was about to berate her, so she cut him off. "No. You are right. I could not get a hold of a *terra angel.*"

The quizzical look inspired her to continue. She adjusted her shoulders, ready for another outburst. "I reengineered an old *terra duster.* Well, not alone. I had a man named

Wando help me. We designed the ion drives so that they would have enough power to make the trip, but in order to get it all to work we had to fabricate a vacuum, and now I'm afraid that—"

The anticipated laughter at her folly was not there. Heck, he wasn't even smiling. *Was he angry?* No, she studied his pensive expression and challenged, "What?"

Hunched on the edge of the stone altar, with his chin in his hand, Zak looked like a statue in a Greek courtyard. Perhaps she was biased, but she didn't think any artist could sculpt something so grand.

"Well," he spoke and jarred her, "I'm not sure what amazes me more—the fact that you redesigned one of those old crop mowers, or that you convinced that obstinate old man to help you do it. You really are a—" he squinted his eyes, thinking, "—charmer, aren't you?"

"You think I'm charming?" She batted her eyelashes.

Every time she expected to goad a laugh, he sobered.

"You said, *now I'm afraid that*—" His eyes pierced her. "What are you afraid of?"

"Oh." Her smile faltered. She waved her hand as if she could dismiss the comment, but Zak seized that hand and held it in both of his.

She wanted to cry at the simple touch.

"It was a great collaboration to get us here," she explained, "but I'm afraid that we exhausted all we had. I'm not sure we have the method to create a sufficient vacuum—" Her head cocked as she contemplated the vaulted ceiling of the cave, "—although a cave might help."

"Us?"

"Huh?"

"You said, us. Who came with you?"

"Oh," she glanced over her shoulder. They were still secluded inside this nook. "Gordy came with me."

"Gordeelum?" Zak's eyebrows vaulted. "I thought I imagined him. So, you and Gordy shot out into space on your own, in a relic—" he shook his head again, "—and you actually made it here?"

"Well damn, you don't have to sound so surprised. Have a little faith in me."

He rose and approached her. Aimee's breath hitched in her throat and her skin tingled in anticipation.

Zak clasped her shoulders and looked into her eyes. "I do."

Honestly, she wanted to say something, but it felt like a basketball was lodged in her throat.

"You went back to school when you got home?" he prompted quietly.

"Y-yes."

His smile turned her kneecaps into noodles.

"I bet you excelled."

"I did alright."

I got straight A's because all I ever did was study so I could take my mind off of you.

"Good." There was a quick nod of approval and then, "As soon as I finish berating you for this reckless trip—and as soon as I finish kissing you the way I want so desperately to do—" his eyes dropped to her lips, "—I have something I need your help with."

"Ohhh-kayy." Where had her command of the English dialect gone? Oh, right, it flew away as soon as his eyes landed on her lips.

"Zak?"

"Hmm?"

"Can we skip the berating part?"

The familiar cleft scored his cheek. Warm palms slid down her arms and tentative hands circled her hips.

"Come here," he whispered.

Tears blurred her view. She reached for him, her hands inching up behind his neck.

For a maddening moment his mouth hovered over hers—a warm breath tickling her lips—and then he was there, kissing her in a way that felt as if all the worlds in all the galaxies had ceased to exist, and the only universe prevailed in this embrace.

With a reluctant last caress, Zak broke away, but he kept his forehead against hers and spoke in a hoarse voice. "I missed you. Every day, every *ren*."

"We're together now." She touched the back of his neck, and inched her fingers into the lustrous hair. "We're together."

He hauled her into a tight hug as her arms linked behind his neck. After a few moments of this bonding, Aimee set her hands on his shoulders and pushed her way back so that she could look into his eyes.

"Are you okay?" She squeezed his shoulders for emphasis. "I hear—I hear that the solar ray can make you mad?"

"The Korons have taken much from me. I won't let them take my mind."

"Then why did you not think I was real? Why has Zuttah been so concerned?"

Zak sank back down on the rock and this time Aimee noticed the fatigue drawing shadows beneath his eyes. Still, he managed a smile.

"I thought I was the one who was supposed to do the berating here."

Not to be dissuaded, she ducked to meet his gaze. The suns there were vibrant, but something in their dark nucleus troubled her.

"Tell me," she pleaded.

"I haven't gone mad, Aimee. I just have trouble seeing in the light. That cursed beam nearly caught me dead on."

"But your shield—"

"—is not infallible. It prevents blindness, yes—but you can still end up with side effects. Right now, I see every beautiful inch of you, and I know you are real. Out there—" His hand flung towards the entrance of the cave. "My sight is limited, and what I do see deceives me. Eventually those phantoms start to get to you. They mess with your mind. And once your mind starts going, so does your strength. I can't let the light stop me. There are people to save out there, and every time I go out, it saps my strength. But I won't stop until they are all free." He nodded, "—so yes, Zuttah has been concerned. I'm not the most jovial guy outside—but in here I am sane."

"You liked the dark long before this," Aimee recalled his childhood tale of being trapped in the cellar for three days straight. And then, being cloistered with her in that tight cave on Bordran...the day she knew she was falling in love with him.

"Aimee." His hands gripped the edges of the rock slab, and he was staring at her intently. "I am damaged. I am not good in the suns. I may not be able to protect you. I may see things that are not there."

"Well, then it's a damn good thing I got here. Someone has to look out for you, and someone has to tell you when it is time to rest."

"Dammit," he chuckled.

"Dammit," she repeated.

He reached for her hands and drew her in between his outstretched legs. Looking up at her, he commanded softly, "Kiss me again."

Without hesitation her hands cupped his warm cheeks and she dipped to press her lips against his. She could feel his sigh of relief mingled with pleasure. She would never grow tired of this.

"Ehh-hemm."

Aimee snapped back and Zak grabbed her waist for support.

Gordy poked his head around the corner and flashed his white teeth. "I don't mean to interrupt, but I wanted to say hi to Zak too." Pink tinged his cheeks and he cleared his throat. "Well, not like that, but—I was thinking more of a handshake." He scratched the back of his head, falling deeper into embarrassment.

Zak rose. His first few steps bore a limp, but he gained equilibrium by the time he reached Gordy and extended his hand towards the young man.

Gordy grabbed it and pumped it enthusiastically. The ghost of the child was still stamped on his face.

"Zak!" he blared. "I knew they couldn't get you."

One of Zak's eyebrows dipped. He propped himself against the cave wall with his palm.

"Gordeelum," he said, "What do your parents have to say about you coming here?"

"Well," Gordy stammered, "I figured we'd all be back before they even noticed that I was missing from classes."

Warped logic, but Aimee hoped he was right.

"You're lucky I'll be putting in a good word for you when I see them."

"For saving you?" Gordy beamed.

Zak looked at Aimee. "No, for keeping her safe."

Gordy glanced back and forth between them. "Right," he nodded slowly, but then plodded on to the next subject. "Hey Zak, is your ship still intact? Because that will be a lot easier than trying to get that fat elephant up in the air again."

Fat elephant? Zak mouthed with a questioning look.

"You'd have to see it to understand." Aimee inserted.

Zak smiled at her, but then swung his glance back to Gordy. "No, my ship was destroyed not long after I landed. I watched as the Korons dissected it and then later learned that it had been reduced to a useless pile of *alorium.*"

Aimee's heart ached for him. She knew how special that *terra angel* was to him.

"Oh—" Gordy interrupted her thoughts, "—because some guy out there has been talking about it."

"What?" Zak's hand fell off the wall. "Who?"

Under that intense scrutiny Gordy turned edgy. He hitched his thumb towards the front of the cave and said, "That old guy. He looks like he's gone lame from a solar ray blast, but he did say something about the *Zari.* Isn't that your ship?"

CHAPTER TEN

Zak tensed. *Could it be?*

He had been told by Zuttah that his ship was destroyed. Zak had seen the abuse it had taken from the Korons, but he had never actually witnessed its final destruction. Maybe it could be repaired and provide Aimee with safe transportation off this planet.

A few feet away, he caught her watching him. There was a maturity to her face now. Youth still hugged her lips, but her gaze was dark and incisive. What had once been a tumble of auburn hair around her face was now sleek and molten, like the desert sand as the suns began to set. The garments she wore molded a body that was tall and toned. She had lost weight. He wanted to feed her, and he wanted to run his finger down the long curve of her neck and feel her pulse to make sure she was real.

But she *was* real. As impossible as it may

be, Aimee was really here, standing before him with her lips parted on an unvoiced question. She always had questions. She always wanted to learn. It fascinated him. She was so beautiful and if he could get her back to safety—if this stranger knew anything about his ship—

"Over here." Gordy waved.

Before following, Zak reached for Aimee's hand. Inside his calloused palm, hers felt so smooth. No force could motivate him to let go. Her mouth may not have moved, but her eyes flashed him an encouraging smile.

"Hey," Gordy called to the man who sat hunched against the cave wall, staring listlessly towards the glow of the entrance.

"Hey," Gordy repeated, reaching the leather-swathed feet. "You were telling me about the *Zari*. Have you actually seen Zak's ship?"

The man's head snapped up. Mottled brown eyes gaped at Gordy. Arms caked with dust trembled. The man's hair was dark and threaded with gray strands that dipped around a salt and pepper beard. His face was drawn, but there was still some semblance of muscles beneath his *Zull-skin* vest.

Zak recalled the regal white outfits worn by his people, beautiful garments crafted from a textile trade that had been destroyed by the

Koron invasion. Now, all that was left was the skin and fur of the indigenous creatures. He pressed closer to hear the man's response.

"Zari."

"Yes," Zak injected, "how could you possibly know the name of my ship? I do not recognize you as a Warrior."

Of course he was not a Warrior. With the exception of Zak, Warriors were descendants of Anthum—traditionally blond and blue-eyed as most Anthumians were. This man showed hints of once being tall and possessing great strength, but those were ghostly attributes now.

"Zari," the man repeated.

Zak crossed his arms and frowned.

"He's not right, Zak," Aimee cautioned softly.

No, the man had been damaged by the Koron's ray. It was such a tragedy to witness...as if Zak was looking at a reflection of what could have happened to him with one more shot.

Zak stooped to his knees and touched the man's shoulder. The dark eyes narrowed on him, and for a moment he suspected there was clarity there.

"Zari," the raspy voice repeated.

"It is okay," Zak eased. "We will talk again after you have eaten and regained some strength.

To Zak's surprise tears began to well in the man's eyes. "Zonda," he whispered with desperation.

Zak froze.

He lurched upright and swayed until Aimee's touch stilled him.

"Zak, are you okay?"

Focused on the man, Zak watched his vacuous gaze shift to the cave entrance. Dry lips moved in a silent conversation. Once again Zak crouched down, hoping to hear some of that soundless litany. He leaned in close and whispered into the man's ear, "Zonda."

A tremor coursed through the thin frame and his head swung back. A war for cognizance waged itself on the bronzed face. Chapped lips parted again, and a voice no greater than a wisp of air pleaded, "Where is my wife?"

Zak staggered backwards, almost toppling onto his rear. Taking a swipe at his face, he hoped it would clear his clouded thoughts...but it didn't. He stared hard at this bedraggled man and challenged, "*Who are you?*"

Whatever clarity illuminated the old man's eyes now faded. His lips moved again, a silent conversation with people who were not there.

"Zak," Aimee crouched down beside him.

"What is it?"

Undeterred, Zak reached forward and cupped the man's shoulders. They were thin from starvation, so he kept his touch light. Again, he prompted, "Please tell me who you are."

It was futile. There was no cracking the shield of obscurity imposed by the Korons.

Zak needed air.

The sun was setting. It was safe to go outside.

He rose and used the cave wall for support as he made his way towards the twilight. Sensing Aimee at his side, he felt her gentle touch on his elbow. She remained silent, for which he was grateful. He was not ready to speak. It was doubtful he could even be coherent right now.

Determined, he marched through the narrow fissure between the granite ramparts until they emerged on the earthen precipice overlooking the desert. For this brief time, both suns had parted ways and left this portion of Ziratak in darkness. Shadows crawled across the desert floor like spilled *Anthumian* oil.

Zak leaned back against the mountain wall and lifted his face into the cool breeze. It clashed with the perspiration on his forehead. Beside him, Aimee slouched against the slate. Her eyes sought his, but he evaded them. There had been so little time to absorb the fact that she was here, and still he had to delay assessing that miracle.

"It can't be," Zak whispered aloud.

"Tell me," Aimee encouraged softly.

"I don't think that man was talking about my ship." He drew in a long breath filled with the moisture of the mountains. "I think he was talking about my sister."

Her quick gasp leaked from the shadows.

"I am lucid, Aimee. As much as Zuttah would want to tell you otherwise, the only side-effect I've really suffered is some tampered eyesight. I'm not making this up. You heard him say Zari's name—and—"

"He said something else, Zak. He said another word...it meant something to you."

Head cast down, Zak stared at the scuffed leather toes of his boots. "Zonda was my mother's name."

Aimee charged in front of him, stooping to capture his eyes. It made him nervous because this was a narrow ledge. He reached out and clasped her arms—probably too tight. There was no way he would chance losing her.

"Zak! Oh my God, are you thinking that man is your father? I thought he—I thought he—"

Right. He couldn't say the word either.

"I guess I never really knew for sure. Everyone *told* me that my parents were killed. When the HORUS came, there was no one to save. They searched for survivors—they used their life-tracker, and I was the only signal they found."

The gravity of that fleeting memory crippled him. It was so long ago. He was a small child hiding in a cellar the day his parents died, the day his sister died...the day his planet died. But, the very reason for him being back here was because not *everyone* had passed away. There was a small band of survivors—these rebels who tried to evade the Korons, and endeavored to prevail.

Could it be?

"Do people have the same name on Ziratak?" Aimee questioned. "On my planet there are thousands of Aimees."

"Huh? Oh. Sometimes they are named after a great relative in honor, but it is rare. I was too young to know if my mother or sister were named after someone else." Zak pounded his fist against the slate behind him. "If only I could communicate with this man. Those Korons *always* present me with obstacles...even when they're not standing before me."

"Curse those piles of rock," Aimee

commiserated.

Aimee was quoting him. Their first meeting aboard the HORUS occurred during an attack of a Koron ship. He had been tasked with the responsibility of getting her safely to the Bio Ward. She was so scared, but so strong and so damn curious. Even in the midst of that chaos he was fascinated by her, and as he cursed the *piles of rock* that were shooting at the HORUS, she watched him with wide green eyes...just as she was watching him now.

Zak smiled.

Aimee frowned.

"What?" she asked, seemingly suspicious of his state of mind.

"You're here," he whispered, his hands sliding up her arms.

"Yes, we have established that."

His Aimee. So literal.

"I need to hold on to that," he sobered. "I need to hold on to you."

Some of her anxiety softened and he hated that the heavy shadows of night stole her face.

In the encroaching dusk, her hair turned a deep shade of purple, mirrored off the majestic evening sky.

He felt her hand on his arm and the cool touch of her palm against his cheek. He leaned into that caress and closed his eyes.

"You hold on to that," she whispered. "And together we will go learn what this man knows...and find out *who* he is."

Admirable words, but not realistic.

"Aimee, he has been damaged by the solar ray. Somewhere deep inside his head, his life plays over and over again, but he does not have the ability to share it."

"But—"

Always a but with this one. She never accepts defeat. It is why I love her.

Yes, time might have passed, but time seemed negligent now that Aimee stood before him. His feelings had not changed. He dropped his hands to her hips and hauled her closer, smelling her hair and dipping to inhale the fresh scent of skin at the base of her throat. Raising his head, he kissed her. It was a soft kiss—a means to convey what was in his heart. When her lips parted and she made a quiet sound of pleasure, he kissed her again. Longer.

Aimee entwined her arms around his neck and whispered his name against his mouth. The cold mountain air slipped between them, reminding him of the chill that accompanied the night at this altitude.

"But—" he repeated, smiling.

It was getting too dark to see her expression, yet he could feel her tremble.

Did she still love him? She had just kissed him with the same passion he possessed. Yet, in all fairness, he was not the man she had left. He was not a refined Warrior dressed in a regal uniform—a master of the *terra angels*—a man many on the HORUS considered a hero.

No, now he was a survivor—a man whose sight was hampered by the light—a man who *saw things* under the suns.

"But," she cut into his thoughts, "what about the serum? The serum to ease the mental side effects of the solar ray? It is supposed to sharpen your cognizance. Do you have some here? I know Zuttah showed me that you still have many key supplies."

Zak frowned. "There is no such serum."

"There is," Aimee asserted in the dark. "Raja gave it to me in case Gordy or I were struck."

Surprised by this news, Zak leaned back against the rock wall, feeling the bite of cold granite against his bare skin.

"Raja was working on something before I left," he mused. "She completed it? Good for her. She is always underestimating herself."

"Zak," Aimee squeezed his arms. "We can

use this, and you can find the truth."

The truth.

Could that disheveled man really be his father? Could it be that some of his family was still alive?

"Come on," she urged.

Backing up her plea with an urgent tug, she wrapped her fingers around his forearm and pulled. "Zak."

Zak stared at that touch on his arm and smiled. His Aimee. If she wanted something, she would tug until she got it.

"Aimee," he hated to temper her zeal. "Raja was right."

The warm glow of firelight cast marionette shadows on the walls. Aimee held on tight to Zak's hand, casting a look over her shoulder to make sure he was still with her. She pulled up short of the entrance, into a spot where she could study the pensive shadows across his face.

He gave her chills. In a good way. Chills of anticipation. Chills of desire.

"Right? What was Raja right about?"

"That the serum is for you and Gordeelum. If anything happened to you—"

Aimee stepped in and crowded him. "That

man—" she pointed towards the cave entrance, "—may be your father. And—" her look was enough to curtail his interruption, "—even if he isn't, he is someone who can be saved. He is someone that we have the power to restore sanity to."

Zak's lips parted, but she hastened on, severing any interruption. "If I came here and found you in that state, do you think for one second I would keep that serum on the off chance that me or Gordy were shot?"

"May I speak?" he smirked.

Crossing her arms to the chill that wove through the crevice, she consented.

"I pity any Koron that tries to take you on," he grinned.

"But Zak, what if he knows something? What if—" she hesitated, "—your mother is still–"

Zak looked like he had been slapped.

"I'm sorry," she bit her lip. "I'm just—I just care about you so much."

"Good." His smile was pensive. "Alright, we can give him some—but just a little bit."

Aimee launched at him, wrapping her arms around his neck. "Let's go do this," she whispered into the crook of his shoulder.

With darkness closing in behind them, the

cave represented an oasis with its warm fire and the camaraderie of its dwellers. These were not beaten people. Yes, some were haggard, some were injured, but none were scared. None had the look of a race that had been hunted. There were smiles and loud-mouthed jokes from the big man spitting a rock into crackling flames. The projectile stirred up a fountain of sparks.

These were survivors. Take their home away, take their dignity, and their health...but they would restore it all.

Aimee wanted to help them. She always fought for the underdog.

Tucked into a rut in the rock wall, the old man sat with his knees up under his chin, his arms wrapped around his legs. He rocked a little and stared at his traveling companions. There was no recognition in his eyes, he was simply fascinated by the banter of the man and woman—the way the man caressed the woman's hair and dipped to whisper in her ear. When she giggled, the old man's head cocked in fascination.

As Zak stooped into his line of vision a frown crossed over the haggard face. For a moment, his gaze shifted to Zak, but he wasn't really looking at him—rather, *through* him.

"Zon?" Zak's voice was husky.

Other than a flinch, the old man did not

register the comment.

"Zon?" Aimee whispered, crouching down alongside Zak.

"My father's name."

"Oh." It dismayed her that there was no reaction to the word. Perhaps this *was* a stranger. Maybe a family friend.

She reached into her belt to extract the vial.

"What's that?"

Aimee saw Gordy's shadow just before he spoke.

"It is a serum to counter the effects of the solar ray."

"Wow. I didn't know you had that on you."

The accusation in his voice waned as he leaned in with interest.

Zak extended a clay mug towards her, mouthing, "*Just a little.*"

She swiveled the vial and felt the suction release. The liquid was odorless, yet it produced the impact of smelling salts when she held it beneath her nose. Tears welled in her eyes as blood surged into her head. Pinpricks of sensation assaulted her scalp and heat flushed her cheeks....all from the whiff of an odorless liquid.

"That packs a punch." She backed the vial

away.

"Packs a punch—" Zak repeated and shook his head, holding the cup up to her.

She reached over and tipped the capsule so guardedly, that only a drop or two slipped out. Simultaneously, they glanced into the base of the cup, their heads colliding.

"Okay," Zak smiled, "maybe a little bit more."

The equivalent of half of a shot glass was poured. Zak offered the cup to the man. He stared at it, his eyes narrowing. Looking to Zak for affirmation, Zak nodded his encouragement.

Tremulous hands reached around the cup as Aimee noticed scars scoring the fingers. As all watched in expectation, he lifted the clay mug to his lips, and his throat bobbed as he swallowed. There was a slight jerk of his shoulders. His eyes widened enough that a white halo eclipsed the dark pupils, and then his expression fell back into submission as he shook the cup and held it up, looking for more.

"Must be good stuff," Gordy inserted.

Poised in anticipation, Aimee watched as the man blinked like he had a hair caught in his eye. Rocking in place, he hugged his knees up tight against his chest.

"I don't think it's working," she said,

dismayed.

Zak stepped back. "I think we need to give the poor man some room."

Gordy took a step back.

"No, I mean, we need to leave him alone. We're crowding him. When Raja was first tinkering with this serum, she too thought that it didn't work, but the patient took a—" Zak hesitated, recalling the translation, "—a *day* before signs were exhibited."

"Oh," Aimee backed up.

Well, what had she expected, instant recognition? A dramatic reunion of father and son?

As she looked at this bedraggled man, could she even detect any similarities? His dark brown hair, albeit infused with gray, was similar to Zak's, but then again, everyone in this land possessed dark hair of some variety. Speckled with cataracts from the solar ray, this man's eyes were darker—almost bourbon, whereas Zak's were—well, Zak's were like looking into the two suns of Ziratak. Gold. Bright. Beautiful.

The facial structure might be comparable, but many men had strong jawlines and high cheekbones. This man had not smiled. If he had exhibited that same cleft under his cheek, then she would have felt more confident.

Sluggish, she trailed after Zak, but kept glancing over her shoulder at the stranger. He had stopped rocking, and now seemed fascinated with his hands as he held them up and wiggled them like newfound toys.

Work!

Raja will be so upset if it doesn't.

"Aimee," Zak's voice broke into her thoughts. "Time will tell. For now, you and Gordy need to eat."

Oh no. Local cuisine. It had taken her forever to get used to the food aboard the HORUS. What did Ziratak have in store for her?

"This one is too skinny," Zuttah boomed, waving his hand at Aimee.

Zak followed his glance and tended to agree. Aimee's legs looked long and sleek in the shimmering blue pants. The pants were a new design for the HORUS, a contemporary take on the outfit Aimee had initially boarded the ship with.

"What is that?" Aimee leaned towards the fire and wrinkled her nose at the pot of *Zull* milk suspended across the flame.

"Pudding," Zak interpreted.

"Did we skip dinner and go straight to

dessert?"

"We're going out to the desert?" Gordy's head popped up from his cross-legged squat on the floor. "It's dark out."

"*Dessert*." Aimee enunciated. "It is the meal that comes after dinner—or the meal that comes after *sumpum* and *crup*."

"Bah," Zuttah scoffed, "we used to have *crup* when we had fields, but those walking stacks of boulders killed the river, and the fields dried up. So now—" he nodded at the metal bowl, "—you get—*pudding*."

Aimee leaned in, sniffing. "For the record, I like pudding."

"Let us all rejoice." Zuttah laughed and then took a long look at the ensemble around the fire. "It is good to see smiling faces around my fire. I am so used to this sour man." He tipped his nose at Zak.

Zak flashed a grin.

"You show up, Aimee—" Zuttah ladled some of the viscous liquid into a smaller bowl, "—and Zak is smiling again. That makes me happy."

In the firelight, Aimee's hair glowed. She reached for the small bowl and slipped a spoonful of pudding between her lips, her head bobbing as she gushed, "Not bad. Not bad at all."

Zuttah beamed, his woolly beard looking like a pair of wings stuck to his face.

So attuned with Aimee's every move, Zak noticed when she grew alert. Her head elevated slightly and keen eyes scanned her periphery. She caught his glance and gave a slight nod.

Behind him.

Zak curled his fingers around a handful of dirt before chancing a look over his shoulder.

The old man was on his feet, staggering towards them. He appeared disoriented, but that made him no less dangerous. A mad man bore the strength of ten civil men.

Zak's muscles tensed. He swiveled and rose, making sure Aimee was behind him.

With the dirt still cupped in his fist, he addressed the rebel.

"Are you okay? Are you hungry?"

In the reflection of the flames Zak swore he detected a hint of clarity in the shadowed eyes. It jolted him. Something about that look...

Standing immobile, the man drew himself up from his slouched posture. He stared hard at Zak and asked with hoarse sincerity, "Do I know you?"

That grasp for reality tore at Zak. This was someone perched on a precipice. Insanity and damnation lay on one side, while enlightenment beckoned on the other.

"No. I am Zak. I am here to help you. To help all of us." He extended his arm to the curious stares of others who sat huddled in groups along the cave walls.

"Zak." The man tested the word. He blinked and swayed slightly before righting himself.

"What name do you go by?" Zak asked.

Dry lips parted and then clamped shut. Dark eyebrows dipped together as the man stared at the floor before lifting his head.

Zak realized in that second that he was staring into lucid eyes.

"Zon."

Could it be?

"My name is Zon." The man repeated in the native language. This time the voice was stronger and his shoulders were drawn back in challenge. There was a flicker in his gaze, the talons of doubt and insecurity attempting to haul him back to the land of the damned. But the man blinked hard to abate them.

"You—" he searched Zak's face, "—your name is Zak, you say?"

Zak felt Aimee's hand against the small of his back, a silent signal that she was there for him. It pained him how much that tender gesture meant.

"Yes," his voice was husky. He cleared his throat.

The man studied him a moment. "I had a son named Zak."

Strength fled Zak's knees, but he focused on the soft touch on his back.

"That is not a common name on Ziratak," he mentioned. "Where is he—your son?"

Pain lanced the dark eyes. "Dead." He shook his head and then raised his hand to it as if the pain of a thousand swords assaulted him. "My family—the Korons—"

Zak nodded in sympathy, but did not reach for him.

"How did you come by your name?" Zon asked with another frown, lowering his arm.

"My father gave it to me. He told me—" Zak swallowed, "—he told me that it was the name of a monarch in a story his mother used to read to him."

Zon's eyes reddened as water pooled in them. "That's impossible," he rasped. "My mother read me the tale of the great monarch, Zak, who lived high on the mountaintops in a temple—"

"—made from the color of the suns," Zak injected. "The suns, Zot and Zor once connected, and a shower of fire fell onto the mountaintop and Zak was born—"

"—in his temple made of stars, where he tried to lure the beautiful snow goddess—"

"*Zari*," Zak barely voiced the word.

In that moment, Zak was acutely aware of the silence. Even the flames seemed to suspend in anticipation.

"It cannot be," the old man took a tentative step forward, his hand outstretched— not necessarily to connect, but almost to ward off, as if Zak was a demon.

"When I was five rotations," Zak recited, his voice now void of emotion, "my parents told me and my sister to stay down in the cellar because a dust storm was coming. They told us not to open the latch unless we recognized their voices."

Zon's body trembled. A tear spilled onto his cheek, drawing a path in the dust caked there. He parted his lips to speak, but shook his head in frustration at the inability to do so.

Zak continued. "Someone came to the latch and Zari lifted it. She was—" *such beautiful, sparkling dust*, "—disintegrated on impact."

Plunging to his knees, Zon dipped his face into his hands.

"I didn't know what to do," Zak proceeded, trying to remain indifferent. "So, I listened to her last command. She instructed me to hide under the table against the back wall."

"My workbench," Zon croaked, his voice muffled. "I was building you a model *terra duster* to play with."

That news rattled Zak, but he continued. "I stayed under there for several days I am told...until the HORUS showed up and attacked the Korons. They said that I was the only life-form to register on their sensors. How can that be?" his voice cracked. "How did they not find the others? You survived. I know others survived. Did my—mother—?"

Zon dropped his hands and stared up with bloodshot eyes. "We had very little warning about the attack. It was speculation more than anything," he hesitated. "They called an emergency meeting in the town hall."

Zak vaguely recalled the grand building with pillars and wide steps stacked high along the river. He had seen a theatre presentation there once. A performance with puppets.

The hall was gone now—reduced to rubble—just like everything else.

"Though they didn't believe the attack was imminent, I was not going to leave my children's welfare to chance. I wanted to make sure they stayed underground and safe until we returned.

With them secured, Zonda and I hurried to the town hall to hear the latest news. We had not even made it to the grand steps when the first ship struck. I watched as the couple before us were charred into black shadows on the staircase—permanent ashen stamps of their existence. Another beam immediately spiked the ground beside me."

Zon paused, rubbing his eyes. Zak could not bring himself to offer solace. Paralyzed by confusion, he stood and waited.

In time, Zon stared into the fire and continued in a hollow tone. "I put my arm around Zonda to shield her, and to encourage her up the steps. If we could just make it into the hall we would be safe—" He faded for a moment. "A ray struck from above, knocking both of us to our knees. At that moment, over the chaos in the sky, I could hear the march of the Korons. They emerged from behind the rotunda, flanking it on both sides. They just began firing at anything that moved."

Zon shook his head. "I—I grabbed Zonda and dragged her up the stairs and into the Great Hall. It was pandemonium in there. People screaming, crying, bleeding. It was complete madness. Yet, we had a goal. If we could make it behind the altar, there was an underground passage concealed there."

There was?

Zak frowned trying to recall the wreckage of the Great Hall. He had sifted through the debris once, but it had been in an attempt to locate life. There was no life in that pile. Just as there was no life in all the mounds dotting the shores of the Zargoll.

"Finally, we reached the altar and started down the ladder just as the Korons blasted through the front doors. Not many of us made it to the tunnel. Most were still outside. We had to—" he swallowed, "—we had to close the hatch—and there was no way for the others to open it from the altar. Even the Korons tried to blast their way through it, but our architects had fabricated the door of an impenetrable composite, similar to the composite used in our very own hatch at home."

The very same hatch Zari had innocently opened, expecting to find their parents.

"Adrenaline kept me moving," Zon explained, now sounding very coherent. "I was so focused on getting us deeper into that tunnel— distancing ourselves from danger—getting us back to our children."

A new crop of tears filled the man's eyes. "That was when I realized that I was dragging my wife. At first, I thought she was leaning on me for support, but at some point she had stopped leaning and her feet failed her. I was so consumed with moving—" his fist curled up, "—I didn't even notice. I stopped and eased her down onto the ground, against the tunnel wall. It was dark down there, with only sporadic lighting. We were in a thick patch of shadows, so I couldn't see her wounds. I looked up—searching for anyone to help, but they had all charged on ahead. Behind us lie darkness and the portent of danger."

Zon looked directly into Zak's eyes and Zak felt a tug of recollection. Yes. Those eyes had gazed down upon him before. He remembered them now…but they were never filled with this angst that tore at his soul. In his heart, he knew the conclusion to this tale.

"Zak—" Tears spilled, dripping down onto dry lips. "Your mother died right there—in those shadows—with no one around. She deserved so much better. She deserved to watch her children grow old."

Zon sat back on his heels. "I carried her out of that tunnel. I wanted to bring her back home. I wanted our family to be together again— but I emerged to a wasteland. Our home was gone. I tried to get back to it, but I was blocked by the Koron troops. I had to—" The composure he had struggled so hard for now collapsed, and his voice cracked. "I carried Zonda all the way to the foothills. I did not want to bury her in the desert. The desert had become *their* land. Zonda always liked the foothills. She liked the brush of grass against her bare feet, and the sound of the wind through the trees…"

His words faded.

Zak envisioned the foothills, where the heat of the desert collided with the chill of the mountains to produce a lush perimeter, an area that was seasonally beautiful, but where the winds could crop up and shear exposed flesh. That was Ziratak now. A dramatic land of paradox.

"The Korons had moved further down the Zargoll," Zon broke into Zak's thoughts, "and I finally made it back to what was left of our house."

There was nothing left of their villa. Even as he was being pulled from that cellar hatch as a child, Zak saw what remained above-ground. Once a two-story manor with impressive pillars suspending a grand wrap-around balcony, all that endured was a portion of a Doric-styled column.

"It was all gone," Zon confirmed. "I found the hatch, but my children—*you*, were gone. Can you tell me?" he pleaded. "Can you tell me what happened?"

Zak glanced around. Every set of eyes he met jerked away. Silence prevailed, a milieu of curiosity and sympathy amplifying the snap of the fire. Its heat warmed his back as did the soft hand still resting there.

Stepping up to the man stooped on the dirt, Zak cupped his shoulder, feeling the protrusion of bone. He squeezed. "Come," he said. "Let's talk."

CHAPTER ELEVEN

Perched high on the precipice overlooking the thin scar of the Zargoll, Zak sat with his hand draped over his eyes.

The suns were rising and their illuminated fingers pointed at him as if to alert the Korons, *here he is*. Pain from their persistent digits stabbed him. He closed his eyes and listened to the cry of the wind as it scurried around the mountain in a vicious chase of its own tail. Over its wicked peal, he heard the tread approach. This was not the lumbering gait of the rock creatures. This was the light, but confident march of a female. A female who had curled up against him in slumber for the past few hours. He could still feel the warm imprint of her body.

Zak's lip hefted into a quick grin. In Aimee's usual obstinate manner, she had refused to leave his side, and could care less what others thought if she lie next to him. Holding her had been absolute divinity, and for as troubled as his thoughts were—for those few hours he slept the best he had in half a *ren*.

He wanted more of her, though. More than just that slumberous embrace. Yes, he wanted what came with bonding—the testimony her people referred to as marriage. It was a lifetime commitment. Would she want that with a damaged man?

The brush of boot against rock, followed by patient silence inspired him to look up. Fiery hair, aglow from the rising suns cast that shower of diamonds upon him again. This was how he had seen her. Now he wondered if all this time it was his failing eyesight...or a prophecy.

"Good morning," she whispered in deference to the silence.

He smiled and reached a hand up to draw her down to his side so that he did not have to look up into the suns.

"You're up early," he commented.

"I was up the moment you left."

So much for a discreet withdrawal.

Aimee sat down on a boulder next to him and stared out at the vast copper ocean.

"It's beautiful," she exhaled.

He stared at her profile. A small nose, a rosy cheek, soft lips and a heart-shaped jaw hugged by the hair drawn behind her ear.

"It is," he agreed.

Vibrant green eyes converged on him. In them, he witnessed a warm mixture of empathy, pain, and dare he hope, adoration.

"Are you okay?" Her voice was husky.

Zak hooded his eyes again with his hand. His shield circled uselessly around his neck. He didn't want to wear it. He wanted to see the world without a tainted lens.

"Yes," he nodded. "I just wish I could have had more time alone with you. I have waited a *ren* to see you and—"

"Zak—" Soft eyebrows knitted into a frown. "This is me you're talking to. I know what a blow it was for you to find your father alive." She hesitated and cocked her head. "Was it your father? Do you know it for sure?"

"One day, you're going to grow up and live in a palace high in the mountains."

"Will I be able to come down and see everyone, father, or do I have to live up there alone?"

"Yes, he is my father." A huge fist had clenched around his heart last night as he spoke with Zon. In the light of day that grip eased. "But—"

"—but it's been so long" She filled in, softly. "You were a young boy, Zak. You had so few years with him, and they were a lifetime ago." She squeezed his fingers and dipped her head to capture his downcast gaze. "It is okay to not have the feelings you think you should."

"*Gayat*," his curse was subdued. "You claim your people have no powers, and yet you get into my mind sometimes."

"Intuition." Aimee sat back and smiled. "All women on my planet possess this power. We don't always know how to channel it though." She sobered. "What bothers you here?" She leaned forward and flattened her palm over his heart.

Zak held her hand tight to his chest when she would have withdrawn.

"You," he stated.

She looked dismayed. "I hurt you there?"

"It is a good pain." And it was. The best. But the fact that it was pain at all meant there was something missing. *Dare he ask?* Dare he ask her to spend the rest of her life with him?

No. Not until he knew she would be safe. Not until his mission here was complete and he could come to her as a whole man...well, mentally. His eyes were another story.

"Come with me." He stood up, startling her.

With a quick tug, he hoisted her up, the

impetus propelling her into his chest. Immediately, his hands wound around her back and his face dropped close to hers. Every muscle in his body grew taut in anticipation. She was so soft and so feminine. She was like hugging the wind. And just like the wind, he feared she would slip through his fingers.

As she looked into his eyes, her glance fell to his lips. *Hah, the rugged Warrior.* He could no more deny that temptation than he could deny breathing. He kissed her, and the wind became solid, something he could wrap his arms around and claim for his very own.

"Zak," she whispered his name against his lips as he felt his stomach clench at the sound.

In the distance a loud screech pierced the morning air. Zak snapped his head up, wincing against the suns. Damn. Yes, he saw the blue sky if he squinted against the light...but he could see little else.

"What was that?" Aimee tensed.

Closing his eyes, he listened for the noise to repeat. It came quickly—a prolonged scream, similar to the discharge of a solar ray. But squint as he might, he could locate no Koron crafts in the sky.

"Look—" Aimee cried.

Gayat, he was looking! He saw diamonds.

"It's the Warriors," she shouted as the sound ricocheted off the mountain. She leaned forward to the point of imbalance and announced, "they're—they're *leaving*."

Oh no. That was not good.

"How can you be sure?"

"Well, look—" She pointed and then turned his way. She was close enough that he could make out her confused glance. For a moment she stared hard at him and then the realization that he could not see dawned in her eyes. *Curse that comprehension.*

"I studied their planned flight route in order to avoid it," she explained. "They were to come into the desert from the south and leave to the north to avoid the winds. When they first approached, the suns were sitting low on the horizon, so I take it that direction is south." She pointed deep into the desert where the line between sand and sky blurred to obscurity. "And that," her arm swung past the mountains, "must be north—and there they go—"

As he could not actually see the *terra angels*, he watched her eyes instead. He heard the crafts, though. It was a bad sign. It meant that they had exhausted their stint away from the HORUS, and that the Guardianship was pulling out of range. They had very little time left to be able to reach it.

"Aimee, I need to show you something," he said, setting her back away from him.

Curious, she dusted her hands over her rear to rid herself of the tiny pebbles. It was a motion that arrested his eyes.

"What?"

"Huh? Oh." Zak cleared his throat. "I need your help."

The fine lines around her mouth eased and she offered a smug smile. "What a refreshing change."

He couldn't help but to snort at that.

"Come on." He offered his hand.

She was no fool.

It didn't take a rocket scientist to realize that Zak was impaired.

In eyes that she could entrench herself in, she detected brief spikes of pain. Pupils shrank to mere pinpoints to escape the suns.

Aimee gripped his hand tighter.

He was leading the way, but his head was down, focusing on his feet. On each step.

Her heart clenched.

This was a man so tall and so strong, climbing rocks with his thighs bulging and the muscles in his back rippling. Yet, she was certain he had not seen the Warrior's *terra angels* fly by.

None of that mattered to her. Being with him and ensuring a lifetime together was what mattered.

"You're breaking my hand, *Zer-shay*."

Zer-shay. Zak had called her that once before. He said that it meant, *pretty one*.

Aimee slackened her grip.

"How is it that I am able to understand Zuttah and your fa—Zon? Do you think Raja tinkered with the translator in my shirt?"

"Probably," Zak mused.

"Good." She smiled at his back. "Now I'll know what you say when you curse."

He tossed a grin over his shoulder and she thought he looked so damned hot at that moment.

"You're going to have to let go of my hand for a minute so we can squeeze through this channel."

Indeed. The tight fissure between the two granite walls not only called for single-file, but she had to inch sideways, her chest scraping against the abrasive rock face.

"How in God's name does Zuttah fit through here?"

Zak chuckled. "He doesn't. There is

another entrance into this valley, but I prefer this shortcut. Besides, wait until you see the view on the other side."

On cue, he turned and strode shoulder-width through the mountain walls into a clearing. His broad back concealed her perspective until he stepped aside.

"What do you think?" he asked.

She might have felt the ground scrape her chin—that's how jaw-dropping the view was. It was like stepping onto the magical set of a Hollywood Wizard of Oz-type fantasy. Snow-capped peaks flanked a lush clearing with rolling green knolls of grass that sparkled like Easter basket stuffing. Puffy white clouds tickled the mountain faces, playing a game of peek-a-boo with the austere barricade. A sapphire ribbon dissected the gentle slopes, its source a series of pools cascading in shelves down the face of the mountain. From that natural staircase, rainbows bloomed in an ethereal splash of color.

More crags lined the sheer rock walls of the crater, but these overhangs were surrounded by caves, shadowed alcoves like an ancient Indian burial ground.

Children dressed in fur played "tag" on a terrace fifty-feet up the crater wall. A woman cooked over a fire in front of a cave, while another grotto revealed a trio of men engaged in conversation—and from the quiver of their shoulders, it appeared to be a funny one. A small group of children charged through the fine grass hand-in-hand. The one in the lead was singing, and the one in the rear, yelling.

"Zak," she gaped. "Where are we?" She didn't give him time to answer. "It looks like another world—I mean—in comparison to the desert."

"No one knows how old this crater is. Maybe a meteor struck the mountain long ago. Over time, the melting snow from the mountain peaks poured into this basin, and the floor became fertile."

Eyesight hindered or not, he gazed out into the valley with a sense of peace. "I was not even aware this valley existed. The rebels discovered it as they fled to the mountains. Not long after the initial Koron attack, when the rebels realized that the Korons would not venture up here, they started building dwellings and have lived here ever since."

An unvoiced question clung to her lips. Noticing it, Zak added, "But this is not their home. Their home is down by the river."

Holding a hand over his eyes, he scanned the lush valley. "I wonder now if my father knew of this basin. If this is where the mythical king lives."

Aimee's throat tightened. "Now you can ask him," she observed quietly.

Still pensive, Zak shook his head. "Come on, I need your help."

Intrigued, she followed, wishing she could feel the green satin blades of the meadow against her bare skin. Brushing her hand through them, it would be like running your fingers through silk spaghetti. Nearby, she heard water surge through the brook, its source a slim scar in the mountain wall—as if the mighty peak was crying.

Zak stepped up to the bank of the creek. Crystal clear water flashed starbursts of light as the rapids collided against rock. Following along the stream's edge, Aimee saw the velocity begin to dissipate as a stagnant pool formed beneath a patch of saplings with spiky blue needles.

"Here." Zak pointed just beyond the thicket.

Passing through the branches for a better view, she anticipated the sharp pricks of needles, but it was more like fur. It tickled her.

Once through the trees, she clapped her hands in delight. "Look, a bridge!"

As quaint as the idea was, she thought it was almost unnecessary. At its narrowest juncture, she could simply leap across the creek.

"No." Zak frowned. Stepping up alongside her, he added flatly, "It's a dam."

"Oh."

Indeed, the haphazard structure impeded the natural current. That was the reason the small pool had formed beneath the trees. But, this contraption was only a slight deterrent. Water was the strongest force in the world...*errr*...universe. Water was not content sitting still. Water wanted to move. It was like the Terminator. It would never stop. And when it wanted to move, only drastic measures could contain it.

"What are you trying to do here, Zak? Is this creek not enough to supply the people living in these mountains?"

Aimee looked up at the dwellings clinging to the rock face—nature's architecture.

How many rebels did it accommodate?

From Zak's expression, she could tell he was dismayed by her reaction to the levee.

In lieu of answering, he offered, "Will you take a walk with me?"

Anywhere. Anytime. Forever.

"Sure."

In no less than three strides, Zak claimed her hand. A warm jolt heightened that connection. She was not a little girl anymore, and yet he made her feel the same way she did the first time he touched her.

They were traveling through the meadow, approaching the far side of the crater. It was an intimidating wall of charred rock capped at the peak with a crooked crown of snow. Aimee's focus, however, remained on the creek, which seemed to care less that there was a massive granite wall in front of it.

"Where is the water going?" she asked.

"Patience, *Zer-shay*." Zak tugged her to a halt and into his embrace. "Always looking for answers." Warm eyes smiled down at her. "You and JOH are very similar."

It wasn't something she would have ever considered, but now that Zak stated it, maybe she really was like JOH. Was her thirst for knowledge a turn-off? Did Zak want someone a little more vacuous?

Judging by the mouth that dipped down to caress hers, she guessed not. It was all she could do not to sigh at the sheer pleasure of being kissed by this man. It was as if no time had passed—as if they had not been apart for five years. Maybe he was brawnier. Maybe the arms around her back were like bands of steel now. Maybe the cheek rubbing against hers was a little stubblier—but this kiss was something that all the galaxies, and all the worlds could never alter. It aligned planets. This kiss was home.

Aware that she was melting in his arms, she tried to recover her posture, but Zak seemed reluctant to release her.

"Aimee." His forehead dipped down against hers, locking out the glare of the suns.

"Hmmm."

"I—I have missed you so much."

Was that really what he wanted to say? There was a delay. Did he want to say the words that were pumping through her veins?

She squeezed his shoulders and kissed lips that were dry, but soft. "I am here. And the only way to get rid of me is to literally pry me off of you."

Zak reached for one of her fingers to peel it away from his shoulder. After consideration, he let her finger snap back into place, and grinned. "Not a chance."

Enjoying another moment of indulgence, he reluctantly backed away. "But for now," his voice was husky, "I need you to show me what you learned when you went back to Earth. Please tell me that they taught you how to build a proper dam."

Not exactly.

"Maybe it is better if you explain what you're trying to accomplish, and we'll work backwards from that."

"Good idea."

With his hand warm against her back, he urged her along the water's edge as they drew nearer to the mountain wall. It was then that she noticed the hole.

There was a classmate at NC State who was from Norway. Wenche Gullorsen. Over coffee in the library, Wenche would tell her about life at home near Torget Island. That island possessed a mountain with a natural cavity carved straight through it. Norwegian legend stated that a troll was chasing a beautiful girl, and upon realizing that he couldn't catch her, he released an arrow, intending to kill her. The Troll King threw his hat in front of the path of the arrow and the hat struck the mountain and created a hole.

Not satisfied with the logistics of this tale, Aimee later did her research on Torget Island, and concluded that ice and water had most likely eroded the looser rocks, while the harder ones at the mountain top resisted the erosion.

Turning around to scope the area, she realized that the natural phenomenon that occurred on Torget Island was not necessarily exclusive to Earth. Here in this crater, the snow from the mountaintops melted. It channeled into the lowest groove of the craggy face. This steady stream of water created a nook in the land below—a nook that meandered through the meadows...looking...seeking...an outlet. It ran up against the crater wall on the far side, and through years and years of pummeling that rock, it eventually bludgeoned its way through to create a cave.

Aimee marched to the cave entrance. It had a low ceiling—maybe only four feet high. She crouched down and started inching her way under it.

"Aimee, dammit, be careful. Wait for me."

Zak's hand encircled her arm, but he didn't stop her. Together they crept beneath a pyramid of bedrock, listening to water cascade against the sheared walls, sounding like shattered icicles inside this tight pocket. As daylight stung her eyes, she caught a glimpse of the coral desert in the distance. It was an arid realm with a slim track running through it. A scar sustained by the very water that slipped off of this cliff into a cataract, a waterfall that could be heard pounding the mountain wall below.

"Cool," she whispered.

Still hunched, she pivoted to face Zak and saw him wince in pain. He ducked his head and grabbed his eyes with his free hand.

"Zak," she cried. "Hurry, let's get back."

There was no argument on his part. When they returned to the shadows of the crater wall, Zak leaned against a boulder with his hand over his brow.

"It's a lot worse than you let on, isn't it?" she whispered.

He would not look at her. Not even after she touched his arm to draw his attention.

"I don't want pity."

"Pity?" she snorted. "Do I look like a person who pities people?"

Zak glanced up. Gone was the military-styled man from the HORUS. Perhaps *that* Zak had been a Warrior, but this Zak, with his tousled hair and leather pants, was rugged and sexy...even with his poor eyesight.

"No," he chuckled. "You look like someone who is going to give me a *zentram* to rest and then you're going to kick me back into action."

Aimee quirked an eyebrow.

Hefting off the boulder, Zak took a deep breath. "Okay, here is my idea." He squinted against water's glare.

"This might seem like a small creek, but it is fed continuously by the snows of the Zorgon peaks. It pours into a waterfall that runs down the foothills and out into the desert. It is a cycle that has evolved over thousands of *rens*. And from this cycle, the river Zargoll was created."

"Erosion," Aimee concurred. "Water flows through the land and erodes a path to form a channel...and eventually a river."

"Right." Zak crouched down at the stream's edge, running his fingers through the current. "And the Zargoll was a magnificent river, but the Korons have spent years filling it in with rock and sand, effectively reducing it to less than half the length it once was."

"They hate water," she pointed out. "How did they work with it?"

Jaw clenching, he muttered, "With slaves. They have been capturing rebels that are still out there." His head jerked towards the desert. "And forcing them to do the labor."

Fingers curling into fists, Aimee could feel heat rise to her cheeks. "What is your goal here?"

Whatever it was, she was in 100%.

A look of conviction hardened him. "I want to build a dam. I want to stop this flow and let it accumulate. The people living inside the crater walls are high enough to remain safe." He glanced up at the rock terraces. "The banks of this creek can overflow into the valley for now."

Zak rose, his frame rigid with

determination. "Down below, the Korons keep close to the river because they know that is where they will catch any stray rebels. If we were to destroy the dam and release the water all at once, it would flood the Zargoll, taking out all the hideous rock people with it. Maybe we won't get them all, but from my missions down there, I can tell you that we'll get most of them."

Trudging through the knee-high grass, he gazed upon the feeble collection of wood and rock that impeded the creek's flow with the same deterrence of a meshed net.

"But, as you can see," he offered her a half-smile, "my engineering skills are lacking when it comes to dams."

"Bah." She shot up to join him. "You are capable of whatever you set out to do. You don't need me." A sly grin crept over her lips. "But, I like pretending that you do."

He reached for her and hooked his arm behind her back. Aimee's breath caught and her heart pounded.

"I need you more than you will ever know." His head dipped and his lips touched hers. Against them he whispered, "I love you."

Everything—every insurmountable obstacle to bring her to this point—it was all worth it. No matter what transpired from here on out, this moment brought her peace and clarity.

With tears in her eyes and a grip on her throat, Aimee responded, "I was afraid that so much time had passed—that you moved on—that your feelings would have changed. I would have understood." *And I would have died.*

Zak drew back. For a moment he remained silent as her anxiety escalated.

"I had the same fears," he shared. "More than anything, I feared that you would not want a damaged man."

"Damaged." She tested out the word.

Anxiety and emotion flashed in his eyes.

Planting her palms against his chest for stability, she hefted up on her toes so that she could press her lips to his and whispered, "I love you too."

Before there was a chance to come back down on her feet, both of Zak's arms were around her, holding her aloft as he kissed her with a passion that made this world spin.

Damn! Do I love you? Are you kidding me? Yes. Yes. Yes.

Settling her back on the heels of her boots, Zak eased his hold enough that he could gaze down at her. His lips were curled up into one wicked grin.

"So," he drawled quietly. "What have I

done wrong?"

Blinking, Aimee gulped. "What?"

"The dam. What do you suggest we do?"

I have a few suggestions.

"Well," her mouth opened and closed like a guppy before she finally concentrated. "We could—"

She had to look away from him. It was impossible to think straight when his gaze was fixed on her mouth.

There sat the dam.

What he had constructed was admirable. The structural dilemma was that it was built to the width of the original creek. That had probably worked for a while, until the reservoir began to build up. As the reservoir grew, it leaked around the perimeters of the dam until the stream adapted and continued its normal flow as if there was nothing more than a stray boulder in its path.

Following the stream, Aimee focused on the cave that it charged through in an effort to reach the outside world. Flashes of sunlight from the other side danced inside the cavern like a Disney laser show.

"If you're looking for a temporary dam—" she was plotting while she was talking, "—*that* is where you want to build it. Obstruct that cave wall so that the water can't get out of the basin—" she paused. "Do that and you'll have one helluva lake here. And when you release the plug, the Korons will be doing the backstroke down the Zargoll River."

Zak stepped up alongside her. "Sometimes I don't understand your words," his profile revealed a grin, "but I understand your enthusiasm. And, if *doing the backstroke* means that those rock barbarians will get wet, then I'm all for it. How do we start?"

Pour the concrete.

"We need some rebar—umm, sturdy posts that we can hammer down into the creek floor."

"Okay." He nodded. "We can get that. I don't know what rebar is, but we have sturdy posts."

"Great!" Warming up to the idea, she reevaluated Zak's efforts.

"You had the right idea," she offered. "But, the problem was that you used too much wood. It is porous and susceptible to the pressure."

Zak crossed his arms.

Lord help her. He had no shirt on, and those biceps were a sight to behold.

"We didn't have much material to work with," he defended. "When I was young, we had stone temples as high as this crater—" He sported a sheepish smirk. "Well, maybe they looked that big to me at the time. Our architects had resources I would kill for right now. My father used to build–"

His words dropped off.

Aimee walked up to him and reached for both of his hands. "He's alive." She smiled and squeezed. "Hold onto that."

Blazing eyes clashed with hers. "It's just that—it's just—I feel guilty, Aimee."

"Guilty? For Heaven's sake, why?"

"I accepted so readily the tale that my parents were killed. I feel like I failed him. That I neglected him. When I first came back to Ziratak all those years ago—when I—"

When he found the sparkling specks of his sister's dress on the floor of that cellar and scooped them up to forever carry in his terra angel.

"—I should have put in more effort to search—to find answers. What type of son was I?"

Oh Zak. Her heart twisted.

"A son who grew up to be a hero," she remarked. "A son who has spent his whole life saving the lives of others. Even now," she swept her arm towards the creek, "you are battling the demons to save the innocents. No father could be more proud of you."

"Dammit, woman. Why do you always know the right things to say?" He smiled, but desperation still plucked at the corner of his lip.

"Because I always speak the truth."

"Always?"

"Absolutely."

His head dipped. "Then you really do love me?"

Aimee grinned even as she kissed him. "Absolutely," she whispered.

"Okay." He kept his forehead to hers. "Then let's go build a dam."

CHAPTER TWELVE

"Here! No, no *no*! *Here*!" Gordy waved like a host of *zurillion* bugs swarmed around his head.

Zuttah grunted and dropped the burly rock at the young man's feet.

"I am not your servant," his deep voice threatened.

Frustrated, Gordy scratched the back of his head. Kicking the rock, he tried to conceal that the action hurt his foot.

A fur-skinned boot appeared beside his, dwarfing it by several inches. Zuttah exerted very little effort and nudged the rock with his toe towards the shadows of the cave.

"Now, let me ask the person *in charge* where this goes."

Ignoring Gordy's annoyance, Zuttah swung his focus towards Aimee who was thigh-deep in the stream, guiding a petrified trunk into place with the assistance of two rebels who had climbed down from the terraces above to assist.

Zak surveyed the entire scene with a keen,

but shuttered eye. Behind the crater wall, the suns began to collapse and his sight improved with each crack of rock against wood. He watched Aimee busily directing everyone. Damp from perspiration, her hair looked darker, but her eyes were bright—with a zest for the task at hand. Water licked her long legs, and it was hard to pull his gaze away from them. Luckily for the mountain men working with her, Zak was the only one staring at her so blatantly.

Reluctantly, he turned his attention back to the limb he was stripping with a stone-carved axe. In the background he listened to her litany and kept his head ducked to conceal his amusement.

"You know," she spoke aloud to men who understood only pieces of what she was saying, "when a beaver builds a dam, nothing will stop him from finishing it. Would you believe that beavers have even used *beaver traps* to construct their dams?" A snort snuck out of her nose. "How is that for irony?"

When no one answered, or even chuckled, she continued. "Did you know that beavers build dams to raise the water level so that they can swim to tree limbs that they normally can't reach? Crafty little buggers, those beavers are."

No one understood her, but they

comprehended the tasks she doled out. They were compliant—grateful and eager to be productive, and under their deference she was the consummate engineer.

"We need to account for the speed of the water and the width at which it will hit the cave. We want the wall to be an arc rather than just slap some boards against this hole. We'll use everything we can get our hands on. This petrified wood is awesome. It's not porous, and it will be a sturdy foundation for everything we'll pile up against it. Rocks, mud, grass, leaves—"

"*Zull* dung?" Zuttah offered.

This time Zak could not conceal the quiver of his shoulders as he laughed. The fallout was immediate.

"*Zull* dung in fact would work wonderfully," there was a bite to Aimee's tone, "if you can find an abundance of it. And, when I say abundance—I mean enough to ply every tiny gap in the wall."

"You find that much every time Zuttah talks," Zak offered.

In return, he suffered the big man's threatening frown. "Well, look who crawled out of the cave and developed a sense of humor," Zuttah chortled. "You and your newfound mirth can go collect the dung from the valley." A flash of white teeth emerged behind the heavy beard.

Zak just smirked in return. There was no way he was leaving Aimee alone here.

"I'll go," a voice offered.

Startled, Zak turned to see Zon approach. He looked much stronger, with his posture erect, and his chocolate eyes sharp and honed in on Zak as if he expected a denial.

"You need to rest," Zak warned, still not comfortable with how to communicate with the man. So many years…

Zon cleared his throat and even managed a negligible grin. "For the first time in I don't know how long, I feel good. I feel strong. I can think straight. Even the prospect of picking up *Zull* dung sounds exciting because it is something I can accomplish, while comprehending the ultimate goal."

A smile cracked Zak's lips. He could relate to that. On some subconscious level, he felt as if he were being watched. Sure enough, Aimee stood in the water, a small rock clutched in her hand. She met his eyes and he understood the message there.

Go with him.

Evidently eager to begin, Zon had already pivoted, his knees cutting through the high grass with newfound agility. Torn, Zak remained rooted in place.

Across the way, Aimee jerked her head in Zon's direction. Sensing his indecision, she added a convincing smile as if to assure him, *I will be fine.*

Zull roamed the western pastures. It was an area close enough to reach with a shout. These *Zull* were an adapted version of the original breed which flourished in the warmth of the desert. Acclimating to the higher altitude when the rebels first guided them here, these *Zull* had shrunk in bulk, and the fur on their haunches grew thick and lush. And according to one beautiful engineer, their dung was a viable material in dam construction.

Zuttah stepped into his line of sight. It was only the briefest tip of the head, but Zak recognized the meaning. The brawny Ziratakian would look after her.

Zak mouthed to Aimee, "I'll be right back."

She just smiled and held her thumb up in the air... *whatever that meant.*

"You are feeling better?" Zak inquired as they trudged side by side through the shimmering grass.

The blades undulated in the wind, making it look like a vast ocean.

"Every minute I grow more coherent. I don't think I was ever hurt or malnourished. I was just too—incapacitated by my thoughts to recognize the status of my health." Zon glanced sideways. "And you–" he nodded, "–I see the mark of the solar ray on you."

"I'm fine." Dusk was coming. He *would* be fine.

There was an awkward pause filled with a breeze that whispered tales of the ancient heroes of this land. In the distance, Aimee's voice continued to dictate, but she undermined her authority with an occasional laugh.

"Did you know about this crater when I was—?"

"When you were young? Yes. I was going to bring you up here one day when you grew old enough to make the climb. I wanted to show you where the monarch lived."

"You were building me a model *terra duster* down in the cellar," Zak winced at the recollection of that dark chamber. "I was so young—I don't even know your trade."

Swallowed in the dense shadows of the crater wall, Zon tread carefully. "I was involved in the design of several of our transportation-class vessels, but by trade—I was just a teacher," he grinned.

"A teacher?" Zak halted.

"Somebody had to instruct our future generation on how to build reliable transport. I worked in a classroom, and when I was through, the students engaged in hands-on training. But, I admit—" he looked up to the stars, and Zak saw that his beard climbed down his throat, "—that I missed the hands-on factor. So, your little *terra duster* was as much a present for myself as it was for you. It was going to be something we could have fun with together."

In the purple hue of twilight, Zak met his father's eyes.

Zon spoke quietly. "I had so many aspirations for you. From everything I see and hear around here…you exceeded my expectations. You have become a hero, and a man that commands respect. I could not be more proud."

Zak cleared his throat. "I just wish I had known—"

So much could have been different had I known.

"When I was faced with the fact that I lost my wife, and then my children—I welcomed the ray of the Koron. Maybe I was purposely reckless—hoping to draw their fire."

"And if we had not met here would you have continued down that path?" Zak challenged.

Contemplating this for a moment, Zon nodded. "In the state of madness that I was in, suicide was something I considered, but was not lucid enough to attain. That serum. It brought back my mind."

To Zak's surprise, Zon reached out and clasped his shoulder. Hard.

"If I was struck dead today, I would die a happy man knowing that you survived. You have no idea how much it means to see you alive."

Emotion clogged Zak's throat.

"But—" Zak coughed to clear it, "—you will not die today. Instead you will pick up dung."

For a moment Zon froze, and then he let loose a barking laugh. "I see you have inherited your mother's sense of humor."

That thought pleased Zak. "What was her trade? Did she have one? I just remember her smelling like *zynther* flowers. And she always had food for me. And she *always* told me to listen to my sister." At that he rolled his eyes and his father joined in his laughter.

"By trade, your mother was a seamstress. But between you and me, her secret desire was to be an entertainer."

"An entertainer?" Zak's eyebrows vaulted.
A distant memory of his mother standing in the
yard under a canopy of vines with the sun
filtering through her lustrous dark hair flashed in
his mind. She was singing, and the melody was so
peaceful, he curled up in the grass and fell asleep
listening to it.

"Yes," Zon grinned. "She told me that as a
child she wanted to join the *Zirithay* choir tour,
but her parents wouldn't let her. Instead, she
used to perform for me and it was quite—" Zon
cleared his throat. "Well, anyway. She was a
talented woman."

"Zari sang too, but not so good."

"Hah—no. Your sister didn't quite have
her voice. But your sister was very smart. Like
you. We knew you both would excel in whatever
you took on."

Their mood grew somber at the mention of
Zari. A throaty growl nearby drew their
attention. The listless *Zull* swayed its heavy
frame atop spindly legs, as if the limbs were
about to collapse under the girth. It was a hump-
backed animal with excessive fur on its posterior.
Half of its head belonged to its nose, and through
those enormous nostrils it snorted its contempt at
being disturbed.

"Ack. Hush," Zak berated the creature. "We will be gone soon."

Zon was already hunched over, using a stick to scoop a pile of excrement into his pail. Busy with the task at hand, neither spoke, and in that silence the distant sound of voices carried to them. Gordy's laugh traveled far enough to agitate the *Zull* as the herd began a collective gait towards the crater wall.

"Who are they?" Zon's voice was muffled by his stance.

"Who?"

"The strangers in the fancy suits. They aren't from Ziratak."

"One is from Anthum, and one is from—Earth."

"Anthum?" Zon looked up. "I thought everyone had fled that planet. I heard they built an elaborate ship to get away from the virus."

"Yeah. They did." *And it was quite elaborate.* "That ship and those survivors are the ones who rescued me from here."

A crestfallen look possessed the older man. "Which one is from Anthum? I will extend my gratitude...if I could put it into words."

Hearing Gordy's guffaw, Zak smiled. "That would be the one laughing right now."

Zon gazed at the blond head for a moment

and then nodded. "And Earth? Where is Earth? It's not in the *Arkaron* galaxy, is it? I always suspected they were going to venture our way."

"No, it's much further away than that."

Something in his voice caught Zon's interest. "The girl," he mused. "She has traveled a long way then?"

"Yes."

Uncomfortable under the prolonged stare, Zak crouched down to continue his work.

"That serum has allowed me to grasp many things. I see the way you look at her. I see how she looks back." Zon paused. "You are in love with her."

Zak felt like a fist was lodged inside his windpipe. "Yes," he whispered. "It is a long tale."

Next to him, the sound of a stick scraping mud blended with Zon's voice. "They usually are. As long as they have a happy ending, all is good."

"I want only for her to be safe." Zak did not look up from his hunt in the shallow dirt. "She should not be on this planet. She came here to rescue me."

"She must really care for you if she travelled that far."

The fist was now twisting inside his rib cage. "If we succeed here—if by some miracle we can destroy the Korons—" the thought that tortured him from the moment he heard of her transportation now manifested itself, "—I'm not sure how to get her off this planet. I don't want her spending the next *ren* here."

Zon stopped digging and leaned against his stick. "Have you asked her? Maybe she wants to stay here with you."

Standing straight, Zak looked into his father's eyes...*his father.*

There—he acknowledged it. It had been so hard to accept—such a mental obstacle. But when he looked into those eyes, and took in the high cheekbones and wide smile...memories of that face besieged him. And so, he felt compelled to speak the truth.

"This is not my home anymore. I don't want to stay here."

A hint of pain pinched his father's lips.

"And where is your home?" he asked.

Zak looked across the field. In the chorus of masculine voices, one bright flower bloomed. Her voice brought him peace.

"I see," Zon whispered. "Then we will find a way to get you off of this planet."

Zak closed his eyes. This had been missing in his life. Vodu was the best replacement for a father that any boy could have, but there was something different. This was a connection that could withstand the test of time.

"I take it your ship was destroyed," Zon probed.

"Yes."

"And you said she came here to rescue you?"

"Yes."

"What about her craft?"

Laughter bubbled up in his throat. It really was absurd when you thought about it. "She came here in a *terra duster*."

A thud sounded as Zon dropped his pail.

"A *terra duster*? In space?"

This time Zak let the laugh escape. "Yes. Believe me. I have the same questions as you."

Zon stooped to pick up his pail. Wrinkling his nose against the odor, he announced, "We have enough for tonight. Let's go talk to the pretty woman about her vessel."

They fell into step alongside each other.

"Ahm-ee, right?" he asked.

"Aimee. Yes."

"I think I am going to like your, Aimee. She did save my sanity, after all."

"You're lucky," Zak grinned. "She tries her best to destroy mine."

CHAPTER THIRTEEN

Aimee heard their laughter long before the profiles emerged from the dark. These shadows were no threat. These shadows carried with them a scent...and it was not pleasant.

When they emerged into the ring of firelight, the bait of their smiles was infectious. Her brooding, handsome hero wore a frown since the day she first met him. This mirth suited him.

"Judging by your smell," she goaded, "I'd say you came back with enough dung to seal this entire mountain."

To her surprise the older man strode up to her with his hand extended. Arching an eyebrow, she stared at that hand imagining all the places it had been in the past hour.

"Ahm-ee," he stated with his palm still proffered.

This was Zak's father. With only the slightest hesitation, she reached out and clasped it, tempted to haul him in for a hug.

Zon beamed and shook her hand.

"I did not get to properly meet you, or thank you before. There are no words to describe how grateful I am to you for restoring my psyche."

He smelled like crap.

It made her smile.

Would it be inappropriate to thank the man for producing such a fine son?

"You are most welcome," was all she could manage.

Whenever she was at a loss for words, purpose kicked in instead. "At first light we'll apply this as the finishing seal. The sun should dry it quickly and our lake will begin to form."

"All business, this one," Zak chuckled. "Speaking of lakes," he mentioned while walking backwards. "I need to head to the water and clean up."

Aimee stared down at her hand. *Yeah, me too.*

In the firelight, Zon's eyes glowed playfully. "Why don't you two go on ahead, and I'll catch up after reviewing the progress. I'll just get dirtier digging into the work."

Aimee gained newfound respect for the man. He was offering them alone-time. With one glance around the crowd seated before the fire, she started to backpedal before turning around and jogging in the dark to catch up with the silhouette ahead.

"Zak," she whispered. "*Zak.*"

He halted. She could not see his face under the night sky, but she had the feeling that he could distinguish her clearly.

"I smell," he declared quietly.

Does he see my smile?

"Yes. You do."

She heard his amused snort.

"Stay there," Zak ordered. "I can see better than you, and I don't want you getting caught in this current."

"That current should be backing up already. By tomorrow morning there will be a considerable-sized pond here...on its way to becoming a lake."

A pond.

Her pond was worlds away. She thought of her parents. Were they okay?

"You miss it, don't you?" his husky question startled her.

"Miss what? No. No. I am thinking if there is anything I neglected with the dam."

"Aimee." Warm hands wrapped around her shoulders. "It may have been some time since we've been together, but I know you. Don't shatter the image I have had all this time—

envisioning you happy and industrious in your home. You can't tell me that you don't miss it...that you don't miss your parents."

It was so dark now. She could no longer distinguish his profile.

"Yes, I miss them, but I missed you more. Does that make me a horrible person?"

Please don't answer that.

The grip on her biceps eased and she found herself engulfed in his arms, her cheek pressed to his chest, where the steady rhythm of his heart lulled her eyes closed.

"If it involves you missing me...no, there's nothing horrible about that," he murmured.

Winding her arms around his waist so that she could hold him tighter, she accepted that there wasn't anything she would do differently if she had to do it all over. She loved her parents very much. But Zak was her destiny.

"You're cold." His lips dusted across her hair as he drew her in closer.

"Warm." With her head tucked into his collarbone, her words were muffled. She withdrew enough to warn, "Zak, we need to get everyone away from the dam now. Either back to the caves or seek higher ground."

"Always thinking," he murmured. "Does your mind ever shut down?"

"Every time you kiss me."

A slight rumble sounded in his throat and then she felt his lips against hers. All coherence was gone and her stomach took a tumble.

"Zak. Zak." A voice called in the distance. "Aimee?"

It was Gordy. It sounded as if his hands were cupped around his mouth for maximum volume. "We're heading back to the caves. Are you coming?"

"I want to be alone with you," Zak murmured softly, his lips touching her ear.

A shiver charged through her.

"I want that too," she purred against his throat.

A gap fell between them as Zak stepped back and hollered, "We'll catch up later."

Wind crackled across the grass. A call sounded. "Okay—" it grew distant, "—be careful."

An edgy glimpse confirmed that the pit of the crater was clutched in a nocturnal glove. For a moment Aimee felt panic well up at the dark. "Let me guess," she uttered. "You can see fine right now, can't you?"

"Well enough to know that your cheeks are red, your beautiful hair that looks like the desert is now blowing into your eyes, which irritates you, and your hands are on your hips, which usually means you're about to make a point."

The wind *was* really ticking her off. She tried to angle her head into it, but that stung her eyes just as bad.

"You think you know it all, Mr. Hot Shot Warrior," she teased.

"My name is Zak. And the only person in all the galaxies that thinks they know more than me is you." He hesitated. "Well...and JOH."

Aimee laughed.

In the dark, Zak reached for her hand. "I need to ask you something, but I want to get out of this wind. Somewhere where you can see me."

That was a marvelous idea on all counts.

Surrendering to the tug of his hand, Aimee trudged through the grass, relying on Zak's grip to guide her in the dark. Developing her own sonar, she listened to the gusts ruffle the meadow, the ebb and flow similar to waves lapping against a shoreline. In the distance muted laughter could be heard. Glancing up, she saw the crater walls dotted with the glow of man-made fires. From this perspective and with so many of those flares, it looked like a posh Tahitian resort lined with torch-lit balconies. Nearby, water lapped gently against a boulder.

The current was already slowing down, met with a barrier it could not penetrate.

Zak's hand parted with hers only to affix itself around her waist.

"Be careful, we have to climb a little."

Before she could even respond she felt the natural incline strain her thighs.

"Stick close to me," he instructed. "It's a narrow trail."

She had no problem sticking close to him, but the uneven terrain had her clutching his hip for support. Continuing in this manner for what she calculated was nearly fifteen minutes, Aimee became aware of the wind shifting. At this elevation it screeched past her ears like the keening whistle of a blizzard—only, there was no snow and she had grown warm from the physical effort.

Zak halted, his arm still secured around her.

"Stay right here, and don't move." He squeezed her waist. "I mean it, Aimee. Don't move. If you take off in the wrong direction you could end up in the valley...below."

Gulp.

"Where are you going?" Her voice was as high-pitched as the siren blasting past her ears.

"I need to light our way."

Panicking when his hand slipped out of reach, Aimee heard a zap over the pitch of the wind. It sounded like one of those bug lamps. Immediately a glow enveloped the ground before her. Rutted with rocks and dirt, the path along the crater wall was indeed a narrow one. Behind her, the path dropped off into shadows that no light could reach. Shadows of oblivion. How far *below* was the valley?

Another zap, and more of the path illuminated. Torches that looked like smoldering mops ignited a trail into the crater wall.

"How did you light those?"

Zak wiggled a small crescent-shaped mechanism. "Just a *terrene* flare. Everyone carries one of these."

A celestial pocket-knife.

Light beckoned. Zak beckoned. It didn't take much coaxing to pry her away from the ledge. Aimee followed him into the cave and felt her ears ring from the cessation of wind.

If your ears are ringing, someone is talking about you.

That's what her mom always said. But who was talking about her? Was it her mother?

Aimee clutched the pendant behind her collar and whispered, "*I'm alright, Mom.*"

"What?" Zak spun around and caught a

glimpse of what was in her hand. His expression softened. He stepped forward and cupped his hand around hers, both of them clasping the tiny sliver from his ship.

"You still have it," he whispered in awe.

"Of course. It kept me close to you." She cleared her throat. "And since I touched it every day of those five years on Earth, it now reminds me of my parents too. Does that make any sense? This pendant links worlds for me."

His fingers rose to cup her cheek, his thumb caressing her jaw.

"You miss them." His voice was hoarse.

"I'll always miss them. But I am where I want to be."

Silence met her words. Humbled by the raw emotion in Zak's gaze, she waited until he cleared his throat.

"You're not making this easy on me."

Easy? What? Wait.

"Making what easy?"

Was he breaking up with her? No. No!

Knowing Zak, he was doing what he felt was best for her.

"Let me show you something." The warmth of his palm dropped from her face to clasp her hand. She was certain her fingers trembled beneath his, but she followed as he moved deeper into the cave. Dread gnawed at her stomach with wicked fangs.

This mountain dwelling distracted her, though. *Cave* was the wrong terminology. As Zak *threw on the lights* by kindling the torches, Aimee witnessed a habitat equipped with rudimentary furniture. A table, chairs, and even artwork dotted the earthen walls. Intrigued, she stepped up to a series of brilliant orbs hovering close to the cave wall. They bobbed with every lick of wind that extended into the grotto. Each globe shimmered with an internal glow, a glow that pulsed in tandem with their fluctuation. One orb was green with golden swirls emulating a cloud pattern, while the other orb looked like a maraschino cherry with a dab of whipped cream on its polar cap. Aimee extended her glance and found more floating spheres, as if someone had dropped a boxful of Christmas ornaments in a gravity-free chamber.

"What are they?" she whispered in awe.

"I like to think—" he took a deep breath, "—that they were left here by the great monarch, Zak." For a moment he fell silent, and then added, "And I like to think that by bearing his name, I was destined to find them."

Imagining Zak as a child listening to his father regale tales of the great monarch in the mountains, Aimee nodded. "You're right, Zak. These are too ethereal even for Ziratak. There is something divine about them."

Hesitant, she reached up and cupped her hand near a floating orb. It emanated heat and shifted the slightest to avoid her grasp. Again she sought to touch it, but it maneuvered beyond her reach.

"Don't disturb them," Zak warned. "They represent peace. They have helped to heal me. I can sit here in the dark and focus on their glow without any pain."

"Does anyone else know about them?"

"Not that I know of."

"You never showed anyone?"

"Just you. I kind of wanted to keep them to myself."

"No one else stumbled across them?"

"Ummm...no." Zak chuckled quietly. "People don't *stumble* up here. Part of the reason I brought you up here at night was so that you could not see the trek to get here. You would have never volunteered."

She didn't want to imagine what that meant. "How did you find it, then?"

"Aside from destroying the Korons and saving my people—for the most part I have been alone. I climb. I hike. I find seclusion...and I found this place."

What a puzzle these orbs were. They hypnotized her. They offered serenity. Standing at Zak's side, she shared in his peace. As much as she didn't want to break that tranquility, anxiety wormed her lips into action.

"You said that *part* of the reason you brought me up here at night was so that I would not see the path," she quoted. "What was the other part?"

"Privacy."

"Oh," her demeanor fell. "Right. You had to tell me something. Was it this? Did you want to tell me about these—planets?"

Zak's shoulder twitched. "I'm not sure they are planets, and no, that's not what I wanted to tell you. Are you hungry? There are *zukee* cakes here, and some juice. I try to keep the cave stocked."

"Zak?" She stared him down, worried when his genial expression faltered.

"Come here." He swept his arm towards a wooden bench. It might have simply been a long plank nailed atop four legs, but the intricate carvings in the wood lent it a regal flare.

He sat and she fell in beside him, close enough that their thighs brushed. As long as she was connected with him in some manner she felt grounded.

Nearby, a golden orb lobbed across a ripple in the breeze and then righted itself.

"Aimee—"

Here it comes. The, *I think it's best if you return to Earth* speech. How was she ever going to hold herself together?

"We don't know if this dam is going to be successful," he began in a husky tone. "It might just antagonize the Korons. It will probably rally them into warfare."

You will be safer away from here.

It was coming. She knew it.

"If anything happens to you—"

Nothing is going to happen to me.

He took both her hands in his and ducked to capture her eyes when she sought to elude him by staring at the floor.

"I love you," he declared with grave finality.

That was it. Those heartfelt words released the torrent.

"No, Zak. No. You can't send me home. You physically can't. I don't even know if we can get off this planet, and we're only at about a *renna*, a half-rotation of the galaxy or whatever. We have two years to go until we reach my solar system...*I think*. And, I have waited so long—*so* patiently to be with you again. I have traveled so far, and battled every obstacle that was thrown in my path—all to be with you. I love you so much—" her voice broke and tears started to pour out of the corners of her eyes. "Please don't send me away. I can't—I can't be without you."

She clutched his hands so tightly she was certain his arms were about to turn blue, but she could not let go. If she squeezed tight enough maybe the emphasis would register, and he would understand.

When he didn't respond, she blinked away the tears so that she could focus on him. To her surprise he wore a soft grin.

"Aimee," he began softly, "I don't want to send you away. I want—" he hesitated and looked down at their hands. "—I want my circulation back, and I want us to become bonded."

"Wh-what?"

Bonded!

It was the Ziratakian term for marriage— except it was far greater than the ceremony of matrimony. Zak had described it so eloquently that night they were trapped in an underground nook on Bordran. *Bonded* was for life. There was no divorce, or un-bonding. It was the ultimate commitment between a man and a woman.

"Aimee—I hate that you are here in this dangerous environment. But—" he hesitated, "—the selfish side of me wouldn't have it any other way. I don't ever want to lose you again. And if this all goes wrong. If a war breaks out. If—"

He didn't have to speak the words. He feared that one or both of them might die in the ensuing days.

"If anything happens to me—I want to know you were mine. I want to spend the rest of my life with you—whether it's a day, a *ren*—or preferably, an eternity."

Aimee sniffled. "You underestimate my dam-making abilities. The Korons will be deep-sea diving very soon."

Zak's smile made her dizzy. With the slightest tremor in his voice, he asked, "Is that a yes?"

Tears fell unchecked now as her head pumped up and down until the word finally broke free. "Yes!"

"Do you think you can let go of my hands so that I can touch you?"

Glancing down at their clenched fingers, she slowly relinquished her grip. In one surge, Zak's fingers were in her hair and his lips were on hers, and the kiss was an explosion, as if a new solar system had been formed right here—right in this magical cave high on the crater wall.

Leaving her mouth, his lips brushed against the tears rolling down her cheeks. Strong arms hauled her in closer until she felt their hearts race in tandem.

This was her man. Hers to love and cherish for the rest of her life. Joy bubbled up inside her and manifested in more sobs.

Zak drew back with concern. "Tell me that you're crying because you're happy."

Her trembling lips were pretty much useless, so she just nodded and smiled.

Warm palms still cupped her face. "I can still see you...that first time on the flight deck of the HORUS." His tone was nostalgic. "You were scared, but you tried to act so strong in front of me. And I still remember when you crashed into me in that linear transport. Here I was about to go battle the Korons...I should have been concentrating on that, and yet—all I could think about was how you felt. You marked me that day. I was never the same."

Me too.

"I thought you were trying to get rid of me. You couldn't wait to send me off to the Bio Ward."

"I *was* trying to get rid of you." Zak shook

his head. "It spooked me to know how much you affected me."

Aimee reached up to touch his cheek. There were a few lines around his eyes now, side effects of the suns and age.

"Do I still spook you?" she whispered coyly.

There was a shift in his glance. The gaze smoldered and he responded in a husky tone, "More than you'll ever know."

And he kissed her.

Warmth.

Zak felt warm from his neck down to his toes. He drew in a breath, but instead of dirt and stale air, he smelled the meadow and a trace of flowers. The source of heat shifted and he smiled contentedly. Aimee was stretched out alongside him beneath a fur blanket. Even in slumber, her arm was cinched around his waist as if she was afraid he might slip away. He dipped his head and touched his lips to her temple. It made her stir as sleepy eyes fluttered open.

"Hi." It was a breathy greeting.

"Hi." He kissed her and she latched on even tighter, which made him rethink his plans for the day.

"What time is it?" she murmured against his throat.

Dammit, she felt good.

"It is morning," he rasped.

"Ummm." Her eyes were half open, and then they were wide, and she sat up so fast her shoulder smacked his jaw.

"Oww."

"Zak! Come on, we have to go! We have to see if it worked."

This was what he was in for the rest of his life. It was a notion that made him ridiculously happy.

Aimee bolted towards the cave door, her shirt askew as she rushed to straighten it against the gust of wind.

"Aimee, wait!"

He scrambled upright, tripping over the bed of furs. As he charged towards the cave entrance, the shining globes bobbed in agitation.

"Wait!" he called again just as her silhouette filled the threshold.

Aimee stumbled backwards and fell on her rear before he could catch her. Her mouth was opening and closing like one of the creatures in the atrium pond.

"Wh-wh-wh-" She was crab-walking backwards, away from the light.

In one swoop, he hauled her up from the ground. Her chest pumped with adrenaline as he soothed his hand down her back until she began to calm some.

"Whoa," she gasped, her fingers clamped around his arms like shackles. "You weren't kidding about bringing me up here in the dark."

"I know." He gritted his teeth, angry with himself. "I should have never risked that climb with you. I just—"

The vice around his arm eased up. "When we get to the bottom," she said, "I will remind you that coming here was worth every step."

Her smile eased his self-condemnation...for a moment.

"I will remember this cave forever, Zak." She pointed at the floating orbs. "These beautiful enigmas."

Her gaze shifted to the ornately carved bench. "The place where you asked me to spend the rest of my life with you." She glanced towards the floor and the heap of fur blankets as heat bolstered the color in her cheeks. "Wh-when," she stuttered, "we get back to the bottom, I will tell you that this cave is the best place I've ever been to in my entire life."

"You know I'm not going to let you fall." His throat was dry. "You know that, don't you?"

Trust lit up her eyes, making them sparkle—or maybe it was a ray of one of the suns poking into the cave.

"I know that." She smiled. "But I should probably inform you that even though I have no problem flying...I'm afraid of heights."

If he could physically kick himself in the rear, he would be doing it right now. How stupid to take her somewhere so perilous. It was selfish, and yet—now, it would also be the best place he had ever been in his life.

Reaching down between them for her hand, he drew it up between their faces, emphasizing, "*Don't let go.*"

Aimee snorted. "Yeah, you're not going to have to worry about the whole letting-go thing. You may need a surgeon to extract me from you."

With a squeeze of assurance, Zak started first towards the cave entrance. He paused on the threshold and heard her troubled breathing at his side. This dwelling sat three-quarters of the way up the crater wall, with nothing more than a thin lip of rock carved out of the mountainside as access. The path was about a foot wide—not even wide enough for him to walk alongside her. Having hiked it hundreds of times, it was no more stressful for him than mounting a staircase. And in the cloak of night, with his enhanced vision, he could maneuver Aimee easily up the narrow trail. Now, however, the suns were about to creep over the crater wall, which meant he had to move fast. The last thing they needed was for him to lose his sight on this treacherous hike.

"Ohh, Zak," Aimee's gaze was wide. "I don't know if I can do this."

Pivoting her to face him, he asked earnestly, "Do you trust me?"

Still locked on the treacherous drop to the valley below, Aimee spoke out of the corner of her mouth. "Of course."

"You need to look at me," he urged.

Terror was like a magnet. If you were anywhere close to it, it was going to reel you in. Aimee was being reeled in by that harrowing view.

"Aimee," he called.

Her head rocked, and then she was looking at him, her lips parted on shallow breaths.

He let go of her with one hand to reach for the solar shield dangling around her neck. Working it up over her eyes, he pressed the side of the frame and triggered the obstruction lens.

"What? Wait." She balked in his arms and he reached up again to steady her. "I can't see," she cried.

"People rely on their eyes too much," he

allayed. "If I were to close mine right now, I could still tell that you were beautiful."

"This is not the time for charm, Zak," her voice pitched.

"Easy," he soothed. "Take a deep breath, and—"

"—and *what?*"

"And have faith in me."

At that command, her shoulders sagged and she gave up the struggle.

"You hit below the belt, Zak."

Alarmed, he searched her thighs. "I didn't hit you."

"It's a saying on our planet," she chuckled. "Never mind."

Turning her head towards the light, he could see the reflection of the crater rim in her lenses. The suns were close.

"Okay. I just want you to know that I intend to slide my butt along the mountain the whole way down," she proclaimed.

Zak's hand slipped down her back and lower. "Mmmm. I'd rather not see that damaged."

Somewhere behind that shield he knew her eyes were smiling. His levity vanished as they stepped out into the wind, engulfed in its vortex. It was difficult for him to acclimate to the light and his sight blurred. A few blinks and he could see again.

"Alright," he raised his voice to battle the gusts. "We have to march single file. There's plenty of room for that, and the incline levels out about halfway down. You can take your shield off once we get there. I'll go first, and you hang onto my belt, okay? I mean *hang on to it.* If you feel yourself slip at all, you'll have a hold of me, and I'm not going to let you pull me over."

It was a feeble attempt to keep the atmosphere light, but he knew she could identify the worry in his tone.

Already, he felt her fingers groping his waist until they latched onto his belt.

"Good. That's perfect. If you want, you can let go with your left hand to keep it against the face of the mountain—palm flat."

"Yes, I like that. If I feel it, then I know I'm close to it."

Zak nodded, but realized that she couldn't see.

"If you need to stop for any reason, yell, or tug on me."

She held her thumb up.

He glanced up the rock wall, but had no idea what she was pointing her thumb at.

"Okay," he hollered into the wind, "let's go."

It wasn't that the hike was extremely hazardous. It wasn't that it was insanely steep, or rugged. It was simply that the ledge was so narrow, and that if you dared to glance over the precipice into the yawning chasm mere inches away, you would be lured to your death by vertigo alone. Visually-challenged, and often traveling by night, it was a vista that had never disturbed Zak. Putting blinders on Aimee was the safest option.

You can't fear what you can't see.

Conscious of her grip on his belt, Zak moved at a gradual pace, one hand flat against the sheer rock face, the other resting atop hers. Every now and then he heard a bleat of anxiety bubble from her lips. He would stop and shift his back against the rock wall, assuring her with word and touch that she was doing great. And she was. Her trust was unconditional. For that trust he would move this mountain if he had to.

Loose pebbles scattered past his feet as he glanced over his shoulder to see if she had slipped. What he saw was a flash of white teeth and pink lips—her bright smile dissected by a lock of copper hair.

"You're doing great," he yelled.

The first sun cracked the crater wall, and with it a burst of pain assaulted him, like a knife through the eye. He doubled over in reflex.

"Zak!" Aimee cried, tugging on his belt. "Are you okay?"

Using the rock wall for leverage, even the granite glowed under the sun's brilliance. There was no relief from the assault.

"Yes," he assured. "Hold on tight. We're almost there."

Encumbered, the path grew hazy. He took a step forward, but was not sure of his proximity to the ledge.

"Hug the mountain, Aimee. Hug close to it," he ordered as he brushed his shoulder along the rock.

"If I hug it any tighter I might be bonding with *it* rather than you."

Damn woman. Always making him laugh during a crisis.

Below his fur-lined boots the path started to glow, the fine granules illuminated by the rise of the second sun. Each shiny piece of quartz was like a miniature solar ray, taking aim at his damaged pupils. Zak dropped his eyelids to mere slits and continued down the path. In time he felt the grade level off. They had reached the mesa, a wide plateau that possessed a natural staircase down to the valley floor.

Aimee must have sensed it. Her fingers

relaxed their hold and he pivoted around, pulling her into his arms.

"We made it to the bottom?" she asked, her voice muffled by his shoulder.

He pulled her shield up to rest atop her head. Impressions from the device scored her forehead and cheekbones. She was trying to glimpse around him, but he had her locked in an embrace.

"I'm so sorry, Aimee. I thought we would be out of there before the sun rose, but this morning, I just wanted to lie there with you—"

"Hush." To his surprise, she kissed him. Her lips were cold but warmed on contact. It was definitely a distraction when he was trying to make a point.

Just as quickly she withdrew and stepped back, lobbing her hands on her hips. "Well, would you look at that."

Zak winced against the reflection of water in the valley. "It's working!" He stepped forward. "Aimee, you did it, the stream is backing up."

Backing up was an understatement. A lake had formed at the foot of the crater. The body of water was wide enough to reach the far meadow where the *Zull* roamed. The creatures would stay safe by migrating north, away from the reservoir. Still, the rapid pace in which the valley gorged was alarming. It accelerated Zak's strategy as he realized that the rebels would have to act quickly to spare the wildlife that the Ziratakians relied on.

"Ummm, it's working alright," Aimee agreed. "A little bit too well. Zak—" She joined him, now fearless of the remaining descent. "If you were looking to orchestrate this—if you wanted a definitive moment to set off an explosion—" she shook her head, "I'm not sure you're going to have that luxury. This lake is building up fast and furious, and it is causing a lot of pressure against that dam. I don't know how much longer it's going to hold up. You need to get everyone ready—*now.*"

Sunlight glared on the stagnant surface below, but its placid, innocent face harbored a powerful punch. It was exactly what he wanted— but like any supreme force, it could not be controlled.

"Alright. We need to get everyone together—armed, and in position above the desert."

Preoccupied with strategies, Zak jolted when he felt Aimee's touch. She reached up and hauled the shield off her head, some of her hair snagging in it. Hefting onto her toes, she fitted the shield over his head and drew it down to cover his eyes. The relief was immediate. It did not stop the pain, but it diminished it greatly.

With her hands still cupped on the sides of his head, her fingers wormed into his hair as she gently admonished, "And where the hell is *your* eye shield?"

"I had other things on my mind." He grinned. "I must have forgotten it."

"What was on your mind?" she teased so close to his mouth.

A growl sounded deep in his throat before he dusted her lips with his own. The shield prevented him from kissing her like he wanted to. "You're lucky we have a crisis on our hands or I'd carry you back up that cliff on my back and—"

"Bah, all talk," she teased.

And then, just as her hand slipped from his skin, she sobered and declared, "I love you, Zak."

Dammit. He never could predict what would pop out of this woman's mouth next. At least the shield hid exactly how her words affected him.

"What are the chances that I can get you to stay safe in our supply cave while this all goes down?"

Okay, well, he predicted her snicker.

Aside from that, she voiced no answer. She

just grabbed his hand and started down the slope.

"Come on. You're moving like an old man."

CHAPTER FOURTEEN

"How long are we talking?" Zuttah's stride was wide enough that Aimee had to jog to keep up.

"Imminent. Seriously—" she huffed from the exertion, "—it could break at any moment. Everyone is clear, right?"

To her left, Zak marched with a *solar ray* gripped tight in his hands. There was no time to ask why he would be carrying the enemy's weapon. Judging from his demeanor, he knew damn well what he was doing.

Walking between these two men she felt like a dwarf.

"The valley *should* be clear—" Zuttah sounded anxious.

"Our last trek out there," Zak inserted, "the one where we found the couple—and—my father," he glanced over his shoulder at the small army in tow, "—that was the last of the captive rebels that we were able to locate. Everyone had long since moved up to the mountains."

His declaration lacked conviction.

Aimee clutched her *star laser.* It seemed such an insignificant piece of weaponry when battling ten-foot-tall granite soldiers. Glancing behind her, she made eye contact with Gordy who also clasped his laser with such force she could see the tendon protruding from his thumb. With a stern nod at the shield resting around his neck, she conveyed her order. He rolled his eyes and hefted the reflective ring up over his ears.

You can roll your eyes all you want.

Beyond Gordy, an army of nearly a hundred men and some women—none of which possessed eye shields—marched in determination. The notion that they had no shields terrified her. Many of them could be blinded today—or worse. They would do their best to protect their eyes, but studying the moves of their target was a necessity to stay alive. At least, that is what Corluss had warned. And with that focus you were bound to unwillingly catch a glimpse of an incoming ray.

Within that band of determined rebels toting man-made weapons, Aimee located Zon. In the clenched lines of his jaw, and the intensity of his stare, she saw the likeness of his son.

Please don't let this man have survived all this time only to fall on this day.

It had been years in the making, but today was the day these good people would finally go to war. Yes, there had been battles, but now they would rally—united—with the power of their own resources as the ultimate soldier. On her last evaluation of the dam from outside the crater, it revealed pockets of water bleeding through. Every step she took, she awaited that explosion— that powerful tide that would not relent until it had depleted.

This band of soldiers marched down the foothills, giving a wide berth to that latent source of doom. Aimee was not concerned with their logistics. When that water burst out of the mountain, it would project forward in an angry torrent with a single-minded goal to rendezvous with its final objective. The Zargoll.

"When we reach the desert we will fan out towards the east," Zak instructed. "The Koron troops have mainly camped on this side of the river, and even though it is such a small stream now, they do not dare cross it."

"Right," Zuttah agreed. "We box them in against the river. Lock them in place so that they cannot escape the path of the surging water."

Aimee felt a tingle in her limbs. *Fear?* Yes,

she was afraid.

Always in tune with her, Zak slowed his pace and touched her shoulder. "What can I say or do to make you fall back?"

He wore his shield so she could not see his eyes. But the grooves of worry around his lips, and the twitch of a muscle in his jaw revealed his anxiety.

"Nothing." There was not a chance she would leave his side.

"This is a battle, Aimee." His voice was low, for her ears only. "There will be casualties."

His grip restricted and he came to a halt, heedless of Gordy colliding with him.

"Whoa, sorry Zak."

Ignoring the interruption, Zak bent his head and whispered near her ear. "I don't want you to be one of them."

Arguing that she was a trained Warrior seemed awfully feeble. To her dismay, Zak's intensity was causing her eyes to tear up. Dammit, she couldn't even reach up to clear them with the cursed shield in place.

"And I don't want *you* to be one of them," she countered with a tremulous tone.

"Zak!" Zuttah bellowed. "Get up here."

Zak's shoulder flinched, but he did not turn away from her.

"Then we better be damn good today."

There was no grin to accompany his testimony, and the gravity enforced her fear.

"Of all the words you could pick up from me—" she tried to joke.

A shout emerged from the crowd as Aimee whirled to locate its source. Faces swung, cast towards the mountain where the first band of water shot through. It was a small geyser in comparison to the portent of danger to come. At best, it resembled the stream of water from a fire hose on a burning building.

Another torrent broke free.

"Zak," she cried, grabbing his arm. "It's starting to collapse."

In his hands, the bulky profile of the *solar ray* looked like a charred exhaust pipe. Instead of aiming it, he hoisted it over his shoulder and glanced across her head at Zuttah.

"We won't have enough time to get down there to flank the Korons. If they escape the deluge, they could break free to the desert."

Zuttah's profile looked grave. Perspiration trickled down his cheek and into his beard. It made Aimee aware that the temperature was increasing. They were nearly at the bottom of the mountain range where the two suns escalated their assault. A slight breeze—a ghost of the winds born in the higher elevations dusted across her exposed collarbone, but the sand was ahead, and with it, the soaring heat.

Zak halted and lifted his hand into the air, bringing the troop to a standstill.

"Listen," his voice amplified to the farthest reaches.

Heads bobbed for a better perspective.

"We may not have the length of time that we anticipated, so I need to speak to everyone now."

A few men in the rear shouldered their way forward for a better vantage.

"I need you all to ask yourselves if this is *your* battle." Zak's voice was strong. "Do you want to risk your life today? Yes, you have lost your land, but the mountains have been good to you, and they are safe. You *do not* have to fight."

"And what of you, Zak?" Zuttah reasoned. "You have not been to this planet since you were a child. Ask *yourself* if this is your battle."

Aimee held her breath as Zak searched the faces in the crowd. His wandering gaze stopped on her. Though he remained locked there, his voice carried to everyone.

"They took my mother," he began. "They took my sister. They took my sight—and they tried to take my mind." More soldiers pressed in.

"But they didn't take my heart. I may have left as a child, but Ziratak was always here." His palm tapped his chest. "We may be outnumbered. Hopefully, this dam will even that tally. But what we lack in a head count—in weaponry—we compensate with will and pride."

Emotion agitated his throat. "Some of us will fall today. Others will pick up the fallen and carry on. This is Ziratak. This is our land. *Our land.* You should not have to scurry into the mountains and exist in seclusion. You should live where you grew up—where your family before you was raised."

Drawing the *solar ray* off of his shoulder and into a contentious grip, Zak called out, "So I ask you. *Is this your battle?*"

From the ranks, Zon stepped forward. In the soft breeze his unkempt hair ruffled like a lion's mane. "Yes," he said.

"Yes," Zuttah echoed.

"Yes," chanted more voices.

Fists rose into the air, pumping with each cry of "*yes*" that echoed in the shade of the mountain.

Caught up in the zeal, Aimee whispered, "yes." If this was Zak's battle, then this was her battle too. "*Yes,*" she vowed softly and touched his arm.

In the reflection of his sun shield, she saw her hair whip in the breeze. Tension tugged at the corners of her mouth. In the gap of her collar, the pendant flashed. *Zari.*

Resolve pumped in Aimee's veins.

When Zak called out, *"Let's go!"*, her legs charged as fast as his, and those of the giant beside him. Today, she possessed the speed of a stallion—and the strength to accompany it.

Today, she was a Warrior.

From this distance the explosion was muffled, as if the mountain heaved a grave sigh. They had made it as far as the desert basin, but the resonance drew the corps to a halt. En masse they faced the peak. A plume of black smoke arose, but it wasn't actually smoke—rather a rush of mud and water surging from that elevated perch and cascading down the crevice. Even now Zak could hear the thunderous approach of a tsunami as water swallowed land in its haste to extend.

At a safe enough perspective, he saw it connect with the Zargoll in a vicious torrent. Though their plan had been to stay back and wait for any surviving Korons to charge out into the desert, many men hastened towards the river. He understood their motivation. There could be no risk of assumptions. They could not chance that this flood was successful. They wanted to witness first-hand the annihilation of the creatures that sought to abolish them.

"Stay back," Zak called to Aimee who had already starting jogging alongside him. His warning was stolen by the zealous cry of the rebels, and the encroaching rumble of the tide. Even if he tried to stop and talk to her, the impetus of the pack bulldozed them forward. No one could counter the momentum of a band of people who wanted their land back. This was an event for them to herald…and not from a distance.

All he could do was try to keep Aimee in his peripheral vision as the clan fell into an all-out sprint. Around him a clamor of footfalls and shouts collided with the epic rush of water. Instinct took over and he became a creature of the desert, honing in on the river banks.

It played out in slow motion as torrents of water crashed through the river bed, elevating the level to heights far greater than its capacity. Zak had hoped that this plan would work, but never had he anticipated success on such a grand level, as if he could have commanded the charging cataclysm with willpower alone.

At a close enough range to witness the melee but still remain safe, Zuttah stood, pointing. Following his hand, Zak locked in on a horde of Korons fleeing the riverbank. Their progress was sluggish from sheer weight alone. Sandstone legs plundered forward with the finesse of drying cement. Black eyes expressed neither fear nor arrogance. There was no soul there. A barrel of a chest did not rise and fall with resuscitation. They did not breathe. They simply existed. And, in one great surge of water—they were gone.

A roar of approval resonated behind him. It was a minor victory. This was only a limited ensemble of rock monsters. Many more lined the riverbed, but their pace could not exceed the acceleration of this water.

"Keep moving south," Zuttah shouted.

Zak nodded and signaled with his hand to motion others on. It was hard to communicate over the roaring thunder, like the pounding hooves of a million horses.

The mountain continued its discharge, far from depleted. Ahead, bright strobes pierced the air. *Solar rays.* Were these creatures so brainless as to believe they could battle the flood with weapons? Regardless of their stupidity, the rays were still lethal, and not to be taken lightly. Zak glanced back at Aimee to ensure her shield was secured. Just behind her, Gordy charged with a grimace of determination.

Zak felt the weight of their safety on his shoulders. He could not fail them.

Shouts erupted as brilliant rays pierced the heart of the corps like ephemeral swords. A man screamed and collapsed onto his knees.

"Down!" Zak ordered, tugging Aimee to the ground.

Packed sand smacked his chest. Working fast, he mounted his refitted weapon deep in the granules for stability. Squinting against the suns and a multitude of prisms from the surging water, Zak bided his time. Around him, turmoil unfolded. They were under attack—from an unseen foe.

Wait.

There. A rock creature lumbered alongside the flooding river, seeking the safety of the arid desert. Behind him another beast advanced, its *solar ray* firing random blasts into the rebel regime.

Zak waited for that moment of clarity when all sound, all motion, even time itself ceased to move. It came. A keen silence that locked out the world. Within this abstract tunnel, only he and his target existed. In that precise instant, he stroked the underbelly of the massive weapon and watched as the stream sought its mark and incinerated it as if no one had been there to begin with.

Another Koron fell under his assault.

Wait.

When the dust finally settled, he realized that they were no longer under attack. A cheer went up through the crowd. Zak rose to his knees and searched the troop, seeing only two men down.

"Casualties?" He looked up at Zuttah.

The brawny man's silhouette provided relief from the suns.

"None. But one or two men have possibly been blinded. We will be able to tell better later."

Aimee reached down for his shoulder. "We still have some serum, Zak."

He felt that reassuring squeeze against his hot flesh. Thank all the gods that she was safe.

Get off your knees, man.

Hoisting upright, he shouldered the *solar ray* and announced, "We keep moving. I think that first blast took out a huge number of them, but I know of camps further downstream. We are not done here."

They continued their march, and Zak spared himself a spot of indulgence to put his arm around Aimee. It offered him balance, and bolstered his resolve—and for just a moment, the severity of the situation eased.

"Korons ahead!"

Before he even had his arm free he saw Aimee raise her *star laser*, preparing for conflict. Corluss was thorough with his training. Zak hoped for the opportunity to thank the man.

A sultry haze hugged the horizon, making it hard to distinguish what was real. Through that mist he observed a band of Korons fleeing the river banks. The rebels circled around them and forced them to retreat. Rays were fired before the Korons fell back as the Zargoll's rushing current lunged out to claim them.

Victory reinforced the group. Shouts. Pats on the back. Boisterous declarations of freedom. A few men sang, while others remained alert. Executing a calculated pivot to survey for injuries, Zak jolted when he could not locate Aimee. Clamping down on his panic, he searched the troop, but there was no desert-haired goddess—and for that fact, there was no fair-haired Gordeelum either.

"Aimee!" Zak cried.

Charging through the crush of curious glances and disrupted celebration, Zak stopped short when Zon blocked his path. His father's face was solemn.

Confused by this obstacle, Zak nearly shoved him aside.

He didn't have to. Zon stepped back with his head cast down.

And that was when he saw her.

Aimee lie inert on the sand. Gordeelum knelt over her, his hands on her abdomen, stalling the fresh blood flow that tarnished her glossy white top. Hauling off his eye shield, Zak dropped to his knees by her side. Knocked loose from her collar, the pendant flashed in the sunlight, blinding him. He reached for it and slipped it back under the material, his hand brushing her flesh, feeling for the drum of her heart. It was there, but it was a feeble cadence.

"No," he whispered.

"Zak," Gordy choked. "There was so much going on. Rays were coming from every direction. I—I saw her—she dropped back because she caught sight of a Koron that had gone unnoticed. Somehow he had circled around us—" he swallowed, "—and Aimee fired at him, but it only clipped his arm. He was close enough to use a—a—"

"We don't know what they are." Zak's voice caught. "We call them *pulse slayers.*"

Nodding, Gordy continued in halting

words. "He—*it*—shot her. I—I fired at him and missed." He looked crestfallen. "But I got him the second time. He's gone. He's a pile of dirt—but it's all too late. I was too late."

Zak placed his hands over Gordy's, infusing his fingers to feel the warm flow of blood saturate them.

"You did good, Gordeelum. You watched out for Aimee when I couldn't. I am indebted to you for that."

It was difficult to speak. Emotion formed a noose about his throat, cutting off his voice—his air—his will.

Hunching over so that his mouth pressed close to Aimee's ear, Zak caught a whiff of her hair. It smelled like the meadow. Fresh, like a crop of wild *zilli* flowers.

"Don't leave me," he whispered. "Not again, Aimee. Don't you leave me."

A hand fell on his shoulder. With tears blurring his eyes he looked up at his father's pensive expression.

"I don't want to lose her," Zak pleaded.

The hand around his shoulder clenched tighter as the man crouched down beside him.

"I know, son." he soothed in a husky voice. "I know."

Zuttah's bulky profile eclipsed the suns as

he stooped over, evaluating the scene with worry in his eyes.

"We have used up our supplies on the wounded. It is a long journey back to the caves." He observed morosely.

The implication that it was a journey she would not survive hung heavy in the air.

Zak felt the pulse thump under his hands as the blood continued to pool around his fingers, but the rhythm was waning. Gordeelum had withdrawn, looking helpless.

"There must be something we can do," Zak shouted. "Nexus elixir, coagulant beams?"

"All used," Zuttah proclaimed. "Most of our wounded have been healed."

Selfishly, Zak could not rejoice over that news. So many men and women had fallen in this battle, and yet all would return. All but—

The blood continued to pour, but what limited sight of it he had was now obliterated with tears.

Who was he to bring Aimee into this world? He should have never disclosed his feelings on the HORUS. He should have loved her from afar. Then she would have returned to her planet and lived to a safe old age, with children and grandchildren...and had never died at the hands of a Koron like everyone else Zak loved.

"Who here can bond us?" He looked up, frantic. "Please," he cried.

The silence was maddening. His sight might be impaired, but he sensed them, the circle of rebels staring down at him with sad eyes. He could feel the weight of their breath, the pressure of their pity.

One voice replied, "I can."

Zak jolted when the hand on his shoulder squeezed again. Wild with grief, he turned towards his father.

"The ceremony was taught to me by my grandfather," Zon explained. "And when I turned of age, I was sanctioned to perform the ritual."

So little I know of this man.

"Please," Zak choked, feeling the beat beneath his fingers wane.

Was this utter despair what his father had felt as his mother died in his arms? *No.* Don't let the past repeat itself.

Rubbing his eye into his shoulder, he was able to clear up enough vision to witness the rebels kneel in an arc around them. Aimee lie still, with only the faintest rise and fall of her chest. Her skin was so pale, when normally her cheeks were infused with a warm blush, especially when she was mad. The wind toyed with the auburn tendrils cast across the sand. He wanted to touch them, but there was no force in the universe that could remove his hands from where they were right now.

As if he was in a bottomless pit, he could hear his father's voice in faint echoes. It was a chant in the ancient language. Soon the soft mantra was joined by the rebels around him.

So deep in despair, he was barely aware of the tug on his waist as his father drew his belt from his pants. Zon took the thick strap and gently weaved it under Aimee's arm and then across Zak's forearm, fastening them together.

Zon touched that binding strip and continued his chant, regaling the tale of the first deities to settle on Ziratak. A man and a woman, whose love was so complete that upon their death they took the form of two suns and forever watched over their planet and their flock of children.

I'm sorry, Zer-shay. I envisioned this being a magical moment between us. I dreamed about it. I never want to be apart from you. I want us to be as one.

Bending close and pressing his lips to her ear, he whispered, "I love you."

On a final summation, Zon drew the ceremony to a close. Traditionally, there would be applause and hugs. On this day there was silence and weeping.

Blood soaked the ground around Zak's knees. If they were back on the HORUS, she could easily be saved. Raja would whip up a serum to coagulate the blood. Fusion rays could reduce the laceration to nothing more than a faint scar.

Raja.

When she had spoken of the healing serum for *solar ray* trauma, she had also been experimenting with another vaccine, a concentrate that could work in minimal doses. With just the tip of a needle she had healed the wounded paw of a *sumpum*, a gaping laceration that spread across the spongy sole of the furry creature.

What if she had infused that serum with the potion Aimee carried?

"You," he heard Zuttah shout over his head. "Take ten men and continue down the river. We can't underestimate them. Make sure they are all gone. If there are survivors, they could not have gotten far."

With no other tangible options, Zak freed one hand and reached into Aimee's pants pocket for the small vial. Parting her shirt at the waist to reveal bloodstained flesh, he opened the vial with his teeth and suspended it atop her stomach.

"Yes," Gordy urged in a whisper nearby. "Please work."

A clear liquid dribbled onto her flesh, leaving a white rivulet in the pool of crimson.

Shaking the vial upside down until it was depleted, he pitched it onto the sand. That was it. Barely three drops.

Reluctantly, he slipped his arm free from the belt that bound them so as to return it to her wound. Her pulse was weak, and perhaps it was his overwrought imagination, but the stream beneath his fingers seemed to ebb as if there was little left to flow out—or the heart just stopped circulating it.

With his free hand, he fisted his fingers in her loose hair, dropping his head until their foreheads connected.

"Come back to me," he commanded.

Her pallid cheek moistened from his tear. The wisp of her breath was so faint.

A hand landed on his back, jarring him, but he ignored his father's support. He also ignored the distant shouts, and the constant drone of rushing water. Paying no mind to the sympathetic murmurs, or the whistle of wind against sand, he pressed his head closer— listening—listening—waiting for her to answer.

Something tickled his cheek. An insect? Had one of the cursed *zing* centipedes crawled up from the sand already to claim her?

No. There it was again. Soft, like a feather. He drew back far enough to study her face and found himself swimming in a tumultuous ocean. Sea-green eyes stared up at him. *Was she gone?*

"Aimee?" he whispered, incredulous.

Long dark lashes fluttered, casting spiky shadows beneath her eyes. *They* had been the source of the brush against his cheek.

"Zak?" she croaked.

It took all the strength he possessed not to weep at that sound.

The hand that was fisted in her hair now cupped her face, while his other remained steadfast in its lock against her stomach.

"*Zer-shay?*" He touched his lips to hers. *Still cold.*

When he drew back, she was staring up at him, her eyebrows furrowed.

"What happened? The Korons? Are they—"

"Shhh—" His throat closed.

Withdrawing his hand from her abdomen with the same trepidation as yanking a stick from the dam, he eyed her wound. There was no fresh blood. *Had Raja's serum worked?*

"You did it, Aim. Your dam worked." It was so hard for him to speak—to get words past the emotion clogging his voice. *Keep it casual.*

Relief eased the lines around her eyes. "Thank God," she drawled weakly.

Her gaze shifted, catching the worried looks of Gordy, Zuttah, and Zon. She hastened back to Zak's eyes.

"What—?" Her stare widened in fear. "Did we lose many? Who—who did we lose?"

Zak's head collapsed into his palm. A hasty prayer was offered to the suns above for restoring this beautiful creature. Rather than answer and reveal his stilted voice, Zak parted her blouse and inspected her stomach.

"That tickles."

It was remarkable. The wound was merely a faint crescent across her sleek abdomen. At the accelerated pace in which it was healing, he wondered if it would even scar.

"Zak?"

Her voice was coming back. And once it did he knew it would not stop.

It made him the happiest man in the universe.

CHAPTER FIFTEEN

"We're bonded?" Aimee looked up at Zak from her reclined position in his arms as he carried her towards the foothills. "And I missed it?"

"Well—yes."

His neck, which her arm was wrapped around, felt hot to the touch.

"But, I know someone who is capable of performing the ceremony again," he defended.

Zak and I are bonded.

Aimee beamed with delight. Her arm hooked tighter around his neck as she leaned in, pressing her chapped lips against it.

Unleashing one hand, she reached down to scratch her stomach. *Damn, it itched.*

"Zak, you can put me down. We'll make much better progress if I'm walking."

"Are you implying that I'm slow?"

Long shadows trailed behind the legs that

trudged purposefully across the sand. Over Zak's shoulder she saw Gordy in an animated conversation with Zon, and beyond them she witnessed the splendor of the Zargoll. Its meandering stream now charged with tiny whitecaps from the current. With the influx from the mountain, it had been transformed to a nearly thirty-foot wide bed. As long as nature could continue feeding it without interference from the Korons, the river would thrive as it once had. The banks would grow fertile again. Life would return.

Images of grand stone architecture and beautiful people dressed in white flowing garments filled her mind, just as Zak had depicted.

Broadening her search, a final indication that the Korons were gone was the fact that anyone possessing a shield had it resting atop their heads. With this barrier removed, she was able to study Zak's pensive profile. Sunlight danced across his eyelashes. Shadows accentuated the straight line of his chin. A muscle pumped in his jaw, and dark hair curled up at the ends from perspiration.

"We're bonded," she repeated in awe.

There it was—that fleeting glimpse of a dimple. His eyes slid down to meet hers and they glimmered with emotion.

"Yes we are."

Scratching her stomach again, she bounced with the urgency of his stride.

"Why are you in such a rush? I thought you had wiped out the Korons. Are you afraid there are others out there?"

The cleft in his cheek evaporated. "We will worry for a time that there are others unaccounted for, but what is left is by no means a substantial threat. We can manage them now, and they won't come near the river. Believe me...they are stupid creatures, but they will avoid the Zargoll now at all costs."

"Then why are we practically sprinting towards the mountains?"

As if suddenly conscious of his wide stride, Zak reduced his pace.

"Maybe I'm eager to get you back to the cave," he nodded towards the mountain. "After all, we *are* bonded."

Aimee laughed and hugged him tighter. A peripheral glimpse of Gordy's anxious expression stole her mirth.

"As much as that notion delights me, I don't think that's why you're in a hurry."

When he did not elaborate, her patience dwindled.

"Zak. I want to walk."

Pain lanced his face. "I can't chance that." His step faltered. "Aimee, you were seriously injured today. Your recovery is a—miracle. I will carry you back to the HORUS where they can examine you properly."

"The HORUS?" She sat up as straight as possible in his arms and felt his muscles strain to accommodate.

"You want to know the urgency?" he challenged. "We are practically past the window to catch up to the HORUS. If we miss it—"

"—it will be five more years."

"More or less. Ziratak has different rotations than your planet, but still, it will be a *long* time. We have to take off immediately."

Aimee's head bobbed with his stride. It jarred the exotic landscape—a horizon rich with a blend of coral sand and lavender foothills. In the distance, the majestic white-capped peaks of the crater mountains loomed like a stockade. The pungent smell of fresh humidity clashed with the heat of the desert as the Zargoll charged by.

This was a beautiful planet.

"We can stay here, Zak. This is your home. You worked so hard to save it."

Amber eyes pinned her. "This—" he gazed into the distance, "—this is not my home. It was as a child, but I spent most of my life aboard a ship. And as much as I am fond of the HORUS, there's still something missing there." He hesitated and his voice dropped. "My—*home*—is where you are."

Aimee's throat clenched. *Bonded.*

"You are my home too," she whispered. "If we don't make it back to the HORUS, we can live happily ever after right here."

"Listen to me," the strain summoned lines around his lips. "You don't know how badly you were injured. The wound may have closed. You may be healing. You may very well feel just fine...but we do not have the resources here to verify that. At least, not yet. Soon they will rebuild here, and the technology will return— but I will not leave your welfare to chance. I want you back under the superior care of the scientists on the HORUS. I want Raja to see what she has done. If she tells me that you are okay— then, *maybe* I'll start to relax."

It was hard to conceal her grin. That was so Zak. Before she could respond, he was talking again.

"And we have to get Gordeelum back to his family. Of course, he's not eager to return because he knows he will be sanctioned to his chambers for the next *ren*, if not the next twenty."

Which was all her fault. She looked over Zak's shoulder at the blond hair gleaming under the suns like a pot of gold. She should have stopped Gordy. She should have tried harder.

"You're right, Zak." Guilt besieged her. "We have to get him back."

Now she was edgy. She fidgeted in his arms. By the sheer virtue of him having to carry her, she was holding up their progress. She wanted to run ahead and get started. Already, Wando's calculations were siphoning through her brain.

"We have a problem," she announced.

"I imagine we have many," he smirked at her expression. "What one are you adding to the pile?"

"A vacuum. We need a vacuum."

A vacuum? His lips formed the words.

"Wando said that old *terra duster* can only take off inside a vacuum—because—because—" she snapped her fingers, "—the area needs to be void of ionized particles. The *duster* would basically choke to death in this oxygen, and never get off the ground. Once in space, it will be fine."

"I understand your concern," Zak mentioned quietly, "but could you lean into me rather than trying to stand up in my arms?"

"You can put me down," she countered with a smile.

Zak grinned back.

"*Terra duster?*" A voice called from outside the scope of Aimee's view. "Did you say, *terra duster?*"

A beard jutted out beside Zak's shoulder. Increasing his gait, the profile of a man emerged. Zon drew his graying hair behind his ear and cast her a keen look.

"I haven't seen a *terra duster* since I was doing my apprenticeship. You know they're not supposed to fly, don't you?"

Aimee leaned forward in Zak's arms and he grunted at the shift in weight.

"Yes," she said. "But we redesigned it. It will work, except for the whole ion drive problem."

Zon jogged to keep up with Zak's stride. The terrain had altered as they reached the foothills and the granular surface made the incline a slippery one.

"Where is the *duster?*" he asked, leaning forward to meet Aimee's eyes past Zak's bicep.

Ahead, a carpet of boulders and bush grass climbed into a thicket of white-trunked trees, and behind that grove, the austere mountain face spouted a waterfall from its core. Shaded ravines carved paths in the slope, like a zebra's hide. And in the distance a grassy ridge rolled like a giant putting green.

When they first arrived, there was so much chaos embroiled in their landing, but she was certain they had set down on a grass plain similar to that field.

"I think it's over there."

"Don't worry, *Zer-shay*, we know where your ship is," Zak assured.

"*Zer-shay*," Zon mused. "I used to call your mother that."

Wincing, Zak continued, "It's just over that ridge."

"And you're going to carry me uphill, on these loose rocks?" she challenged.

Opening his mouth to respond, Zak was interrupted by his father. The man had an enthusiastic gleam in his eyes. "Can the *terra duster* still use its rudimentary skills?"

"What do you mean?" Aimee asked.

"It was designed to hover over the ground, not fly. Originally, its purpose was for farmers to maintain their crops. In essence, it was a utility vehicle to transport equipment. Can it do that? Can your *duster* move if we need to relocate it?"

"Ummm—" Aimee replayed Wando's

endless dialogues over in her mind. Had he mentioned that simple function?

"I really don't know. Our sole intention was to get it into space."

Zak was shaking his head. "I still can't believe you risked your life like that. You didn't even know if it was going to work."

"Oh bah. It worked, and here I am, saving your sorry ass."

There was a delay until she saw him recall the translation of *ass*. Zak's eyebrows hefted and he laughed. "What's so *sorry* about it?"

Aimee rolled her eyes. "Men and their egos."

A commotion ahead alerted her.

"There it is!" Gordy yelled, charging over the knoll.

"Now, if you'll just put me down, I can try to answer your father's question."

The older man's eyes volleyed between them, a smile toying with his lips.

"Actually, I know how to operate one," Zak's father inserted. "Quite well. I can help."

Reluctantly, Zak drew his gaze away from Aimee.

"Really?" he questioned.

"That's great!" Aimee gushed.

Zon laughed at them and patted Zak's

back. "At some point you will need to set her down."

Stricken, Zak uttered, "I can't. Not yet."

Father and son's eyes connected. Zon clasped his shoulder. "I understand," his tone was solemn, "I really do."

Zak lowered his head and she felt his arms constrict around her. In answer she looped hers tight around his neck and leaned into the warm skin at the base of his throat. She tilted her head, brushing her lips along the patch of flesh just below his ear.

"I'm okay," she whispered. "And I love you so much."

Zak came to a halt. He lowered her legs to the ground, but looped his arm tight around her back in case they failed her. With that grip, he drew her against him as he dipped to caress her hair with his lips. "And I love you."

"I'll just go see to that *terra duster*," Zon murmured, backing away.

Unaware of that retreat, Zak continued. "I almost lost you. Do you have any idea how concerned I am right now?"

She stroked the back of his neck in assurance. "Yes. You hold yourself together like a Warrior, Zak—but your eyes can't hide your emotions."

"They used to. It's the blasted solar ray," he mused with a faint smile. "Or maybe I had no emotions back then."

"I'm okay." She squeezed both sides of his head. "I'm *okay*. And we will figure out how to get Gordy back to the HORUS, and then—"

"*You made it here in this?*" Zon's voice pitched in the distance.

Zak glanced over her and shook his head. "You do realize that I would have never let you take off in that."

Aimee craned around to view the tarnished elephant. With its shell burned from the approach to Ziratak, and the series of pockmarks and dents that dotted its hide, it looked like the offspring of a wooly mammoth and a leopard.

"And yet," she murmured, "you're about to board it with me, so you must have some modicum of faith."

"In you—yes." They watched his father squat down and bang his fist on the protruding foot of the craft. "I'm not sure how much he knows."

"Well, his son had to get his smarts from somewhere."

"We have to move it?"

Was his hearing going as well as his eyesight?

Zak waited for his father to elaborate.

"Yes. It appears to be inoperable in a traditional hovering capacity." Zon waved towards the mountain. "We need to get it to that cave that sits up above the ridge. You know the one—it has a wide cliff overlooking the valley."

So that if you take off from it you could plummet to your immediate death.

"Yes," Zak said, worrying that the serum was wearing off. And if it was wearing off on his Father, then what of—

"I think I know where your father's going with this."

The object of Zak's concerns chimed in with a zeal to match the crazy man beside her.

Zak glanced back and forth between them.

"Please," he crossed his arms. "Do share."

"We can create a vacuum in the cave, can't we?" Aimee asked Zon.

"Yes," His head pumped. "We used to keep food supplies preserved in the caves. Just start a fire—cover the entrance with a *Zulli* tarp—and the fire would suck it in, extinguishing itself once all the oxygen was gone."

"Like saran wrap." Aimee said to a host of

blank faces. She shrugged. "Well, that's what they call *Zulli* tarp back home."

"The problem," she continued, "is that once you drop that tarp—will there be enough time for us to take off?"

"That's my concern as well," Zon mulled.

"My concern," Zak interrupted, "is getting the damn thing up there."

Aimee laughed. "You pick up my bad habits when you talk."

There she stood, laughing at him, when only a brief spell ago he was trying to stop the flow of life from leaving her body. He was completely on edge and anxious to get Aimee back to the HORUS. If he had to strap the damn *terra duster* on his own back and haul it up the mountain, he would do it to expedite this process.

"Okay, so just to recap, you need that pile of—" Noting Aimee's raised eyebrow he rephrased, "—that *terra duster* up that hillside and in that cave, and you have confirmed that it can't make the journey up there under its own power?"

Aimee shot a quick glance at Zon and with his hasty nod, she claimed, "Yes. Unfortunately, it was engineered for space travel, with a minimal capacity for atmospheric flying."

"Zuttah!" Zak shouted.

Lumbering towards them with a rock lodged in the corner of his mouth, Zuttah spit it out and bounced his head. "I still can't believe it, but it looks like we got most of those boulder-headed beasts. The last reconnaissance returned with a report that if there are any Korons still out there, they're deep in hiding and they won't venture near the river again."

It was amazing that it had worked, but there was no time to dwell or rejoice on the events of the day. Zak scanned the slope that climbed the mountain face. It was manageable with enough men—of course those men were preparing to engage in an epic celebration once they joined up with their families inside the crater walls.

"We're going to need to move that *terra duster*," Zak explained.

Zuttah's eyes widened.

"Where?"

He followed Zak's hand and shrugged a beefy shoulder. "Alright. I'll gather some men."

No questions asked. That was Zuttah.

"The composite is light," Aimee offered, recalling Wando's description. "Though the frame is bulky, it was designed to weigh as little as possible."

Zuttah snorted and his mustache ruffled.

"We have a skid. We'll have it up there before nightfall."

The two suns rested at opposite angles atop the crater wall. They would drop behind it soon.

Was it even possible that just this morning he had woken with Aimee at his side and the dam was still intact? So much had transpired so quickly. And now the hastened pace was not about to let up. He wanted assurances that the young woman flailing her hands in an animated conversation with his father was going to be safe. He wanted to return the proud and daring Gordeelum to his parents...and if it meant chancing their lives in a vessel that roamed the lands when his father was young...well Zak trusted those around him.

By nightfall Zak was beginning to worry. The *elephant,* as Aimee referred to it, still squatted quite a distance from the cave, and a host of men lingered on the wide cliff that jutted over the slope below. Repeated pleas for Aimee to stay off her feet primarily went unheard. At the moment, she was on her knees drawing graphics in the dirt. Zon stood above her, gripping his forehead.

"Can you fly this thing, Zak?" Gordy

stepped up alongside him.

Eyeing the tarnished monster, Zak mused, "It is a distant predecessor to the first craft I learned. I think Aimee has a saying, *It's just like riding a bike.*"

"Aimee did a great job landing, but she was coached," Gordy added. "We're not going to be coached." He kicked at a stone and watched it shoot off the ledge and disappear into the ravine below. "Maybe we should stay here."

Zak studied the young man. Trouble lurked in the bright eyes.

"You don't want to go back?" he probed.

Gordy stared out into the desert that was now dissected by a resplendent river.

"What we did here," he began tentatively, "it was amazing. I've never been a part of such a monumental feat. I feel like I—I—achieved so much. Nobody back home would have thought I could do this."

"Did you ask them?"

"Huh?"

"Did you ever ask them if they thought you could accomplish something so grand?"

"Well, no," he defended. "But, I could tell."

"Gordeelum," Zak placed a hand on his shoulder and guided him a few steps away for privacy. "When your parents were sick, I visited with them in the Bio Ward."

"When I was locked up?"

"You know you were put in that chamber for protection," Zak reminded in a low tone. "Anyway, they told me that they thought you were the bravest person they knew...that you faced your solitude with that virus with a maturity that made them both so proud."

Gordy's eyes rounded.

"They felt," Zak continued, "that you were capable of anything."

"They—they—" Gordy cleared his throat and his voice resumed much deeper, "–they never said anything like that to me. When they received their serum and were released from the Bio Ward, they smothered me. They wouldn't let me out of their sight. It was a battle just to get them to let me go to school in the R-4 satellite."

"And why do you think that was?"

"Yeah, yeah, we almost lost each other, so they didn't want me to go away to the satellite for such a long time."

"Gordy, do you know how many people want to be loved by their parents like that? How many even *wish* they had parents?"

A quick dart of the eye at the bedraggled man working with Aimee did not go undetected by Gordy.

"Well," Gordy straightened his posture, "maybe they will be even prouder when I return—when they learn what I took part in here. Will you put in a good word for me?"

Zak smiled. "Of course."

"And maybe they will find some clause that will allow me into the Warrior apprenticeship."

"I'll put in a good word for that as well."

Trying to look composed, Gordy's lips failed him and erupted into a white-toothed grin. "Cool."

"Is this going to work?" Zak asked.

"Yes." There was a subtle waver to Aimee's voice. A slight lilt that sounded like, *of course this is going to work—I mean, I'm pretty sure it will work, that is, I hope it will work.*

"Yes," she repeated, seeking affirmation from Zon.

The tip of the man's finger tapping against his bottom lip didn't inspire confidence.

"Well, if I understand Aimee correctly," he started, "they mounted these drives to power this relic. It's been a long time since I was able to tinker with space travel technology, but even in my day, ion drives were being phased out.

However, given the circumstances and limited resources Aimee and her friends had, I think they did a remarkable job."

Heat infused Aimee's cheeks under the praise. Zak's lingering glance also made her feel flush. And the touch of his fingertips against her cheek elicited a fevered reaction.

"We have to do this fast," he proclaimed gruffly. "I'm afraid she may have an infection."

Infection! *It's just your eyes that make me burn up.*

"The craft is in place and the tarp is up," Zon directed. "As soon as you are in the ship and ready, I will start the *Zull* dung fire. With the tarp across the cave entrance, the fire should deplete the oxygen and give the ion drives enough boost to propel you out of the cave and into our lower atmosphere..." The lapse in his words spoke volumes. "I just hope you have enough power to make it *out* of the atmosphere. In space you will be fine, of course."

Zak's eyebrows knitted. "I am not going to chance Aimee and Gordy's lives on *hope.*"

"*Hope* got us here in the first place, Zak." Aimee injected. "There are no guarantees. I learned enough about this elephant on the trip to Ziratak. This will work."

Sharp gold eyes pierced her. "Aimee—"

"Have faith in me, Zak."

His intensity wavered. "You know I do, but—"

"Son," Zon reached for Zak's shoulder and squeezed. "Finding you—alive—has been a miracle. Do you think I would risk anything happening to you?" His voice grew hoarse. "I feel confident that this will work."

Zak's hand clasped the arm that was extended towards him. "Will you come with us? I just found you. I don't want to lose you again."

Misty eyes scanned the desert. "Only a few days ago I lived as a recluse, begging upon the aid of others to feed me and hide me from the Korons. Now, I have my land back...and my mind. There are exciting times ahead for the people of Ziratak, and I want to be part of that. And then—" he smiled at Zak, "—when you return, I will be able to show-off all that you made possible."

"No, no." Zak shook his head. "Don't credit me. The victory here today has been the work of many."

"Indeed." Zon used his grip on Zak's shoulder to draw him into a quick embrace. "But know this," he declared quietly. "When you were young, I always predicted that you would grow up into a fine man. Thanks for confirming my notions."

Stepping back, Zak flashed a grin, "Well, Aimee tells me that I had to get my smarts from somewhere—" Over Zon's head, Zak sought her glance. "—now we know."

"I'm sure your mother was the smartest in the family," she quipped.

"Ahh," Zak's father's laugh was bittersweet. "She speaks the truth."

They sobered and Zak vowed quietly, "One day we will return here."

We. Her and Zak. Bonded. A couple that would travel the galaxies together.

She stepped forward and wrapped her arm around his waist. "Definitely." Her smile extended to include Zon.

A family.

Pain and longing for her own family wormed its way into her soul. Always in tune with her, Zak bent his head and whispered, "*After* I meet your parents."

Oh God, enough with the tears. She crammed her fist into her eye and beamed up at him. She felt so loved by this man.

"And when you return," Zon clapped them both on the shoulders, "we will all climb the crater and search for the temple of the monarch. As the legend has it, all we have to do is find a cave with floating planets in it. It was said that they form the path to the temple gate." Mirth filled his voice. "Of course, it is just a legend, but wouldn't it be a fun adventure to share?"

Aimee and Zak's eyes locked. *A cave with floating planets marking the gate to the temple.*

The trio was disrupted by Zuttah's shout, "We are ready!"

Through the windshield Zuttah waved up at him with a smile short a few teeth. Zak was going to miss this gentle leviathan. Zuttah and Zon would remain and guide the Ziratakians on a new adventure—a pursuit to restore a world of splendor and peace. A civilization abundant with soaring temples, brilliant banners, exotic gardens, ethereal music, and happy families. A world Zak once recalled.

Beside him, Aimee barked into a remote. "Clear out the cave and light the fire."

Anxious eyes met his as their hands simultaneously latched onto the same control.

"What do you want to do?" she whispered to exclude Gordy who was busy communicating with Zon through an earpiece. The young Warrior knelt in the rear, administering to the interior cavity of the giant elephant foot.

Zak contemplated her question, sliding his gaze over the dark hair that dipped before her shoulders as she leaned towards him. Her bottom lip was moist and blushed after being released from her nervous bite. A fur vest replaced the blood-stained blouse. Long, sleek arms were poised over the controls, prepared to launch this behemoth into space.

"I want to be the father of your children," he vowed with a grin.

Her eyes widened, and then she snorted. "Do you think you can wait until we get back to the HORUS, or should I inform Gordy that we'll be awhile?"

On a chuckle, he took his eyes off of her and gave Zuttah a thumbs-up sign through the window. The burly giant frowned and looked up.

"If I have to wait," he quipped, "then this thing better fly at *superluminal* speed."

Aimee laughed and danced her fingers over the hologram.

Outside, Zuttah's hulking frame retreated until he was nothing more than a hazy silhouette behind the diaphanous tarp. In another moment his silhouette disappeared altogether.

"All clear," Zon communicated across all their earpieces. "I will start the fire and then I will move outside," he hesitated, "out of range of your earpieces. You will be on your own after this. When I'm certain the cave has been depleted of as much oxygen as possible, I will wave the banner outside. When you see that—"

"I gun it," Aimee filled in.

"Gun it?"

"We go," she corrected.

"Right." Relief filled the tinny voice. "Okay—I'm heading out. Zak—" There was a lengthy pause. "There is something for you under your chair. I love you, son."

Before Zak could respond, the earpiece was filled with the howl of the wind from the cave ledge. Zon was a murky profile behind the tarp. Suspended over his head loomed the shadow of the banner held in his raised hand. When that banner fell their fate would be revealed.

"There's no time to look." Aimee read his mind as he glanced towards his feet, hoping to catch a glimpse of what was down there.

"Soon," Zak said more to himself.

"Gordeelum," he yelled over his shoulder. "Get in your seat."

"Yes sir!" Gordy's enthusiasm came across loud and clear as he could be heard fastening himself in.

"Zak," Aimee said softly as their eyes

stayed glued to Zon's raised arm, "do you think you found the gateway to the monarch's temple?"

"It's just a legend, Aim."

"Then, what—"

The banner fell.

CHAPTER SIXTEEN

It felt like trying to stand up from the couch with a tray full of cement blocks across your lap.

Aimee struggled to lift the tarnished beast off the cave floor. Beside her, the corded muscles on Zak's arm tensed as he fought with the controls. The elephant gagged on the oxygen still trapped in the alcove, and then it caught an anoxic gasp and lunged forward. For a blinding moment, the tarp hugged the windshield. As they cleared the lip of the precipice the flimsy material slid away, exposing the desert valley below.

The *terra duster* took a sickening dive.

"No!" Gordy screamed.

Aimee was prepared. She initiated the two remaining chemical motors as Wando had instructed. These would power them through the atmosphere until the ion thrusters could resume.

It was an aerobatic maneuver that the best pilots might flinch at, but outside, the imminent blur of sand began to recede as they pulled up into Ziratak's stratosphere...into the blazing path of the suns.

Zak reached up with one hand to shield his eyes. "You're doing it, Aimee."

Looking down at the controls, with his hand still arced over his brow, Zak offered, "two more atmospheric layers to go and we'll be in space."

Perspiration beaded on Aimee's forehead and her stomach itched again, but she could not take her fingers off the panel. The pointer and middle finger pushed higher atop the screen...two small digits urging a massive elephant to fly.

Chancing a glimpse at the windshield she saw the lingering gasses begin to thin out and give way to the dead black of space. But, space was not dead. As the few wispy tendrils of atmosphere dispersed, it was replaced with the brilliance of the cosmos in a dazzling strobe effect. Stars and distant planets gleamed. Mystical clouds bathed the elephant which now glided smoothly in a state so quiet no one dared to speak...or even breathe.

Finally, Aimee broke the stillness. "It is still so beautiful," she whispered in awe.

"It is." Zak looked at her and then beyond into the stars.

"It is *trumpenen*!" Gordy called from the back.

Trumpenen, Aimee mouthed.

Zak shrugged his shoulders and grinned. "Time to reprogram our translator."

Growing serious, she leaned in confidentially. "How do we find the HORUS? Wando and JOH had programmed in the Ziratak coordinates. I didn't do much of anything but sit back and wait until we landed. Now I don't know—"

"I come in handy sometimes, Aim," Zak teased. "Look—" He tapped a display high up on the dash between them. "You see that flashing strobe? That is us."

"Okay, but there's an awful lot of *nothing* around us, and Wando warned that if the charge/mass ratio isn't right, we won't have enough velocity to make it back to the HORUS."

"You worry too much."

Dexterous fingers extended and the blinking spot decreased as the view broadened and a host of flickering specs appeared.

"Are those all ships? There must be hundreds of them." Aimee leaned forward and looked out the windshield expecting to see traffic lights regulating the rush hour. But there were no space crafts in sight.

"They're just beacons," Zak explained. "Some are on vessels—most mark planets and asteroids. Ummm, on Earth do you have a device that identifies you from the person next to you?"

"A driver's license?"

"Okay," he nodded. "Consider all those beacons as driver's licenses. "On the deck of the HORUS, a transport controller is monitoring who or what is in range based on their unique identifier. These are identifiers put in place by Warriors on past missions, so it is highly conceivable there are unidentified entities out there. But—" he tapped on the flashing amber light that pinpointed their *terra duster*, "someone put this on your elephant, and they are watching and waiting to see the signal. Once they latch onto it, they will pull us back in."

She recognized the anxious spasm in Zak's jaw.

"There's a problem?"

Staring at the flashing blip, Zak started. "Well, it's just that the beacon can only be tracked from a certain proximity. It's possible that the HORUS has already pulled out of range. That was our big rush in getting off of Ziratak."

"How will we know?" Her breath hitched. "How will we know if they're out of range?"

For a moment he sat in silence. It was a

quiet filled with certitude. "If we're out of range, then they will never find our beacon. Then they will never pull us in. We will drift out here until the ion thrusters go dry."

And we will just float away with no food or water—and no prayer.

What had only moments ago looked so beautiful with its kaleidoscope of dazzling jewels, now appeared dark and sinister. That profuse void was a boundless belly, devouring those precious gems.

Distracting her from her melancholy, Gordy, who was oblivious to the conversation asked, "What's under your seat, Zak?"

Zak leaned over and reached under his legs until his hand wrapped around a fur sack. He pulled it up onto his lap, unfastening the crude laces. Aimee's view was obstructed by the fur casing, but she saw his cheek plump up into a smile. When he sat back he lifted the item for their inspection.

"It's a *terra duster*," she remarked, her hand extending to touch the finely sculpted wood.

"He told me that when I was young he was working on a functional model for me to play with." Zak's fingertips trailed over the bulbous motors hugging the back of the fuselage, all carved from the very same tree bark used to create the dam. "He must have just carved this in the past few days," he commented in wonder. "It's perfect."

It might have been a crude wooden sculpture and not a fully functional miniature, but Aimee could tell by Zak's smile that he would not trade this model for any fancy operational toy.

"It's perfect," she marveled leaning in close to inspect it. The detail was uncanny, with intricately carved panels, and even a lifelike glint to the windshield from repetitive polishing. It bore the emblem of the HORUS on its side, an emblem depicted on the side of this very elephant.

Aimee jerked in her seat and her head lolled backwards.

"What the—"

"They've got us!" Zak sat erect, his hand on the panel again. "It's a weak tug. A sweeper must have caught us."

"A sweeper?"

"A sentinel craft orbiting the HORUS, rather than the Guardianship itself." He read her anxiety. "Don't worry, they'll pass along the signal, and any second now—"

Aimee flinched as she felt the elephant

jolt.

"What was that?" Gordy leaned forward in his seat, gaping between their shoulders.

"You're going home," Zak announced quietly.

Reaching for Zak's hand, she searched his face. "And you?"

Warm fingers enfolded hers. "I'm already home."

Bleary eyes watched as he tapped on his earpiece and called out to the HORUS. The slight heft of his lip revealed that he got a response. The warm fingers squeezed hers again.

Joining them was a hand on her shoulder, as Gordy announced, "We did it, Aimee. We are going home as Warriors."

A Warrior.

Well, I'll be damned.

It was a much more effortless approach than the first time he had landed here with Aimee, Zak thought as the *terra duster* slipped into the flight deck. Piloting beams guided it in for a routine landing. Outside, a congregation had formed, while inside both Aimee and Gordeelum bore signs of trepidation, certain they were about to be reprimanded.

Grabbing his wooden prize and musing over the man that had carved it, Zak put his arm around Aimee. There was only one goal right now, and that was to get her to the Bio Ward. Until he heard directly from the scientists that she was alright, his demeanor remained subdued. If Aimee truly *was* healed, then he wanted to give Raja the biggest hug in the universe for concocting that serum.

The latch lowered and Gordy exited first, seemingly eager to jump out of the elephant's tummy. As his boots hit the deck, he searched the sea of faces, locking onto the anxious expressions of his parents. His mother broke from the crowd and swallowed him in an embarrassing embrace. Even from this elevated perspective, Zak glimpsed the exuberance on Gordy's face.

"Are you ready?" Zak whispered to Aimee.

Wide blue eyes looked up at him with trust that could sap the strength from the most virile of men.

"Don't let go of me," she warned, latching her arm around his waist.

"Never." He kissed her hair.

Together they descended into the welcoming mass...amicable faces that parted at the shout of a voice from behind. A ripple in the crowd ensued as people were nudged out of the way to let pass the intent figure working his way to the foreground. The last set of shoulders was shoved aside as a platinum head emerged. Stepping forward with his arms crossed, the silver uniform locked into a resolved stance.

"Look who has returned." Salvan sneered. "We thought you were dead. Surely a hero of your caliber wouldn't abandon us for as long as you have. I guess you preferred your own kind over the people who cared for you all these years. You never possessed any devotion to the HORUS, did you, Zak? It was just a means to feed your ego."

Reaching up, Zak applied pressure to his eyes to battle the headache that suddenly assailed him.

Salvan cocked his head. "You are disabled, aren't you?" He leaned in for a closer inspection. "Dare I guess, blinded? Our Warrior hero is now tainted in so many ways, isn't he? You serve no purpose to the HORUS after all." Casting a laugh back over his shoulders for the benefit of the crowd, Salvan added, "What type of hero relies on a woman and a near child to save him?"

Aware that Aimee's posture had grown rigid, Zak patted her side and smiled down at her.

"You should have stayed there, Zak," Salvan carried on. "There is no room or need for a wounded hero on this ship. We don't advocate burdens—"

"Are you through?" Zak asked mildly.

Startled, Salvan hesitated. His pale eyebrows linked together. "No. *You* are through. You will never pass a physical to resume your duties. You are done. What do you have left to offer this ship—janitorial skills?"

Zak handed Aimee the fur sack. "Will you hold this for a minute?"

"Sure."

With his left arm still wrapped around her waist, Zak drew back his right fist and pounded it into Salvan's jaw.

"I'm not *that* debilitated," he declared.

Salvan bent at the waist, clutching his chin in both hands. "Guards!" his shout was muffled.

The crowd poured in around him, reaching out to embrace Zak, Aimee, and Gordy in a united reception. Aimee located Corluss and Wando in the crowd, tugging Zak through the fray until she reached them. Each beamed with pride and collusion.

A blind man. A dwarf. A teenager. A fallen Warrior—and a woman. There was no limit to what they could achieve.

EPILOGUE

"She is completely healed," Raja announced. "It took an extensive internal scan to find any indication that she had been injured to the caliber you described. And well, there's a slight scar."

Zak slumped back against the counter in relief. Regrouping, he stunned Raja by wrapping her in a fierce hug.

"You are a miracle-maker," he proclaimed.

A blush stole over Raja's high cheekbones. "I am a tinkerer, and it was very dangerous for you to have experimented like that."

"What choice did I have?" Looping his arm down Aimee's back, his hand cupped her hip. "I couldn't lose her."

Raja's eyes rounded, but after a second they narrowed conspiratorially. "Would you consider yourself indebted to me, then?"

Aimee and Zak exchanged glances.

"For all time," Zak vowed with an ardent

nod.

"Good." Raja crossed her arms. "Then you won't mind taking me with you."

What? Zak jolted. At his side he could feel Aimee start as well.

"To Earth?" she asked incredulously.

"Yes." Raja strode up to a wall-length window where her slim profile was framed by stars. "I have reached the highest level I can achieve in the science department here. I want to master new sciences."

"*New* sciences?" Aimee squeaked. "Our technology is old compared to the HORUS."

"*Old* is merely a perspective. Your world's approach will be something totally fresh to me." Raja sobered and added, "I have no family here. Sometimes I feel so alone on this ship. Please," she pleaded. "Please take me with you. It's only a *ren*—five years—and then I can come back here and they will have no choice but to promote me with my unique knowledge."

"Who do I need to speak to?" Zak felt anger at the injustice that welled up inside him. "Who is holding you back?"

"I am," Raja explained calmly. "I am my biggest hindrance."

Aimee's hand inched up his chest, arresting his next outburst. She was looking up at him with a wizened expression. He felt that he was about to be schooled by her....yet again.

"Raja wants to go to *college*, Zak. Her time on Earth would be just like me leaving for school. When she returns, she will have degrees that will give her merit." Aimee turned to Raja. "I understand. I *completely* understand. Yes. Come with us!"

At first the idea made Zak queasy. After seeing the enthusiasm on both women's faces, he started to warm to the concept. If they were to have a companion join them on their journey to Earth, who better than the one person who made their union possible...*a tinkerer.*

Following a whirlwind celebration, which included Vodu performing the Anthumian *bonding* ceremony, Zak and Aimee had discussed their future plans at great length. These plans included his introduction to her family, and an extensive tour of the planet Earth. He was eager to experience it all with her, just as she had shared his world.

Raja had already begun calculating a litany of remedial potions to administer to his affliction. But Aimee accepted his impaired sight, vowing to be his eyes on the sunniest of days. What better vision could a man ask for?

Zak looked down at Aimee still secured

under his shoulder, smiling up at him with the tender clarity of love in her gaze. Even if they spent the remaining *rens* of their lives traveling the cosmos...all that mattered was that they would be together.

"Well then," he grinned. "The next stop for this trio is Earth."

BEYOND

SERIES

BEYOND
TWO SUNS
THREE PATHS
FOUR WORLDS
ZON
ZON THE EXPLORER

ABOUT THE AUTHOR

USA TODAY bestselling author, Maureen A. Miller's first novel, WIDOW'S TALE earned her a Golden Heart nomination in Romantic Suspense. A great fan of the romantic suspense genre, she broke from tradition to share the BEYOND series because they were tales that had stuck in her head for many years. After all, who wouldn't want a hot guy in a spaceship to take them away on a great adventure?

You can learn more about Maureen on her website at www.maureenamiller.com

Made in the USA
Thornton, CO
05/24/25 23:48:36

d91a9f78-d385-4c61-826a-2d90a2074359R01